Praise for *The Death of a Difficult Woman*...

"A PRISTINE WHODUNIT."
—*Kirkus Reviews*

"A WINNER!"
—*Murder Ink*

... and the previous Bonnie Indermill mysteries by
Carole Berry:

"BONNIE INDERMILL IS REAL, which can't be
said of very many of today's female leads."
—*Chicago Tribune*

"A SPUNKY YET VULNERABLE HEROINE...
witty, upbeat."
—*Publishers Weekly*

"A MARVELOUSLY INVENTIVE SETTING for
a mystery series ... Brava!"
—*Alfred Hitchcock's Mystery Magazine*

"FAST-MOVING, WRY, AND FEISTY."
—*Kirkus Reviews*

THE
DEATH
OF A
DANCING
FOOL

CAROLE BERRY

BERKLEY PRIME CRIME, NEW YORK

THE DEATH OF A DANCING FOOL

A Berkley Prime Crime Book / published by arrangement with the author

PRINTING HISTORY
Berkley Prime Crime hardcover and trade paperback editions / January 1996
Berkley Prime Crime mass-market edition / October 1996

The Putnam Berkley World Wide Web site address is
http://www.berkley.com

ISBN 0-425-15513-7

Berkley Prime Crime Books are published
by The Berkley Publishing Group,
200 Madison Avenue, New York, NY 10016.
The name BERKLEY PRIME CRIME and the BERKLEY PRIME CRIME
design are trademarks belonging to Berkley Publishing Corporation.

PRINTED IN THE UNITED STATES OF AMERICA

10 9 8 7 6 5 4 3 2 1

1

IT ALL STARTED ON ST. VALENTINE'S
Day.

As holidays go, that one had always
seemed kind of pallid to me. How
commercial and gooey—those silly
heart-shaped boxes of chocolates with
their shiny red cellophane wrappers and
cheap satin bows. Corny! If you'd asked
me a year ago, I would have said that
there was no backbone or real heart to
Valentine's Day. But then came last
February 14, a Sunday, and it packed a
one-two punch that still has me reeling.

Punch number one was a marriage proposal, complete
with diamond ring. It came early in the day, not because
Sam is more romantic in the A.M. than in the P.M., but
because he was going out of town that afternoon. The
proposal itself wasn't a complete surprise—Sam and I had
been playing with the idea of marriage for a while—but
the ring was. The one-karat oval, with smaller stones
called trillions at its side, was very pretty on my finger.
It scared me.

I've never considered myself the diamond type, but that
wasn't the worst of it. The moment that ring took its
sparkling place on my finger, I started worrying that I
might not be the wife type, either. That wasn't a new

worry for me, but the ring gave it a new weight.

Sam is definitely the husband type. He's also pretty traditional, and a shiny red heart-shaped box of chocolates came with the ring. Two layers. Ordinarily I have some self-control. The bugaboos of sugar consumption and tooth decay don't bother me, but the bugaboo of my back-side, which had been expanding, does. The ring threw me for such a loop, though, that I went at those chocolates like a Tasmanian devil.

As I remember it, by late morning, in an effort to keep temptation out of my path, I had stashed the chocolates in the refrigerator. And there I was, ready to yank that door open, when the second blow from the Valentine's Day one-two punch struck.

The note was stuck to the refrigerator door with a mag-net shaped like a moving van.

" 'Eddie called. Will call back,' " I read out loud. And then, louder, "Eddie?"

The only Eddie I could think of was Eddie Fong, known by those who knew him best as "Fast Eddie."

I had last seen Eddie Fong several years before, when he entered my Manhattan apartment through the bedroom window, via the fire escape, and left the same way. And in between this unorthodox entrance and exit, Eddie had stashed a gym bag containing $40,000 cash, stolen from gangsters, in my hall closet.

Sam was at the kitchen counter pouring himself a cup of coffee. "He called while you were in the shower. Who is he, anyway?"

"I don't know. There was an Eddie I used to work with, but it can't possibly be the same one."

"Why not?"

A simple question with a simple answer. That particular Eddie had been one jump ahead of both the police and a nasty bunch of underworld types. I explained that to Sam, adding, "He left the country in a hurry."

"Probably not the same Eddie, then. It sounded like a local call, and this guy didn't seem nervous." Sam carried his coffee to the kitchen table and pulled out a chair. "You must know him, though, because he said he owes you something. A favor. He said to tell you he wants to pay you back."

"Oh-oh. It *is* Eddie."

A vision flickered through my mind—a dark, cold basement in Chinatown, a man with a scar—and I all but choked from the memory of the hateful gag that had been in my mouth.

"You look like you've seen a ghost. So what's the story with this guy?" Sam glanced at the clock on the stove. "If you want to tell me, you better do it now. I've got to get going."

What's the story with Eddie? I didn't answer right away. How do you explain an Eddie Fong to a Sam Finkelstein who has lived in the same house, and made payments on the same mortgage, for over twenty years?

Some of you may not know about Sam, so I will tell you this: He's terrific. He looks good—about five eleven, in good shape, with a full head of salt-and-pepper hair and dark brown eyes—and, more important, he acts good in all the ways that count.

Sam's a widower, and part owner and foreman of a company that does corporate moves, the Five Finkelstein Boys. According to Sam, his family considers him, or used to consider him, their black sheep. What I say to that is, they've never seen the real thing. Sam works hard, comes home when he's supposed to, doesn't drink much, and his gambling is limited to dollar lottery tickets. To my knowledge, Sam has never dealt in laundered money, and I'd bet my life that he's never faked his own death.

"Tell me about this Eddie," he insisted. "I promise not to get jealous."

Jealous? In spite of what the note on the fridge had done to me, I grinned at the silliness of that idea.

I pulled out a chair and sat down. The light snow that had started that morning was heavier now, pelting the window behind Sam. It was the worst winter in years,

Sam was facing a hard drive to Buffalo, and Eddie Fong was back in town.

"Well, a couple of years ago I had gotten a job . . ."

About fifteen minutes later I finished with an abbreviated version of the life and loves of Eddie Fong, and left Sam shaking his head. It was a reasonable reaction from a reasonable man.

"Your friend Eddie sounds like trouble. You should keep away from him."

No sooner had he said that than the phone rang. Sam asked, quickly, "You want me to get it? I'll tell him you're sick or something."

Instinct shouted to me, Don't pick up that phone, but I saw Sam's eyes shift toward the clock again.

"That's okay. Eddie's an old friend. He probably just wants to say Hi and let me know he's alive."

I picked up the receiver. "Hello."

"Bonnie! Great to hear your voice!"

As it turned out, Eddie Fong wanted to do a lot more than say Hi.

I'm not quite sure how it happened, because when I answered that phone I had no intention of seeing Eddie, but by the time the call ended we had a date for lunch in midtown Manhattan the next day. Maybe the thing that egged me on was the chiding tone in Eddie's voice when I protested that I lived way out on Long Island now, and the weather was so crummy.

"Oh, not you too, Bonnie. Don't tell me you've gone domestic and turned into a suburban hausfrau," he said, and he followed this with a scornful chuckle, making it sound as if that state of affairs would be several steps below joining a cult.

I had not gone domestic with a vengeance, not like my friend Amanda, who by the way had given Eddie my phone number. Amanda is working her way through *Mastering the Art of French Cooking*, while the most elaborate thing that comes out of the kitchen in Sam's house is a mean lasagna. I had gone maybe a little bit domestic, though, and you know what? It didn't feel all that bad. Sometimes I enjoyed keepin' the menfolk—Sam's nineteen-year-old son, Billy, lives with us—fed. Still, that "suburban hausfrau," smacking of ruffled aprons and ironing boards, rankled.

"Come on," Eddie urged. "Your feet won't get any wetter than they do when you drive your station wagon to the mall."

"I don't have a station wagon."

"Just kidding. You take the train into Penn Station, catch a cab for a few blocks and you're there. Jaguida's Restaurant. Forty-fifth and Tenth. See you tomorrow at one o'clock."

When we'd hung up, I went upstairs to the bedroom to help Sam finish packing.

Before going further, I probably should say a little about Sam's house. I was spending almost all my time there, and in an indirect way, my feelings about the place may have been partly responsible for my renewed involvement with Eddie Fong.

The house started out as a modest three-bedroom, but has had several additions over the years. It is now roomy, if awkwardly shaped. The living room, which is almost never used, is smaller than the den that was added about fifteen years ago. There's no dining room; all meals are eaten in the kitchen, which has grown to twice its original size.

With all this stretching of the original dimensions, though, the bathroom situation remains exactly as it was twenty-five years ago when some real estate developer saw his chance to make it big off Long Island's growing working-class population: one-and-a-half baths, and the half is in the basement. One and a half was enough bathroom, Sam claims, for him, his wife, Eileen, and their two kids. But it's not enough for me. Sharing a bathroom with a nineteen-year-old aspiring rock star who is obsessed with his hair is awful.

Maybe I lived alone too long. Eleven years of baths in my own bathtub, and a medicine cabinet filled with my stuff, and—please don't think I'm totally compulsive—eleven years of toothpaste squeezed from the bottom.

As for the rest of the house, Eileen's ghost no longer haunted me the way it had when I first stayed there—though the only big change had been new bedroom furniture for Sam and me—but I still hadn't completely adjusted, and that's the problem. The place didn't feel like . . . home.

"I'm meeting Eddie for lunch tomorrow. A place in midtown." I showed Sam the piece of paper with the restaurant's address, and one of his eyebrows went up a millimeter or so, which is about as hysterical as Sam gets.

"That's pretty far west in midtown. Hell's Kitchen is more like it. It could be a rough neighborhood," he added. "Take your Mace."

The Mace had been a Christmas present. In case you're thinking that the man worries about me, you're right, but he also gave me a down parka, and a black nightgown so sheer that if I happen to look in the mirror when I'm wearing it, my skin turns pink.

"The neighborhood's not going to be any rougher than the one my apartment's in," I said.

Sam was quiet for a moment, but then, as he lifted his suitcase onto the bed, he said in an offhanded way, "You don't have to keep your apartment. You live here. Huntington, Long Island. We never use your place."

"Billy uses my place."

That was true to a point. When Billy's group, Crisis, had late gigs in Manhattan, he sometimes stayed over.

"You think it's worth hanging on to it so that the kid can crash there a couple of times a month?"

It probably wasn't, but the apartment in Washington Heights was my safety net. It's not palatial, it's not in the best part of Manhattan, and it's not particularly quiet. The furnishings will never make *The Times* Home section. But it's rent stabilized, it has a water view, and it's mine.

I shrugged and left the subject hanging. Sam didn't press it. He had bigger fish to fry, and I'm being rather literal here. As he played with the latch on his suitcase, he said, "What about a honeymoon?"

"You're asking if we should take one?"

"Of course we should take one. I'm wondering where." A hint of a smile crossed his face. "There's one place I've always wanted to go."

"Yes?"

"Starts with a P."

This coy behavior from a man who ordinarily is not coy should have warned me, but hearing that one letter, P, my imagination took over. Paris. The City of Light. The thought was such a delight that I felt like flinging myself at the man, but if he wanted to make a game of it, I was willing to play.

"P?" I asked.

"Panama."

Sam's smile was full-blown now. I struggled to keep mine from disappearing.

"You mean the . . . Isthmus?"

"The Caribbean coast. Terrific beaches, great water, and there's this charter operation I've heard about. Deep-sea fishing. Marlin, tuna"—his hands, one filled with socks, the other with T-shirts, stretched wide—"this big. Bigger. Think about it!"

I promised that I would think about it.

Sam and Billy left in the early afternoon for a corporate move that was expected to take several weeks. I often work as a move coordinator for Finkelstein Boys, but in this case the company that had hired the movers hadn't hired me. Sam might be flying back on weekends, but otherwise there I was, without a whole lot to do for as long as three weeks. Except think about Panama.

I waved goodbye, then stood in the doorway and watched Sam's Ford leave tracks in the newly fallen snow. When the car had disappeared around a snow-banked curve I went into the den, sank into the recliner, put Panama out of my mind, and gave some thought to serious matters like what color to wear for my second wedding, where to get married, who to invite. Maybe I'd pick up a couple of those bride magazines. . . .

Bride magazines? What was happening to me?

If you know me, you know that my life during the past few years has not been devoted to leisure pursuits. Rent stabilized doesn't mean rent free, and I'd been working as an office temp, and occasionally teaching dance classes. Now, though, I found myself in a situation that boggled my mind.

I didn't have to work!

There was food in the refrigerator and gas in the Chrysler that had been Eileen's. I didn't have to call a temp agency, put on a suit, put on shoes that hurt, and paste on a happy face for some control-crazed bureaucrat in a suit and tie.

You'd think I would have been thrilled. I've certainly complained enough about working. But the truth is, the situation made me feel a little wobbly, as if my feet weren't planted firmly on the ground, and maybe a little guilty, too. When you've taken care of yourself for twenty years—no matter how haphazardly—going cold turkey isn't as easy as you might suppose.

That afternoon I spent some time on the phone talking diamond rings and wedding plans with my friend Amanda, and then with my mother. Later I had a leisurely dinner—grilled cheese sandwich and salad—followed by another attack on the heart-shaped box. If I'd ever had standards, they were gone. Truffles, nougats. I even ate one of those disgusting chocolate-covered jellies.

Unlike me, my cat, Moses, has always been very much involved in leisure pursuits. His meals, however, are something he takes seriously, and he does have standards. He weighs about sixteen pounds, and the fact that he's such a glutton is complicated by the fact that he's finicky. As my fingers hovered over a peanut cluster, Moses circled my ankles, unhappy with the evening's offering of veal stew for seniors.

Three weeks, with nothing to do but feed myself and a picky gray cat, and shovel the driveway and the sidewalk in front of the house. That's not quite correct. I was teaching a social dance class at the local Y Wednesday afternoons and, in addition to lunch with Eddie Fong, there were friends I planned to see. Not only that, but Sam and I had bought paint for the dingy bedroom walls. How hard could it be to paint a square, 14-by-14 room? We had the brushes and rollers, a ladder . . .

I know, now, what I should have done to keep myself out of Eddie's clutches. I should have made myself an ironclad schedule, with no ''maybe's'' in it, and stuck to it. Every minute of the next three weeks should have been planned in advance, even if that meant pounding on a word processor at poverty wages.

Because when I left the house the next day and caught the train into Manhattan to meet Eddie, I had entirely too much time on my hands.

2

JAGUIDA'S WAS ON THE GROUND FLOOR
of a ratty tenement, with its entrance
several steps below street level. The
restaurant announced itself with a hand-
painted sign in the window: an oversized palm print, and the words
"Jaguida. Spiritual Advisor. Reader."
There was no mention of food.

The place was tiny and hot as a furnace, and boasted that bracing combination of scents familiar to many New
Yorkers—grease and roach spray.

Being the only customers, save for an elderly man
drinking tea at a back table, whose eyes darted madly at
us from time to time, Eddie and I were fortunate enough
to have gotten the window table. On the windowsill, a
stack of neighborhood newspapers and a philodendron
fighting for its life partially blocked the view. Not that
the view was so great. The snow that had fallen on New
York City seemed to have come from a different place
than the fluffy prettiness that had fallen on Long Island.
In the city the stuff was sooty gray, punctuated by yellow
ribbons left behind by neighborhood dogs. Along the
curb, directly outside Jaguida's, problems with trash
pickup had resulted in a mountain of black plastic bags

against which rested a truly nasty-looking discarded kitchen sink.

But Eddie? He looked terrific.

"I tell you, Bonnie," he was saying, "I've changed. You're lookin' at a brand-new man."

That was hard to believe, but if looks were an indicator, Eddie *was* a new man. The Eddie Fong from the past had dressed in corporate finery—well-tailored three-piece suits, a Burberry overcoat—and had worn his hair in a cut suitable for the cover of the IBM annual report. The new Eddie Fong, the one sipping tea across from me in Jaguida's, sported a black leather jacket, black jeans and boots, and a baseball cap—worn backward. His straight black hair was long and pulled into a ponytail.

Eddie also looked healthy, which was quite a change from the last time we'd met.

"You're not living on Maalox these days?"

"No way. I'm in great shape," he assured me as Jaguida, a big woman in a gold Lurex sweater, tight gray sweatpants that could have used a spin through a washer, and sneakers, put our lunches on the rickety wood table.

Jaguida was heading toward the kitchen, backside straining dangerously against those sweatpants, when Eddie called over his shoulder, "We want some more tea. Okay? Then you can read my friend's leaves." Turning back to me, he went on. "The stress I used to live with is a thing of the past. All that business with the gangs and the cops . . . finished. It's not like I want to deny my roots or anything, but I'm keeping away from Chinatown."

"And the police aren't interested in you anymore?"

"No. All the charges against me were dropped. I have stress now, sure, but it's more like"—he waved his hands expressively in a search for the right phrase—"creative pressure. That's what I deal with now. I'm feeling great," he said, and thumped himself on the abdomen as if to prove the point.

I took a bite of Jaguida's special of the day, sausage probably made of the parts of animals we don't like to think about, in a pepper-laden sauce, over noodles, and had to believe him. The stuff tasted good to me, but it was not for the sensitive stomach. Jaguida's tea was strong and black, and made the yuppie herbal teas I'd grown accustomed to seem wimpy, but after a couple of bites of the sausage-noodle mixture I drained my cup.

"Is Jaguida's spiritual advice as spicy as her food?"

"Some people say she's got the Gift. Second sight."

The old Eddie Fong had been as cynical as they come, but the new one didn't crack a smile at the notion of second sight. Another change in this chameleon friend of mine.

"So how about that Amanda," Eddie said. "Settled for security out in Queens—with a cop, no less!—when . . ."

"Tony's a good guy. You'd probably like him."

Eddie passed off Tony's virtues with a shrug. "Yeah. I'm sure he calls his mother once a week and pays his phone bill on time, but if Amanda had stuck with me, she could have had some excitement in her life. And some real money, too. Amanda's moldering out there in Queens. You know what she said she spends a lot of her time doing? Experimenting with recipes!"

From Eddie's tone he might have been revealing that Amanda spent her time experimenting with drugs. Cooking doesn't particularly interest me, but I don't find it all that perverse, either.

"Amanda's not moldering." Loyalty to Amanda and Tony kept me from adding, "too badly," or saying anything about the state of their marriage—not precarious, but not so great, either. "Your life might be too exciting for most people."

Shaking his head, Eddie again assured me that he was a changed man. His gambling days were over and he was keeping away from his old Chinatown haunts.

"I've got something new happening and it's already growing. It's going to be *huge*," he said, digging into that peppery sauce as if his stomach were coated with lead.

According to Eddie, his new venture was guaranteed to

make him rich. And he seasoned that pronouncement with something he was sure would intrigue me: I was his friend. He owed me. I could get rich too, Eddie promised, if I wanted to take "a piece of the action." And if I didn't, maybe my fiancé would.

I'd already told Eddie about Sam and Billy, about the house and my newfound security. He, in turn, had widened his eyes appreciatively at the sight of my ring, and had pronounced it "quite a rock."

"It's like," he said, "this business you have—corporate moves—probably makes you enough money, but if you want to go big-time, if you want to be where the people smell sweet—I'm talkin' summerhouses in East Hampton and skiing in Vail—you should come in with me. You do that, and you and your boyfriend aren't just going to be comfortable. You're going to be rich! I promise that whatever you give me, I'll triple it in a year!"

The new Eddie Fong obviously had taken some lessons from the old one.

My initial acquaintance with Eddie had come at one of those not-rare moments in my life when I didn't have much money. I remember him saying, back then, that if I stuck with him I'd need an armored car to carry my money to the bank. That was an exaggeration. I'd been able to fit the $40,000 he hid behind my vacuum cleaner into a shopping bag, and for my efforts I'd ended up tied to a pole in a basement.

The accumulation of wealth has never been a driving force in my life. The beauty of having enough money is clear, but right then I was cushioned by a nice checking account. A piece of Eddie's action, whatever it was, was decidedly unappealing, and even scary. I answered emphatically "No" for both myself and Sam.

To reinforce that No, and to brag a little, too, I gave Eddie one of my business cards. These were the first business cards I'd ever had and I was inordinately proud of them, passing them out not only to people who might someday conceivably have a corporation to move, but indiscriminately to friends and family.

He turned the card over in his fingers and read, with a bare hint of derision, " 'Bonnie Indermill. Move Coordinator.' Sounds fascinating."

"On a one-to-ten job scale, it's a good seven."

"And you're willing to settle for a seven when you can have a ten?"

"Yes."

"Okay, but you've got to remember, Bonnie, there's also a matter of . . ." Eddie began, but Jaguida was back with another pot of tea. By the time she had shuffled off again, he seemed to have thought better of whatever he'd been about to say.

I'm not completely naive. He wanted to talk about the $40,000. Well, he could bring it up all he wanted.

Fidgeting in his chair, Eddie stared through the window out onto Tenth Avenue.

The immediate neighborhood was made up of run-down tenements with small businesses on the ground floors, and an occasional warehouse. It was not what you'd call a "high rent" district, but the pink marble towers of luxury high-rises were visible two blocks east, where a minor renaissance had been taking place. Like the tide, these revivals ebb and flow in Manhattan neighborhoods.

"Take a look at those towers near Eighth Avenue," Eddie said after a few seconds. "Have you been over there?"

"No. What's your new business, anyway?"

Ignoring my question, Eddie went on about the high-rises. "It's not just apartments. They've got restaurants, stores, a health club, a movie theater. This neighborhood is happening." Smiling back at me, he added, "There's another new apartment complex a few blocks south of here, full of professional types with spare change in their pockets."

Eddie was so enthusiastic about these luxury apartment buildings and the people who lived in them that, for a fleeting moment, I wondered if he had become a burglar. I pushed that ugly idea out of my mind and asked him if he lived in one of those complexes.

"Not yet, but I'm working on it, and I won't settle for anything less than a penthouse, either."

"So where are you staying now? With your aunt and uncle?"

Eddie's aunt and uncle live down in Chinatown, and have a little restaurant there. When I met Eddie he was staying with them, but now that notion struck him as so ridiculous that it made him hoot and slam his hand on the table.

"Not hardly! I told you, Bonnie, I'm finished with Chinatown. For right now, because of a . . . you know . . . cash flow thing, I'm living . . ."

Once again, my usually glib companion had to cast about for the right word. I followed his gaze to the restaurant's ceiling, where leaks from the floor above had left a series of overlapping brownish stains. ". . . upstairs," he finished.

Upstairs. The word, once Eddie had managed it, briefly hung like a cloud over our table. He was living in the tenement upstairs from the restaurant.

God knows I understand cash flow problems, not to mention dumpy apartments, but Eddie had always had such high-flying ideas about how he was going to live that I was embarrassed for him. Groping for something nice to say about the place, I happened to glance down at the floor. A fat brown cockroach was ambling across the worn yellow linoleum floor toward us.

"The neighborhood's certainly convenient to everything. All the Broadway shows, and . . ." I couldn't think of anything else the neighborhood was convenient to except the old piers across the Westside Highway, so I shut up.

Eddie spotted the roach and, with a smooth movement, stretched out his leg and squashed it flat with his boot. When he pulled his foot back, the roach's remains blended nicely with the other spots on the linoleum.

"You're right." He nodded. "The location's real convenient. My new club is right down the street."

I said the first thing that came into my mind. "You mean a gambling club?"

Eddie disposed of that notion quickly. "No way. It's like I said, Bonnie: I've learned my lesson. I realize, now, that there's no substitute for hard work. I've opened a dance club. Samba, tango, waltz, hip-hop." He wriggled his shoulders and winked. "You know me. I've got all the moves."

Too many. A dance club, now? What did he know about dance clubs, much less about running one? The Eddie Fong I'd known had been an okay social dancer, but that was all. His interest in dancing had been minimal and, as far as I could tell, his interest in hard work—and running a club had to be hard work—had been zero.

"Are you putting me on?"

"All right, ye of little faith."

Eddie took one of the newspapers from the stack on the windowsill and thumbed through it. "Read this," he said when he'd found the right page, "and *then* tell me you don't want a piece of the action."

The first thing that jumped off the page at me was a black-and-white photo of Eddie. That Eddie's picture had made the paper wasn't all that surprising. It was easy to imagine him appearing handcuffed in one of the tabloids. In this picture, though, his hands weren't cuffed. One of them was around the waist of a tall, pretty young woman, and the other rested on a bar. Eddie was smiling and looking hip and urbane as anything. Another man, his face not so clearly lit, waved toward the photographer from behind the bar.

I read to myself.

Six weeks ago, two entrepreneurs from California, Eddie Fong and Max Breen, opened The Dancing Fool in an old warehouse on 45th Street near 10th Avenue. The club, which has live music four nights a week and a disc jockey on Wednesdays and Saturdays, has already made a hit in the immediate neighborhood and, according to Eddie, who is handling The Dancing Fool's publicity, is starting to attract people from all over the City. Last Thursday night when this writer dropped by, a line of people had formed outside the door waiting to join the crowd enjoying Ballroom Dance Night. Inside, for people watchers, were celebrities like Brad Gannett, the star of NBC's hit series Undercover Squad, *who had stopped by with some friends.*

Eddie, who has years of experience in the club scene on the West Coast, and Max, who formerly ran a club in West Hollywood, pointed out that at The Dancing Fool there is something for everyone from 18 to 80, with every level of dance skill from novice to Nureyev. The partners say that the club fills the big niche between the social dance schools, with their aggressive sales pitches, and the discos, where anyone over 25 feels like a dinosaur. On Sunday the club is open in the afternoon and evening for ballroom dancing, and on Tuesdays, Thursdays and Fridays they alternate Texas Line Dancing, Latin Night (Samba, anyone?), Ballroom, Cajun, or West Coast Swing. On these nights there's live music at The Dancing Fool, and the lovely young woman in the photo above, Dawn Starr, an actress, singer and dancer, demonstrates the latest steps. One turn around the floor with Dawn, whose stage credits include roles in the roadshow of Chorus Line *and a season at the San Fernando Playhouse, had this writer feeling like a budding Gene Kelly.*

Eddie, Max and Dawn hope you'll drop by the club. The cover is a reasonable $10.00 and the drinks won't break you. If my experience at The Dancing Fool is typical, you'll more than get your money's worth.

I was astonished. Maybe I shouldn't have been. Eddie is smart, personable, and imaginative. But he's also very reckless. Impulse control is not one of his strong points. But there was the proof in black and white. He was doing something that required planning, foresight, and lots of work. And also, front money.

"Congratulations, Eddie. It sounds like you've really found something for yourself. Of course, I'd forgotten all about your years of experience on the club scene," I chided.

Lifting his shoulders, he grinned. "So I exaggerated. What's the big deal? It's not exactly brain surgery, running a club. Actually, the whole thing came kind of naturally to me. It's what you'd call a real good fit."

"Wasn't it awfully expensive getting started?"

Eddie flicked his fingers as if money were a mere trifle. "There are always ways to get money. The building belongs to a business acquaintance of Max's father. It had been vacant for years, so we get a low rent. And then, Max and I each kicked in a hundred thou, give or take a few bucks."

One hundred thousand dollars isn't a fortune in the business world, but I was surprised that Eddie had come up with that much.

"Before you stopped gambling, one of your long shots must have come in."

"Nah," he replied. "My aunt and uncle loaned me fifty grand, and I had a little bit put away. Actually . . ."

Lowering his eyes, Eddie stared into the depths of his plate. After a moment he looked up.

"You know what, Bonnie? The Dancing Fool is your kind of place. You'd fit in really well, the way you're into the dance scene."

Eddie was wrong. I hadn't been much involved with the professional dance scene for a long time. When I want to torture myself, I think about my last serious audition. It was about eight years ago. I answered an open call in *Backstage* for a road company production of Bob Fosse's

Dancin'. The memory of being not just *among* the first cut, but the very first cut, still makes me cringe. We hadn't been on stage for more than five minutes when a choreographer's assistant—he looked about sixteen—called, "Girl in the second row in the blue leotard. Thank you."

"Thank you," in audition-ese, means "goodbye." It's not as if I was the only one cut. While I slipped my shirt and jeans over the blue leotard, the assistant was thanking boys and girls dressed in every color in the spectrum. But this time the voice inside me, the one that had been whispering, You've had enough, shouted the words at me: *You've had enough!* Not long after that I took my first full-time office job.

I toyed with my noodles, then said, "My dance scene these days is at a Y near Sam's house. I teach a ballroom dance class Wednesday afternoons."

Eddie looked so dismayed that it might have been comic if I hadn't felt a little squeamish about that admission. I wasn't moldering as badly as Amanda, but I was on the way.

"Teaching the two-step to overweight housewives? That's too bad," he said sadly.

I bristled. "It's an interesting group of people."

"Yeah. Right. Now, you want to see interesting people, at The Fool . . ."

The rest of our time over lunch was taken up with Eddie and his club. Pretty soon the beautiful people would be stopping by. Pretty soon they'd be getting name musicians like Harry Connick, Jr. Pretty soon they'd be putting in a kitchen and serving food.

His enthusiasm infected me. Knowing Eddie as I do, I should never have allowed that to happen.

When we had finished our meal Jaguida brought our bill and then dragged a chair from another table. Perching herself on it, she shoved my teacup at me.

"You want I should read your leaves, you got to finish your tea."

Her voice was guttural, her accent—which hadn't been

nearly so apparent when she was taking our orders—unidentifiable. On top of that, she was a truly amazing-looking woman. Her fingernails were the color of blood and as long as daggers, and her hair a canary-yellow piled-high business that contrasted startlingly with her swarthy complexion and faint mustache.

I smiled at Eddie. "Do I really want to do this?"

"Sure. I told you Jaguida has the Gift. She'll put you on the right path and change your life."

Oh, brother. Feeling kind of nutty, I drank the rest of my tea and handed the cup over to the resident oracle for inspection.

Jaguida took the cup in both hands and swirled it slowly. As she studied the leaves that settled, her eyes widened. They were so dark brown they looked black, and that darkness was heightened by the yellow mass on her head. She glanced at me once, and then back at the leaves, and then at me again.

"The tea leaves say you are at a crossroads. You have the chance for . . . What is it I see?" She cast her eyes into the depths of the cup and narrowed them as if she were actually searching those damp leaves. "It could be something . . . yes." Looking back at me, and clicking her red dagger nails against the cup's side for emphasis, she said, "Fabulous wealth and glamor may be coming for you."

Jaguida had the Gift, all right. She should have been on the stage. I remember the way those words—"fabulous wealth and glamor"—began as a rumble at the back of her throat and slowly came rolling off her tongue until I could almost picture piles of glittering gold coins and closets full of designer clothes.

"You must make the choice," she told me. "There is a man. He is kind but his interests may not be best for you. Your spirit is still young. The man's is more settled, older not only in years, but in spirit. . . . "

Sam is six years older than I am, not sixty, and though his spirit may be quieter than mine, it's a long way from dead. Okay, so a couple of times he's made noises about "when I retire," and I haven't done anything to retire from yet, but I'm sure we'll work it out.

A crash from the kitchen, followed by a string of curses, put an end to Jaguida's soothsaying. Muttering angrily under her breath, she slammed my cup on the table.

"You can leave the money by the register," she barked to Eddie. "Or else sign the bill."

When she had stormed away, I giggled. "What a hoot! You told her what to say."

Eddie drew himself up indignantly. "I did not. Jaguida wouldn't compromise herself like that. It's like I told you, Bonnie. She has second sight. It's a gift."

"It's bullshit." I meant that, but in a tiny corner of my mind there may have been a speck of doubt.

Eddie took his wallet from his pocket, but had second thoughts and borrowed a pen from me. When he had scrawled his name across the bill, he finally said, as if it had just occurred to him, "Hey, Bonnie? Did you ever run across any extra cash in one of your closets?"

He was so transparent I could hardly keep a straight face. "You mean the forty thousand dollars you hid behind my vacuum cleaner? I vacuum occasionally, Eddie. I found it."

"And? What did you do with it? Spend it all on clothes?"

He looked a little sheepish, but not so sheepish that I felt sorry for him. "I only spent a little of it on clothes. I turned the rest over to the police."

His jaw dropped and an almost frantic look came into his eyes. "Tell me I'm having aural hallucinations, Bonnie. I can't have heard you right!"

"You heard me right."

That Eddie and I have a different view of the police didn't surprise me, but his reaction to my news did. Sure, he had always wanted to make money the easy way, but he'd also had an "easy come, easy go" attitude about it.

Now, though, from the way he hunched his shoulders and hugged his arms across his chest, it looked as if he'd have to go back on the antacids.

"I couldn't keep that money. It didn't belong to me."

"It didn't belong to the cops, either," Eddie shot back. "I can't believe you did that." Shutting his eyes, he breathed deeply and rolled his shoulders. It was an obvious attempt to calm himself, and it seemed to work, because when he opened his eyes again they didn't look quite so frantic.

"There's some city agency that keeps unclaimed cash. The Property Clerk, maybe. I don't think anyone would have pocketed the money." Brightening, he added hopefully, "You might be able to reclaim it, Bonnie."

"Not me, but if you want to try, go right ahead. The police would probably love to talk to you about where it came from."

With that, Eddie bit into his lip. I felt kind of sorry for him, but at least the subject of the $40,000 was dropped.

3

A FEW MINUTES LATER WE GOT INTO our coats and walked out into the gray afternoon. Frigid as the air was, it hit me like a tonic after the oppressive heat of Jaguida's. At the curb I stuck out my arm to flag a taxi, but Eddie put a gloved hand on my shoulder.

"Come on," he urged. "We're closed today, but I left one of the local winos sweeping up. I don't trust him with keys, so I've got to lock the door when he leaves. Walk over with me and I'll give you a look around the most happenin' place in town."

A yellow cab veered toward the curb. I've seen clubs before, and bars and dance floors and bandstands and the whole happenin' bit. But I've also seen Penn Station and the Long Island Railroad before, and Eddie was insistent. "What else have you got to do? You're not working and your friend Sam's away. You going to spend the afternoon watching the soaps and eating bonbons? You'll turn into a couch potato." Tilting his head a bit, he added, "And get fat. Have you put on a pound or two?"

That struck a sore spot. Waving the cab off, I fell into step beside Fast Eddie Fong.

When we rounded the corner at Forty-fifth Street, an

icy blast of air coming off the Hudson River whipped my face. A couple of blocks west, on the far side of the highway, old piers lined the river, but there was nothing tall enough to stop the wind.

Much of the block we walked down was lined with five-story tenements like the one we'd just left. Some were better kept than others, but even the ones with plastic daisies poking through the snow in their window boxes didn't look like something Eddie's up-and-coming professionals were going to zero in on. All the first-floor windows were guarded by heavy burglar gates, and the high chain-link fence in front of a vacant lot was topped by coils of New York City's variant on English ivy, razor wire.

Eddie walked purposefully, then cut across the street at an angle. Snow had frozen in the gutters, and eyes streaming from the cold, I made my way carefully after my companion. He seemed to have no trouble with his footing until he reached the opposite curb. Once there, however, he hit a slippery patch and his feet flew from under him. Only a desperate grab at a convenient parking meter kept him from going down. That's the thing about Eddie: everything always looks easy for him, until it suddenly all goes to hell.

The building we stopped at was different from its neighbors, but no more glamorous. Less so, in fact. There's some grace and symmetry to a row of old tenements. This building was twice the width and about one-third the height of the tenements, with concrete walls and only a couple of small windows, high up. The plain black door was at the building's side, up a short driveway. No street address was visible, and no sign announced The Dancing Fool, though graffiti indicated that ''Killer 147'' and several other ''artists'' with the price of a can of spray paint had passed that way.

''How does anyone know your club's here?'' I asked while Eddie manipulated a ring of keys with his leather-gloved fingers.

He had gotten the door open when a delivery truck with a ladder mounted on its side pulled into the driveway. Eddie waved at the two men in the front seat.

"Lots of people have been finding us already, Bonnie. When these guys get through with their magic, the whole world's going to know The Dancing Fool is here."

As Eddie ushered me through the black door, the two men from the truck were unloading long, flat boxes. On the truck's side were the words "Neon Magic, Inc. Lets The World Know You've Arrived."

If The Dancing Fool had arrived, it had done so with a minimum of expense. When my eyes had adjusted to the dim light inside the club, I saw that in one form or another, plastic ruled. Smart black and white plastic in most cases, but plastic. The dance area, which occupied most of the ground floor, was a checkerboard of oversized synthetic tiles. Around its periphery were three-legged black plastic tables and white chairs which looked suspiciously like garden furniture. The walls behind these tables were covered with a grayish, waffled-looking synthetic material that Eddie explained was there for sound absorption. I tapped on one of the wall-mounted shell-shaped light fixtures and it gave under my touch. Not only plastic, but cheap plastic.

Tacky it may have been, but Eddie showed me around as if it were a palace. A coat-check area had been set up by the main door, and just past that, narrow stairs led down to the restrooms and up to the second floor. A portion of that second floor was open to the first, and what little natural light there was on the dance floor came through a skylight.

The club's bandstand, a low platform, continued the black and white scheme. So did the bar that ran along a side wall, but the bar offered its own special twist on the colors: white background, with black spots of varying shapes and sizes.

"I like the Dalmatian print," I said.

"It came out of a restaurant owned by an ex-fireman.

We got it for almost nothing. When you don't have a lot of money, you make do with what you can find," he added self-righteously, as if explaining this to an heiress.

At one end of the bar, next to the rows of liquor bottles, I spotted a television and VCR.

"You put the TV on when you're open?"

Eddie shook his head. "But when we're closed and working around here, it's nice to have."

Above the bar, behind the shelves of bottles, there was a big mirror, and dead-center on that mirror someone had taped a small photo of the actor the newspaper article had mentioned, Brad Gannett.

I stepped behind the bar to examine the photo more closely.

Gannett had one arm around the shoulders of a young woman with short, spiky dark hair and an appealing smile. There was a third person in the picture, a man, on Gannett's other side, but the actor had lifted a drink as the shutter clicked and the lower part of this man's face was hidden. What showed were thick bangs falling over his brow and close-set, sleepy eyes.

As for Gannett himself, who in America but a recluse wouldn't have recognized that longish wavy hair, that slightly off-kilter nose said to be the result of a street fight, and those heavy, sensuous lips.

"I took that picture upstairs in the Celebrity Lounge," Eddie said. "One of these days we're going to have a whole wall of pictures like that. We keep a Polaroid camera in the office. I'm glad it had film in it the night Gannett was here."

"Why didn't the reporter take his picture for the paper? That would have been good publicity for you."

"Yeah, but by the time the reporter got here I'd already taken this. I told Brad that there was a reporter downstairs, but he said he was tired of posing. Brad's an okay guy, by the way. Men like him and women love him. But I don't have to tell you that."

I grinned. "Who are these people with . . . Brad?"

"His girlfriend—she's an actress—and another friend of theirs. Real down to earth, all three of them."

A clanking noise came from beyond an open door at the side of the bar, interrupting Eddie.

"What's back there?"

"A storage room and the back exit. Is that you, T'Bird?"

In response, a janitor's bucket rolled through the doorway. A second later—after Eddie whispered, "They call him that 'cause of the wine he drinks"—a man with a mop over his shoulder followed the bucket.

You see men like T'Bird all around Manhattan, not just in the funkier neighborhoods. They're on the Upper East Side; they're on Central Park South. They're all over the subway to the point where you see them not as individuals but as a faceless shambling army of unkempt gray men. And so I was prepared to hardly give T'Bird a glance, to recognize him simply as "one of them." Yet when this man wearing a faded plaid shirt and worn jeans two-stepped gracefully through the door after the bucket, I couldn't take my eyes off him.

He was about six feet tall and slender, with wide shoulders and the kind of posture my mother admires. His complexion was ruddy under two or three days' growth of beard and his dark brown hair hung sloppily over his collar, yet his eyes, when he spotted me, were alert and attractive.

He nodded at me, and then winked at Eddie.

"Another girlfriend? You trying to put a scare into the lovely Dawn Starr?"

The man's smile was marred by a chipped front tooth.

Eddie answered stiffly. "This is my friend Bonnie. You about finished here, T'Bird?"

"Ten minutes, Massa Eddie," the man responded. Lifting the mop from the bucket, he twirled it, positioned it wood end down, and tapped it smartly onto the floor in unison with one of his feet: TAP-pause-TAP-TAP.

My breath caught in my throat. There was something so familiar . . .

"What's his real name?"

Eddie, who glared at T'Bird until he had pushed the bucket onto the dance floor and started mopping, shook his head and said, under his breath, "Who knows. He's just a bum with a smart mouth. If he doesn't watch it, he's going to have to look somewhere else for his spare change."

His expression softened as he nodded toward the mixing board on one side of the bandstand, and then at the speakers mounted high on the walls. "A lot of our money went into the sound system."

The speakers were huge. Up on the second floor it had to feel pretty wild, especially on Disco Nights. As I mentioned, a portion of the second floor was open to the club below, and the black and white paint job on the wood slat railing around the balcony indicated that it was part of the club scene.

"Our offices are in the shut-off area upstairs," Eddie explained. "The open area is our Celebrity Lounge. That's where the 'beautiful people' hang out. Come on. You're going to love it up there."

I climbed the stairs behind him. At the top there were two doors, but one, covered with the same soundproofing material that was on the walls, was barely noticeable. Eddie told me it led to the office. The other door, the one Eddie opened, was painted black and white.

"You have to give celebrities privacy, you know," he tossed off nonchalantly as he unlocked the door and led me into the Celebrity Lounge.

A little more money had been spent up here. The tables were real wood, had four legs, and sported ceramic-tile tops. Maybe the white banquettes along the wall weren't really leather, but they weren't the cheapest grade of Naugahyde, either.

"When Brad Gannett and his friends dropped by last week, they hung out up here for about an hour. He's really getting big, you know. His acting career is taking off.''

Eddie sounded almost like a proud parent. From the little I'd seen of the star of *Undercover Squad,* Gannett's success had come about not because of his acting ability but because of his well-developed physique, which photographed nicely in tight, sleeveless T-shirts and jockey shorts. Many women were wild for him, but I wasn't one of them. Not that I shut my eyes when Gannett paraded his macho stuff across Sam's twenty-one-inch screen, but having someone's manly apparatus thrust into my face doesn't do it for me. A furtive type myself, I'd rather take surreptitious peeks.

I sank into one of the banquettes and tried to put on a tough face. "Don't push your luck, punk," I growled in the style Gannett was famous for.

Eddie smiled, but he was taking this club so seriously that he bounded to Gannett's defense. "Brad's a better actor than people realize. He's just been signed for some big action film that's going to make him bigger than ... Stallone."

"Wow! We'll get to admire his tush on the wide screen."

Eddie ignored that. "It's only a matter of time before Mick Jagger shows up here. And Bobby DeNiro. He's into the club scene. They go out with models, you know, so we'll probably get some of them, too. And if Tina Turner's in town ..."

As visions of Tina and Mick and Bobby and all sorts of other beautiful people danced through Eddie's head, I nodded toward the doors at one end of the balcony. On one of them was a poster of a man and on the other a woman, both in full flamenco garb. "And when Mick and Tina do show up, they'll have their own restroom."

"Of course," Eddie responded. "I mean, you can't expect people like that to go down to the basement and get in line with everybody else. Privacy is important to them, you know. We want them to feel at home here."

Moving to the edge of the balcony, I peered over the

railing. If and when Eddie's club did become home to privacy-seeking celebrities, they could enjoy staring down on the bobbing masses below.

"Impressed, aren't you?" Eddie said, beaming.

I nodded. I was impressed. While I've never been, as Eddie had put it, "into the club scene," I've been in enough of these places to know it's not the money spent on decor that counts. It's the creativity and energy of the people who run the clubs. And Eddie, for all his faults, had never lacked either of those qualities. I would have sounded like such a Puritan—or maybe a suburban hausfrau—if I'd said this, but if he managed to keep his crazier impulses under control and his fingers out of the cash register, he stood a good chance of achieving exactly what he was after: making it big.

"I'm proud of you," I said as we left the Celebrity Lounge.

"But you still don't want a piece of the action?"

"Nope."

Eddie shook his head in wonder at my foolishness, and then, unlocking the door to the enclosed portion of the floor, surprised me by asking, "Then what about a job?"

"I have a job."

I followed him down a hall, past a closed door with a formidable-looking lock on it, and into the not-very-office-like office. It held a couple of rickety wood chairs, a metal filing cabinet and two metal desks, one of them supplied with a phone and the other with an ancient adding machine and a battered manual typewriter. File folders and papers were all over the floor, piled in corners and against walls. As we moved into the room, Eddie's booted foot accidentally hit one of these stacks, toppling it. He kicked some of the papers out of the way and walked over the rest of them.

"Great filing system," I said, idly staring at the adding machine. "And your office equipment makes my fingers just itch to go to work here."

"The office could be better," he admitted. "We

haven't had time to set up files or any of that. That's why I asked if you wanted a job. We couldn't pay you much, but it would be off the books and you could do all the dancing you wanted. Free admission, any night or every night.''

''No thanks.''

The room's one dirty window was painted shut and blocked by a rusted window gate. I peered through the grime at a rusty fire escape that looked as if it wouldn't support the weight of a pigeon.

''What do you do if there's a fire? Your celebrities could be trapped up here.''

''Soon as we get some money we're putting in a sprinkler system.''

Nodding at the doors on one of the inside walls, I asked Eddie where they led.

''This is our private restroom.''

He swung a door open, revealing something the likes of which I haven't seen since I traveled in rural Greece twenty years ago. I wouldn't have gone in there wearing chain mail.

''Yech!''

''Beats working at the YMCA. And—'' Eddie opened the second door, frowned into an impossibly tiny, crowded closet, and slammed it again. ''And that's a mess. We could really use your organizational help, Bonnie. If you still have that cool apartment in Washington Heights, that would be convenient.''

''I don't know how 'cool' it is, but I've still got it. Sam's son uses it occasionally.''

''Then you wouldn't have to worry about commuting from Long Island.''

''I'm not going to worry about commuting, Eddie, because I'm not going to do it. This isn't for me.''

''Still beats the Y,'' he said caustically.

Back downstairs we found T'Bird waiting near the door to the street. As Eddie counted out some cash, I couldn't help staring at the janitor again. It wasn't that he was especially handsome, or for that matter particularly disreputable-looking. He was simply . . . familiar.

When we left the club, the workers installing the neon sign high on the building's front were finishing up. The sign was big, covering an area of maybe a dozen feet. As the men tested it, bright dancing feet flickered across the concrete. There were feet in high-heeled pumps, and a few seconds later in boots, and then in saddle shoes and bobby socks. Watching those feet dance on the wall, I experienced a rush of excitement. That excitement's for Eddie, I told myself. This kind of place isn't for me.

Eddie walked me back to Tenth Avenue and tried one more sales pitch while I flagged a cab. "Bonnie? Why don't you come by Tuesday night? Texas Line Dancing starting at eight. Or Wednesday for Disco. You don't have to pay. And you can bring a friend. Amanda, maybe."

"Do I detect a little wishful thinking there?"

A yellow cab pulled toward the curb. "A little," he said, "but not much. I've met the woman of my dreams."

"Really? Is it the 'lovely Dawn Starr'?"

Eddie grinned sheepishly as he opened the cab door. "You saw that picture of Dawn? Well, wait till you see the real thing. She's astonishing. I'll tell you, Bonnie: I'd cut off my arm for her. Or at least a finger."

I laughed as I climbed into the back seat. "Which finger? Never mind. It sounds like love or something."

"I'm crazy about her. Right now things are on hold between us, but I'm hoping we're going to work them out. Anyway, you should come by with Amanda. It will be good for both of you. Get her away from the recipe books and you away from the Y."

"I like the Y. But maybe."

Slamming the door, I waved goodbye through the window. My cab pulled into traffic and immediately stopped for a light. I shifted in the seat and watched Eddie disappear through the door that led to the tenement above Jaguida's.

Without having seen it, I knew what his apartment

looked like. The walls were pockmarked, the floorboards warped, the floor itself slanted. The kitchen was a windowless little roach-hole with a rusty sink and a stove you lit with a match. Or maybe there wasn't a stove. Maybe there was just a hot plate. Without a doubt, the bathroom was a horror.

Eddie may have been poised on the brink of fame and fortune, but that afternoon I did not envy him in the least.

That night after I talked to Sam on the phone I settled back into the ruffled throw pillows on the sofa—Eileen had been into ruffles with a diet soda, a bowl of popcorn, and my shiny heart-shaped box of chocolates in easy reach on the maple spool-legged coffee table—ditto Eileen's feelings about Early American–style furniture—and watched *Undercover Squad*. Brad Gannett's manly assets were displayed in fine form.

4

BY TUESDAY AFTERNOON THE PRETTY white snow that kept falling on Sam's sidewalk didn't look quite as pretty to me. When you live in a rental apartment in New York City, someone else shovels it for you. Maybe I was getting exercise hefting that shovel, but there are more fun ways to work those muscles.

Painting the bedroom wasn't one of them, either. That's something else that's taken care of for you when you rent an apartment. The part of the day I had not spent shoveling, I'd been balanced on a ladder with a dripping paint roller in my hand. Most of the ceiling and part of a wall had gone from drab nothingness to the delightful Pearl Drop. A change for the better, but by late afternoon I'd had it. My entire body hurt.

After taking a hot shower and washing my hair, I turned on the television. Tuesday's a bad night in TV land, and I was thumbing through the program guide looking for something to entertain myself with. I had the volume on low and was hardly listening to the evening newscast when a familiar name grabbed my attention.

"... found dead this afternoon in his West Side apartment. Although the autopsy has not been completed, the police are calling Gannett's death a suicide."

Snatching the remote control from the coffee table, I turned up the volume.

"People close to the popular actor say that he had been in good spirits and excited about his career. Another source, however, has said that Gannett was subject to mood swings, and in the past had sought treatment for problems with drugs.

"Recently Gannett had been linked romantically with actress Katharine Parker, shown here leaving the Medical Examiner's office earlier today."

An image of a young woman with spiky dark hair came onto the screen. It was the same woman whose smile had radiated from the photograph on the mirror in The Dancing Fool, but she wasn't smiling now. A microphone was thrust toward her but she waved it away.

"Miss Parker had no comment," the newscaster continued. "Gannett, who was a member of the Hell's Kitchen Actors' Workshop, first came to public attention with his role as the brawling, womanizing cop in the popular TV series *Undercover Squad*. He had just signed with Tri-Star Pictures for the lead in an action-romance feature film opposite sultry film star . . ."

I was stunned, almost as if someone close to me had died. It wasn't because Gannett as an actor had touched me deeply, or that I'd identified with him. In some way my sense of loss may have been for Eddie. He'd liked Gannett, and he'd been so proud of the actor's visit to the club. Who knows? I might have liked Gannett too.

As a short clip from *Undercover Squad* ran on the television screen, the picture of Gannett and his friends over the Dalmatian-spotted bar floated through my mind. He'd looked so happy. Funny, how well people can conceal what's going on inside.

"That's actor Brad Gannett, dead at twenty-eight." The TV anchorwoman was shaking her head sadly. Two fellow newscasters picked up her cue. "A shame," one of them said. "Gannett was just starting to make it big." The other agreed: "His life was too short."

On that unhappy note, the news faded into a commercial break—a perky song and dance about a fast-food restaurant. I flicked off the set.

Gannett's life was too short. Life *is* too short. For a few minutes I sat there, surrounded by the trappings that added up to plenty of free time, enough money, and lots of love, brooding about a man I'd never met.

Finally prying myself from the recliner, I looked out the window. The street lights had already come on and their yellow glare glanced off the snow. Next door, a neighbor was trying to coerce his car up an icy driveway. The squeal of spinning tires tore through the usual quiet. He made it finally, and the street fell silent again. For a moment I felt incredibly lonely.

Our neighbor on the other side, a pleasant, plump woman with two chubby children and a hefty husband, had said something about getting together for dinner one night while Sam was gone. Was it too late to call her and say, "What about right now?" Probably. But there were a couple of movies I'd been wanting to see, and Amanda's husband, Tony, was working nights that week. Maybe I could talk her into meeting me at a theater.

Or . . . at The Dancing Fool on West Forty-fifth Street, Texas Line Dancing Night would be starting in a little while.

Life is short, and then you die. I picked up the phone and dialed Amanda's number.

She's my dearest friend, and I love her, but . . .

"You know that Tony and I are working on our marriage," she said piously when I asked if she wanted to go to The Dancing Fool.

Whenever I suggest anything to Amanda that doesn't involve hearth and home, she never fails to remind me of the work she and Tony are doing on their marriage. I've heard so much about this work that it's starting to sound like pure drudgery.

"So? Are you working on it right now? I thought Tony was on swing shift."

"Well, yes, he is."

"Then come with me. You can't very well work on your marriage when Tony's not home. It's Texas Line Dancing tonight. You won't even have to look at another man, much less touch one."

Our cab rounded the corner, bringing The Dancing Fool into view, and Amanda said softly, "Wow! I wasn't expecting that. It's fabulous!"

The Dancing Fool looked like the happenin' place Eddie wanted it to become. It was darkness that had made the difference. The trash-filled gutters, the graffiti, the shabby tenements, had faded into a picturesque urban backdrop. What we focused on—what everyone coming around that corner would focus on—was the neon sign, the feet dancing across the front of the old concrete building. These feet flickered through the dark, beckoning us with a kaleidoscope of inviting colors.

The bright beam of a spotlight mounted atop the club's roof fell on a red velvet rope draped between brass stanchions on the sidewalk, focusing attention on those who passed between them, made their way up the driveway, and walked through the door of The Dancing Fool.

The stanchions were there for effect, not function. There wasn't a line, which considering the below-freezing temperature was understandable. But there were people. That was the surprising thing, or at least it surprised me. There weren't enough of them to be called a crowd, and they didn't look as if they were ready to climb over each other's bodies to get inside, but The Dancing Fool had customers moving through its door, eagerly waiting to pay hard cash.

Amanda's decidedly mixed feelings about coming with me were causing her no end of anxiety, and as the cab pulled to the curb she gripped my arm. "This is so exciting, but remember, I can't stay long. I hope Tony never finds out about this. I told him we were going to the movies, you know. . . ."

"I know. I know." I was a little miffed. In Penn Station

when Amanda and I met, my ring had gotten a quick look and a "Very pretty." That out of the way, she'd started talking about her damned marriage again.

"I don't plan to stay long, either," I assured her. "This is a show of support for an old friend."

I was kidding myself. The moment the beat of the music coming from inside the club reached my ears, I started keeping time with my feet. As we passed between the velvet ropes and walked through the black door, energy seemed to surge through me and all my shoveling and painting aches disappeared.

There was a small clot of people just past the coat-check, waiting to hand money over to a golden-haired, chiseled-cheekboned young man who, for the record, would have struck me as flat-out gorgeous if he had not been wearing leather pants, which I loathe. Amanda and I fell into line behind two couples. They were madly faddish and all set for Texas Line Dancing in their Western-style shirts and cowboy boots. One of the women had on a black leather skirt at least ten inches long. They were also madly young, and had a cultivated "hipper than thou" look to them. After giving us a supercilious once-over, they ignored us.

I wouldn't have given that a second thought if Amanda hadn't leaned toward me and said, "How embarrassing. We're not dressed right for this."

The thumping rock-a-billy-type music was so loud that I thought I'd misunderstood her.

"What?"

She put her mouth near my ear. "Our clothes are wrong. We look out of it."

How does a New Yorker dress "right" for Texas Line Dancing? My answer to that question had been black corduroy pants, a white shirt and, my *pièce de résistance*, a purple vest. Cowboys wear vests, don't they? My heavy boots were more appropriate for an ice slick than for a cattle drive, but hey! I live in New York, I don't drive cows.

"You can take the woman out of the suburbs, but it's hard to take the suburbs out of the woman," I quipped.

I meant to kid my friend, but when Amanda heard that, her mouth sagged. This was no laughing matter for her.

In the right circumstances, Amanda is stunning. That's not just my opinion. Men of a certain age and type can be depended upon to worship her, and I know at least two women who made not very successful attempts to copy her look. But these circumstances were wrong. For the very young and trendy, Amanda was, I'm sorry to say, not worthy of a second glance. Her yellow silk dress with the flared skirt had been the right length two years earlier, but now it was too long to be hip and too short to pass as a daring fashion statement.

There was also the matter of her hair, which for several weeks had been giving her almost as much trouble as her marriage. In the grip of some hellish need for change she had let a lunatic beautician talk her into a permanent. It wasn't a complete disaster, but the mass of too-tight ringlets changed her appearance, and not for the better. Her features looked smaller and, under certain lights, pinched.

Taking up one of her curls, Amanda twisted it like a cord and held it in front of her face. "Frizz. I have to get a trim." She sounded apologetic.

As we approached the beautiful young man collecting money, it seemed as if I might have to apologize too. I'd promised Amanda a free evening, but the young man— Did he have the most perfect cleft in his chin or what? It looked as if Michelangelo had pressed his thumb there— smiled his million-watt smile and I almost forgave him his leather pants. "Good evening, ladies. That will be ten dollars each."

"I thought . . ." began Amanda.

"Don't touch their money, Steve!"

Eddie's shout from near the bar carried over the music, and the music was loud. Dodging a line of dancers, he trotted across the floor and grabbed the two of us in a bear hug. After that we got separate hugs, mine first,

Amanda's next and longer, and probably harder.

Eddie had dispensed with the black leather and jeans and was all set for the cattle drive in a blue Western shirt with beaded trim. With this, he wore a black shoestring tie and a big, gleaming silver tie clasp in the shape of a steer's head. The silver settings of two turquoise rings shone from his fingers, and his silver belt buckle was bigger than my fist. I would have bet my pile-lined boots that not too far away there was a Stetson hat to top off this outfit. When Eddie plays a part, he plays it to the hilt.

He was so clearly a person of importance in The Dancing Fool that, having been on the receiving end of his public hug, I felt quite special. I wouldn't have thought it possible that Steve the gatekeeper's knockout smile could get any bigger and more welcoming, but damned if it didn't! And it wasn't my imagination that the snotty trendettes who had been in front of us turned and ogled. When Eddie held Amanda at arm's length and said, "God, you look great," and then said to me, "and so do you," we were no longer two suburban hausfraus in the wrong clothes. We were part of the in-crowd.

Eddie led us to a table—his table—and I grew warm under the gazes of the people around us. As Amanda slid gracefully onto one of the plastic chairs, she forgot about her split ends and tossed her head so that her springy curls went all over the place. Her flare for drama was back, and I was glad to see it.

Amanda pronounced the brandy alexander Eddie brought her "perfect." She's a brandy alexander kind of woman. I'm beer. In this case it was domestic, on draft, but it went down like champagne as I took in the scene at The Dancing Fool.

It's the crowd that makes the party, and this crowd was lively and good-looking. Their excited smiles, the garish Dalmatian bar, the thumping music, the rhythmic stamping feet, all thrilled me. What had been tatty in the bleak light of a winter day had become, with the help of energetic people, subdued lighting, and a four-piece band in

Western shirts—Tex and the Tone Rangers—terrific. I couldn't sit still. Even before I got on the floor, my shoulders were swaying, my feet tapping.

It's a funny thing I have about dancing. I love it in a way that seems almost primitive. Maybe it is. Maybe a couple of million eons ago when my fish forbears grew their rudimentary legs and climbed out of the primordial stew, the first thing they did was a quick shuffle-ball-change.

I'm pretty good on a dance floor, too. It beats me why. I'm not especially musical. The violin my mother forced into my hands when I was nine might as well have been a chainsaw for the sounds I drew from it. As for sports, I'm just adequate in some of the gentle ones, like swimming and badminton, and in the tough ones—tennis, skiing, the ones requiring strength and coordination—I'm a mess. But give me a decent beat, show me a step once or twice, and I've got it. And I even manage to look good doing it. With a terrific partner, or surrounded by a chorus line of terrific dancers, I can look . . . pretty good.

Pretty good, but not wonderful. It may have something to do with my body type, or speed, or grace. For a long time I tried to cross the divide that separates pretty good from wonderful, but I never did acquire the elusive thing that makes Broadway casting directors fling their arms wide and yell, "She's the one!"

I did acquire something else, though: a good eye. I know a wonderful dancer when I see one. The leggy young woman with the shoulder-length red hair standing in a spotlight in front of the other dancers was one of those.

She appeared to dance almost without effort, and made it seem as if what she was doing was totally spontaneous. Watching her, I knew that wasn't so. Every part of her— feet, arms, head—was perfectly in synch—and every moment had been refined until the final product was an act she could have taken to Broadway. Nevertheless, she made it look as if *anybody* could do what she was doing.

From the efforts of the people following her lead, you could tell they all believed her.

I recognized her from the photo Eddie had shown me. "That's Dawn?"

Eddie was lapping the woman up with his eyes. Infatuation isn't a rare state of affairs for my friend, though. There was a time when he would have thrown his Burberry trench coat over the nastiest puddle in Manhattan for Amanda.

Catching me looking at him, Eddie grinned self-consciously. "Just . . . call it Starr-gazing."

I leaned close. "You said your relationship is 'on hold.' What does that mean?"

"Dawn wants to concentrate on her stage career. She's spending a lot of time taking acting lessons and going to auditions, so we've . . . um . . . cooled our romance. Just for a while," he added.

I'd never thought that the two—a stage career and a romance—were mutually exclusive, but then again my stage career never went very far, so maybe I was wrong.

"She's the best, isn't she?" he said.

She was also the best-looking. Oh, I know that beauty is relative and in the eyes of the beholder and all that, but to put it simply, the god of conventional beauty—the one who bestows perfect features and creamy skin and shiny hair—had smiled long and hard on Dawn Starr. And the little devil who fills out the rest of the package had smiled too and given her a real statuesque showgirl body.

Show business is tough and there are no guarantees. For every performer who gets a call-back after an audition there are probably a thousand who get a "Thank you." But there was a chance that if Dawn Starr ever had the good fortune to be in the right place at the right time, some casting director just might look at her and shout, "She's the one!" It wasn't only that she was exceptionally pretty, or that she was a magnitude better than anyone else with a sense of rhythm, a graceful body, and the willingness to work hard. Dawn had that rare thing called "star quality." Regardless of who else was on the floor, she was the one who held your eyes.

I nudged Amanda. "That's Dawn Starr. She's an actress-dancer type. Eddie's in love or something."

Amanda sniffed. "That name's made up."

Well, well. There was a snide remark that said as much about the remarker as the remarkee. Before Amanda married Tony LaMarca, she was Amanda Paradise and people sometimes said the same thing about her.

When the band took a short break, Dawn joined us at our table. From the way Eddie stumbled over her name introducing us, you'd have thought he was introducing someone from his Celebrity Lounge.

I'm big on handshakes. Sure, they're dumb. They probably date back to some weird cautionary routine like making sure the Lord of Fife didn't have a dagger in his hand when he crossed your moat. Nevertheless, when I meet someone new my hand automatically goes out. It's the legacy of too many interviews.

I stuck out my hand.

Seeing it, Dawn Starr smiled as if I'd offered a sweet, soft puppy across the plastic tabletop. Lifting her pale hand with its perfect pink nails, she brushed it over mine so softly that my skin might have been skimmed by a dewy rose petal.

Amanda, who hasn't run the interview gantlet so often, didn't offer a hand and so didn't get her palm anointed. Instead, she got a blue-eyed smile that looked warm enough to melt the ice in the gutters outside.

"It's such a pleasure to meet Eddie's old friends. I hear you all go back years and years."

Three years don't add up to years and years. Had Eddie, trying to impress her with his stability, exaggerated, or was Dawn simply the gushy type?

The beauteous young Steve who had greeted us at the door was on bartender duty now. He brought Dawn a drink which looked suspiciously like diet cola, and as she cooed her thanks at him, Eddie confirmed my suspicion.

"Dawn doesn't often drink alcohol."

He was drinking alcohol. For that matter he was selling alcohol. Nevertheless, he made it sound as if for her abstinence Dawn was a whole lot closer to heaven than the rest of us.

"It's just that it's so fattening," Saint Dawn said. "I have to watch my weight."

I pushed what was left of my beer aside, but Amanda, generally a stalwart member of the fat police, surprised me by killing off what was left of her brandy alexander in one long swallow. Steve, who was standing by our table, smirked when she thrust her empty glass toward him and said, "Would you please bring me another one of these?"

"Sure."

His hazel eyes were lazy and suggestive, and what they suggested was, *I will do this for you, and maybe later you will do something for me.* He reached for the glass and at the same time positioned himself so that he could take a not-very-surreptitious look down the front of both Dawn's shirt and Amanda's dress.

Eddie had rested his arm across the back of Dawn's chair. Almost as if he couldn't help himself, his fingers began combing the red fringe on the shoulder of her shirt. It was an intimate gesture. Dawn appeared not to notice, but when Eddie's hand brushed her curls, the little smile that seemed built into her lips grew wider.

As we waited for the music to begin again, conversation around our table was strained. The problem was, we all had different things on our minds.

Eddie wanted so much for us to like Dawn—and for Dawn to like us, and of course for Dawn to like him—that I think he would have agreed with anything any of us said. This fawning quality in Eddie was hard to take.

Amanda, on the other hand, stopped just short of being rude to Dawn.

"You're from California? Where in California?" she demanded of the redhead.

"Southern California. Anaheim, near Disneyland."

"You lived there all your life."

If Dawn noticed that she was being grilled, she didn't show it. Her smile never wavered and her answers were anything but evasive.

"I was born in Colorado. My father was in the Air Force," she explained, "and before he retired I had lived in half-a-dozen states. But since I was sixteen, I've been a California girl."

"This is her first time in New York," Eddie said. "And she loves it here. Don't you, Dawn?"

Dawn nodded. "It's so exciting. I adore the crowds, even on the subways, and the streets are like"—she smiled happily—"theater."

Anyone who adores the crowds on Manhattan's subways isn't playing with a full deck. As for the theater of the streets, the less said about it the better.

So Dawn gushed, Amanda grilled, Eddie fawned, and I waited impatiently for the music to start. Steve returned with Amanda's drink and then, eyes fixed on the third button of my shirt, asked me if I'd like another beer.

"No thanks."

"And you know Disneyland well?" Amanda was asking in a tone that was anything but Disneyland-happy. "You've been to Frontier Land, and the Pirates of the Caribbean?"

Amanda's elbow was propped on the table and her fist was clenched under her chin. Not only is Amanda usually one of the sweetest people around, but I'd never known her to have the remotest interest in Disneyland. Embarrassed, I interrupted.

"I understand you were in a road company production of *A Chorus Line*, Dawn. I tried out for the parts of Cassie and Judy. I would have taken any part, actually. Eventually I got to understudy Judy, but that was a long time ago." And since the woman playing Judy had the constitution of a linebacker, I never once went on.

"It couldn't have been that long ago," Dawn said

sweetly. "You're not that old." She took a sip of her diet soda. "Of course, everyone wanted to be Cassie, with that great dance number. I ended up playing Maggie, so I got to do a little ballet."

"Where exactly did that company play?" Amanda asked Dawn.

I was relieved to see the musicians returning to the bandstand.

"Most of the time we were on the West Coast. Then, last year I did a season at the San Fernando Playhouse. I was Anybody's in *West Side Story*."

"Anybody's," Amanda repeated after a few seconds. "That must have been an interesting role."

The guitar player struck a couple of chords.

"That's my signal," Dawn said, tilting her head prettily. "You guys, too. Come on now."

Dawn and Eddie headed out onto the dance floor. I started after them, but Amanda held me back for a moment.

"She's a phony."

"About what? She looks like a real showgirl type to me. She probably has been in those shows."

Amanda started to say something, but the dancing lines were forming. "I'm going to dance, now. Are you?"

Shrugging, Amanda followed me to the floor and got into line beside me. Within a minute or so, the scowl left her face, and she stomped and spun and jumped around with the rest of us trying to follow Dawn's lead. Eddie had started the set alongside Dawn, but he wasn't in her class. After stumbling over his feet once or twice, he scooted into the line between Amanda and me. "Isn't she fantastic!" he said.

Amanda's lips moved but I didn't hear what she said.

5

I SPLASHED COOL WATER FROM THE sparkling brass faucet onto my face, and dried my skin with a satiny paper towel. Flattering soft pink lights circled the mirror above the black marble sink. The walls and floor of the ladies' room were ceramic tile, pink and black. On a shelf under the mirror were some little goodies a woman who happened to find herself in need of repair in a dance club might find useful: hand lotion, perfumes, cotton puffs, hair spray.

Don't get the idea that all this had been put together for the sweaty masses. The bourgeoisie was lined up two floors down waiting to use the cramped basement restrooms. My celebrity status had been conferred upon me by Eddie. "Treat yourself," he said, graciously handing me the key to the Celebrity Lounge. Would he have been so gracious if any real celebrities had been around that night? Probably not, but maybe. What is it that celebrities do differently than the rest of us in the ladies' room?

The room was big enough to accommodate some substantial furniture. Against one wall there was a slouchy rose-colored velvet settee. Across from it an old-fashioned mahogany side table was flanked by two red brocade chairs—the type called "boudoir" chairs. None of the furniture was new or even newly upholstered, but the effect was nice, kind of funky and comfortable. I could imagine myself lounging on the settee. Maybe Christie Brinkley would perch her size-four self on the red brocade and talk about life after Billy Joel. Tina Turner might join us, and wouldn't she have some stories to tell. She'd probably want the settee for herself, though.

Before leaving the room, I examined the perfumes on the shelf. Giorgio sounded good. I gave myself a quick spritz and the fragrance wrapped itself around me. What a nice touch, and expensive. Then I examined the label on the bottle's bottom. "Marvelous Mimics, Inc." The other perfumes had the same label. Oh, well. It's wonderful feeling like you're getting the star treatment, even for a few hallucinatory moments.

The Celebrity Lounge was almost dark once the soft pink luminescence of the ladies' room disappeared. As I made my way past the banquettes, I paused near the one where, the day before, I'd sat mimicking Brad Gannett. Eddie hadn't brought up the actor's death. Maybe he didn't know about it yet. How awful, though, that The Dancing Fool's best-known celebrity guest had killed himself less than a week after his visit to the club.

The twang of the guitar announced the start of another set. The music rose, and as I stepped into the upstairs hall, the floor began vibrating under my feet. I had locked the Lounge and was about to return to the dance floor when I saw that the door to the back part of the building was open. A light was shining from the direction of the office. It wasn't steady, but rose and fell, one instant illuminating the walls, the next leaving them in shadow.

Perhaps Eddie was back there and I could return the Lounge key to him.

I was partway down the hall when it became clear that the light wasn't coming from the office. It was coming from the room with the formidable lock on the other side of the hall. Someone had left the door ajar. I gave it a slight shove and, as it opened, it squeaked. Then I had a clear view into a little room.

The overhead lights were off and my eyes were immediately drawn to what I first thought was a television set. It was small—maybe nine inches in diameter—and the figures flickering across it were in black and white. My glasses were in my purse and rather than dig for them, I moved farther into the room.

It was the inside of the club the screen was picking up. And the people inside the club. The images passing across the monitor were remarkably clear. There was Steve at the cash register behind the bar, and a second later the woman working at the coat-check. I could actually make out the tweed fabric of a coat passing over her counter. After that I saw the narrow hallway outside the downstairs restrooms. Still a line at the ladies' room. And then, abruptly, I was taken inside the basement ladies' room. There was Amanda, lips stretched wide, applying that glossy crimson lipstick she loves.

A couple of shelves on the wall beside the monitor held rows of video cassettes lined up neat as soldiers at attention. On the floor beneath the shelves there was an old-fashioned safe with a combination lock.

Somewhere nearby a man coughed. The music from downstairs permeated the entire building, but this cough was so close that it startled me. As I turned toward the door it squeaked again and swung wider.

A man stepped into the room.

I couldn't see his face clearly but he was taller than Eddie, with wide shoulders. He stood dead-center in the doorway, blocking it.

Though I don't recall feeling fear at that point, I must have been nervous, because I reacted by stepping deeper into the room, until I was stopped by some cartons stacked against the back wall.

The tall man came closer, until finally he loomed over me. That's when I got that horrible trapped feeling. With the music pounding, nobody downstairs would hear me if I screamed. My heart began slamming against my chest.

"What the hell do you think you're doing?"

The room suddenly seemed airless and I couldn't gather my breath to respond. The man grabbed my upper arm and repeated, angrily, "What the hell are you doing in here?"

He was so close that even in the dim light I could see his clenched jaw and the sinews standing out in his neck. My impression was of a thug. I shook my head and mumbled, stupid with fear, "Nothing, nothing."

"Nothing?" The corner of the man's mouth lifted. "Bullshit! I ought to call the police."

He tightened his grip until my arm hurt. The key to the Celebrity Lounge was in my free hand and I lifted it to show him. "I'm Eddie's friend. He told me I could . . ."

A sound from the hall caused the man to glance over his shoulder. At the same time, someone said, "Hey, Max! Let her go! She's a friend of Eddie's."

Max! It was Eddie's partner who was manhandling me.

"You mind your own business, T'Bird," he said.

He had loosened his grip, and while his attention was diverted I wrenched my arm free and scooted past him and out of the room.

T'Bird, an unlikely knight in shining armor, held a metal wastebasket filled with trash in front of his chest. He might have intended it as a weapon, but I think it was probably more of a shield. T'Bird looked scared, as if he'd inadvertently cornered a rabid animal. Just the same, he didn't back down, and I was grateful.

Max moved into the hall and shut the door behind him, but not before T'Bird got a look at the images flickering across the monitor. His eyes narrowed, and after a few seconds he looked at Max and tilted his head.

"You're watching the restrooms? That seems awfully strange to me."

"The restrooms," Max said, "are where most drug deals go down. We keep an eye on things intermittently.

And I don't think you're much of a judge of what's strange, so mind your own business.''

I was close to the stairs now. I could probably make it to the first floor before this brute could touch me again, but a strong sense of outrage combined with my fear.

"I'm a friend of Eddie's." My voice was shaking but I went on. "My name's Bonnie. You may own this club, but you have no right to touch me."

"Eddie's friend Bonnie?" Max repeated my name, "Bonnie," and his brow furrowed. I could almost see his hot fury start to dissolve. He squeezed his eyes shut tight—"Oh, no"—and wiped at his face with the palm of his hand as if trying to erase the last few minutes.

"Damn! You're the woman Eddie said might come in and make sense out of our office." A rueful smile played across his face. It might have been disarming if I hadn't been so angry. Turning his neck, he said, "Hit me. Go ahead. Or take that trash can there"—he nodded toward T'Bird—"and dump it on me. I'm Eddie's partner, Max, and I'm a jerk."

Max did everything but grovel at my feet. He managed to put on such an engrossing act that I almost forgot that T'Bird was there until he put in, sarcastically, "So kiss the big lug and make up."

Max raised his eyes briefly to the ceiling, and then said curtly to the other man, "It's over, buddy. Get on with your cleaning. If you're through up here, a lot of bottles are piling up behind the bar."

"Here today, back in the gutter tomorrow," Max said softly when T'Bird had disappeared down the stairs. Then he went back into overdrive with the apologies.

In the light of the hall, with Max oozing niceness, I modified my initial impression of him. Or at least his appearance. He was tall and looked like he worked out with weights, but he wasn't grotesquely muscular. His receding light brown hair was gathered into a straggly take on the all-too-familiar ponytail, which emphasized a somewhat heavy jaw, but there was nothing ferocious about the way he looked. His gray eyes were wide and clear, and his smile, which I was seeing much of now, showed a lot of straight white teeth.

"It's just that there's so much expensive security equipment in there," he explained. "Not to mention our safe. We use the room for storage, too. I thought you were casing the place. I didn't realize you might be coming to work with us."

That, of course, was the reason for his profuse apologies. Eddie had told his partner that I might be the inexpensive solution to the mess in their office—the filing, phone-answering equivalent of T'Bird.

If I'd had any misgivings about turning down Eddie's job offer, my meeting with Max took care of them. I didn't want to work for him. I've endured, at least temporarily, employers who were rude, who yelled, who were sarcastic, but I would not put up with anyone who squeezed my arm.

I was waiting at the bar while Amanda said goodbye to Eddie. Steve, who had been stacking glasses, paused in his work when I asked for some water. As he filled a glass for me, I noticed that the photo of Brad Gannett was no longer there.

"I heard Brad Gannett killed himself," I said. "Is that why his picture is gone?"

Steve sighed. "Yeah. Max took it down. Thought it was too depressing. I guess a lot of women are going to be crying tonight."

"I guess so. Did you meet Gannett when he came here last Thursday night?"

"Sure. He seemed like a nice guy, too. Down to earth just like anybody else. I guess none of us ever know what's happening in another man's head . . ."

"That's right."

". . . because I've got to tell you, when Gannett came back on Saturday, he had some nasty attitude."

"This past Saturday? I didn't know he'd been here more than once."

Nodding, Steve went back to stacking glasses. "He and Terry came by."

"Terry?"

"The same young guy he'd been with the first time. They were too early. We open later on Disco Nights. I was the only one around."

"Oh. What did they want?"

He shrugged. "At first I thought they just wanted to hang out, and I would have been happy to let them sit around here and have a couple of drinks, but . . ."

Steve's eyes darted around the room; then he leaned across the bar. Realizing that I was going to hear something juicy, I scooted closer.

". . . If you ask me, Gannett was high. On something. You know what I mean? He was all weird and aggressive, like he was looking for trouble. I wasn't surprised when I heard on the news that he was a druggie."

"I got the impression from the news that he hadn't used drugs for a while."

"Sure, but you know how it is, Bonnie. Where there's smoke, there's fire. You want to know what Gannett said?"

Of course I did.

"Gannett said, 'I need to talk to the ponytailed bozo who runs this dump.' "

Steve's cleft chin tightened in outrage at the memory. "I mean, as nice as everyone had been to Gannett and his friends—free drinks and everything—that was rotten. Of course I didn't take it personally." He ran his fingers through his golden blond hair as if to show me that he wasn't a ponytailed bozo. "But that was cold of him. Don't you think so?"

"It sure was."

Ponytailed bozo. There was a time when I would have done the bunny hop on burning coals for one special man with a ponytail, and to this day I wouldn't call him a bozo. But Eddie and Max . . .

I couldn't help wondering which one of the ponytailed bozos Gannett had been looking for.

Amanda had caught my eye with a "Let's go" signal, but as I turned away from the bar Steve touched my arm.

"Hey, Bonnie? Don't mention to Max that I told you this. Okay? He doesn't want rumors getting around. Says they can ruin a club's reputation. He's trying real hard to keep this place clean."

"Sure," I said.

"You actually liked Dawn?" Amanda asked as our cab bounced over a pothole on its race down Ninth Avenue toward Penn Station.

Glancing across at her, I shrugged. "She's nice enough. She seems more like a showgirl than a ballroom-dancer type, but she's got a lot of talent."

"She's a phony."

"I take it you don't like her."

"She makes my skin crawl. And I'm sure she's a lot older than she looks."

Amanda was huddled into a corner of the cab, and when light from a storefront flared across her face, I was surprised by how unhappy she looked. But then Amanda hadn't had a great night. In the heat of the club her hair had gotten even frizzier. She'd broken a heel stomping on the floor, and she hadn't ever gotten comfortable with jumping, clapping, and yelling "Yippee" simultaneously. On top of that, I think she'd had a few too many brandy alexanders. Her words slurred when she added, "Dawn's not good enough for Eddie."

Being good enough for Eddie doesn't necessarily position a woman at the top of the goodness scale. I put Amanda's sour remarks down to jealousy.

"Did you meet his partner, Max?"

Amanda brightened. "Oh, I liked Max a lot. When my heel broke he took hold of my arm and kept me from falling on the floor. He's a real gentleman.''

So there you go: My arm-squeezing goon had turned out to be my friend's arm-holding gentleman.

It was about eleven o'clock when Amanda and I got to Penn Station. We hugged and started toward our separate trains, but then it occurred to me that I'd forgotten something important.

"Wait, Amanda." I ran after her. "I need to ask you something. Sam and I haven't set a date yet, but when we do get married, will you be my matron of honor? And will you help me with a dress and food and all those other things? I don't know much about weddings."

She squealed with delight, and we hugged again. Even at that hour Penn Station was busy, but no one paid attention to us except a derelict dozing in a nearby seat. Opening one bloodshot eye he growled, "People tryin' to sleep around here."

6

THE BIG CLOCK OVER THE DOUBLE doors had a second hand, and every time it completed a circuit and another minute passed, I became more annoyed. My fellow social-dance instructor, a slickly handsome Realtor named Monte, who always smelled as if he'd been dipped in Brut, was late again. Our class waited, audibly, on the uncomfortable metal folding chairs that lined one of the studio's walls.

The second hand went around again. Seething, I called to my students, "Please get your partners and come to the center of the floor." The heck with Monte! I'd go it alone.

I'd told Eddie that my Wednesday afternoon class was *not* made up of overweight housewives in knit pants, and that was, to some extent, true. Of my dozen pupils, half were housewives, but only a couple had reason to recoil when they got on the scale. What I hadn't mentioned was that my class was composed entirely of retirees who either couldn't afford to winter in Florida, or didn't want to. Knit pants were much in evidence, as were polyester print blouses and support stockings. There was leather, sure, but it knew its place—sensible shoes, not skirts or, God forbid, pants. This was not the Manhattan club scene.

But let me tell you, when I put the needle down on the record, some of my retirees shed their years. The Alonzos—he with white hair oiled until it shone like my sister-in-law's silverplate Sunday best, and she draped in flowing pastel chiffon—moved with catlike grace and with eyes locked like adagio dancers, and the way my retired fireman swept his "lady friend" into his arms and gazed into her eyes almost made me look forward to reaching seventy-five.

On the other hand, there was Mrs. Mintz, who always showed up alone and not only talked nonstop but at the same time did interesting things with her false teeth. She wasn't above removing them for inspection, either. And there was Mr. Bottie, who arrived with his wife but invariably gave her the slip so that he could do interesting things with his hands to any other woman unlucky enough to get within striking distance of the old fool.

That afternoon Mr. Bottie, who was bald as an egg and, come to think about it, shaped like one, zeroed in on my unpartnered status like a bee targeting a hibiscus. Sidling up to me, he slipped his arm around my waist and said, like a character in a thirties comedy, "That bum Monte doesn't know how to treat a lady! I'll rescue you, babe!"

As I gently pushed my ardent septuagenarian back toward his wife, the door at the far side of the room swung open.

I'm nearsighted, but not so badly that I mistook the man who walked in for Monte. This man was thinner and taller, and had longer, darker hair. After glancing around the room, his gaze settled on me. He stared for a moment, then called, "Be right there." Sitting down, he unzipped his duffle bag. "Your other teacher quit. I'm supposed to get a locker, but the woman at the desk gave me a hard time about that," he explained as he changed from his heavy snow boots to leather shoes.

My class—there were no shrinking violets among this group—had turned as one to stare. Mrs. Mintz, whose stream of words was generally delivered in a monotone, demanded sharply, "Who is he? Does anybody know who he is?" Someone else complained, "He's wearing jeans! This isn't right. The Center's paying for Monte. Why would Monte quit? Monte studied with the Fred Astaire Dance Studio."

I stared as rudely as the rest of them but it wasn't out of yearning for the fragrant Monte. Shoes on, the new man crossed the floor toward us, and with every step he took I stared harder, trying to clear what had to be an apparition from my vision. By the time our substitute teacher was in front of me I was totally confused and speechless, too.

"Well, well," he said, with an eyebrow lifted. "This is an interesting turn. I didn't know you were . . . one of us."

I gaped stupidly for another few seconds before saying, "I didn't know you were one of us, either."

"What are you talking about?" one of the students grumbled. "Are we ever going to get this show on the road?"

"You dance?" I asked the new man.

The question made him smile. "A little. My name's John. What do we have for music?"

It was a relief to step away from him even for the instant it took to put on a record. Today he was John, freelance social-dance instructor with a dazzling smile. The night before he'd been T'Bird, freelance janitor with a broken tooth.

And he could dance! A little? No. A lot. My pupils forgot Monte fast. I forgot Monte real fast. I'd put on an old Judy Garland recording that was kind of tricky for my group and for me, too. As I've said, I'm good, but not wonderful.

The record was scratched and the Y's sound system hardly state-of-the-art. Judy sounded as if she was battling a sore throat and the horns were dull, as if they were being played into a mattress. It didn't matter. "Zing Went the Strings of My Heart" had never sounded zingier to me. John moved like an expert and helped me move like one.

As for my class, they had never been so attentive. The Alonzos' concentration level was fierce, and when John said to them, "Quicker steps," they sped up until they looked like a couple who danced for a living. Mr. Bottie was kept so busy that he didn't have time for any funny business with his hands.

Only Mrs. Mintz remained true to form. She'd lowered her voice to its usual monotone, but the patter was relentless: "I know you. Where do I know you from? Are you famous?" she babbled as John demonstrated a basic foxtrot slow-quick-quick step with her. "Who is he? Isn't he an actor?" she asked me when John moved on to someone else.

I had recognized our new teacher by then, but if he didn't want his cover blown, I wasn't going to blow it. Rather than answer Mrs. Mintz, I cut in on the Alonzos. I was feeling less confident than usual with my class, but Mr. Alonzo and I executed a turn that seemed to me pretty nifty and clean. I probably turned red when John called, "Not bad, you two, but keep your knees softer, Bonnie, and go into the turn half a beat sooner. That way you won't be so hard on your partner's back."

John demonstrated this with me a few minutes later, and you know what? Despite what was by then a serious case of performance anxiety, I did it better.

For the last dance, we put on a big-band version of Cole Porter's "Night and Day." When Ginger danced with Fred, did she feel as flawless as I did following John's lead through the tricky steps?

The hour ended with my exhilarated class asking—demanding—that John return the next week, and permanently replace the now-despised Monte.

They were filing out the door a few minutes later when Mrs. Mintz stopped in her tracks, spun, and snapped her false teeth.

"John Daly. That's who you are. You were on Broadway. I saw you in *Isadora*. And *Dance Fever*. You won a Tony. Am I right?'' With that, she put her hands firmly on her hips as if daring him to argue.

''Looks like you got my number.''

''Well? Where have you been for the last twenty-some years?'' she demanded.

''I took a sabbatical.''

He was smiling but there was a bite to his voice. That didn't bother Mrs. Mintz. Satisfied, she clicked her teeth into place and left.

As John sat down to change his shoes, he was shaking his head. ''Ah, how I've missed the roar of the greasepaint and the smell of the crowd. For this I spent the morning in a dentist's chair. Did they recruit those geezers from a geriatric ward?''

''They're from a senior center. Some of them are good,'' I added, defending my group.

''Humph. But what the hell. The job's in the profession, I suppose, though this''—he glanced around the studio—''is at the profession's outer edge.''

I'd defended this job to Eddie, but that had been different. I hadn't really felt defensive. What I mean is, regardless of what Eddie had said, I'd felt like this was a decent dance job. John's criticisms, though, put me in a different frame of mind. I was embarrassed about my students, and about the studio, too.

The place wasn't used only for dance classes. Exercise mats and easels were stacked against one wall, and another wall was covered with posters from the Lamaze childbirth class. Oil paint dappled the floor. John's eyes stopped moving when they came to the area at one side of the studio where I'd chalked *L*'s and *R*'s on the floor. I'd used them to demonstrate to a couple of students who were having an especially hard time: ''Left foot here, right foot there.'' At the time, it had seemed like a reasonable thing to do, and it had worked in a rudimentary way, but now, as John took it all in, I saw things through his eyes, and cringed.

Why was I so enthralled with a man who, in his other life, was a janitor called T'Bird? That required going back to when I was about fifteen.

I had a tendency at the time to develop brief, wild infatuations. I still do, but in those days my love objects were often men whom I had no more chance of getting near than I had of going to the moon. These included the usual rock stars and actors, an Olympic swimmer, and, in a transitory cerebral moment, an English poet with the saddest eyes imaginable. I later heard that the poet was a grubby type who didn't wash, but by then he no longer made my pulse race, anyway.

John Daly had been one of these early, fleeting love objects, but he lasted longer than the unwashed poet. To some extent, John may have shaped my life.

When I was four or five, my mother, new to our working-class neighborhood and determined to do the right thing, enrolled me in a dance class. Tap-Toe-Hawaiian. The triple threat of the suburbs, and I wasn't half bad. There were recitals in imitation grass skirts and crepe-paper leis, and in tutus, but my favorites were the ones in tap shoes, when I really made myself heard.

To my mother's surprise, I stayed with the lessons long after my peers had dropped them. The hula gave way to something known by the vague term ''interpretative'' dancing, which meant that I got to writhe around in a long tunic, and by the time I was in my early teens there were flirtations with jazz and ballroom dancing. But through all this, I never thought of dance as a career possibility. Dance was for fun, for exercise. For career there was that other triple threat: typing, steno, bookkeeping.

Then, when I turned fifteen, my mom took me to *Isadora*.

It was the first ''adult'' Broadway musical I'd seen. By adult I mean that it wasn't the Radio City Easter Show or a *Peter Pan* revival. The audience was . . . grown-up. On the stage there was drama, passion, sex, dancing. And, with third billing there was John Daly, in his early twenties and already being talked about as an heir to the great musical stars from a decade earlier. The two leads were more famous, and John's tenor voice had been described by one critic as "weedy," but he was the one I couldn't take my eyes off. Perfection. As for the young woman John partnered on that stage, I would have taken her place in an instant. And *could* have taken her place. That's how I felt when the show was over and the audience burst into thunderous applause. I belonged on the stage.

I saw the show twice more, using my babysitting money, and when *Dance Fever* opened with John in the lead I spent so much time in the audience that I learned the entire show by heart. On the night the Tony Awards were handed out and John Daly stepped to the podium to accept his, I was in front of the television set cheering. My father and brother both thought I'd lost my mind, but my mother understood.

Hollywood followed Broadway for John, but somehow his first movie, the film version of *Dance Fever*, didn't affect me the way the Broadway version had. By then, more tangible love objects had entered my life and I spent most of the movie's two hour running time necking with someone whose name and face have faded from my memory. I do remember that the film was blasted by the critics and didn't do well at the box office. These days the only place it ever turns up is on cable TV at four A.M.

The rumors about John's out-of-control behavior began when he was making his second film. Musicals were dead forever, Hollywood had decided, and John somehow ended up playing the self-sacrificing young father of a dying child. The role didn't suit him. Some of the gossip columns mentioned difficulties on the movie set and problems with drugs and alcohol, but this was the mid-seventies, and rumors of drugs and alcohol went with the territory.

And then John Daly was gone. *Disappeared* is too dramatic a word. If there were any "Whatever happened to John Daly?" stories in the media, I don't remember them.

John wasn't really that big a star. He'd burned brightly, but not for very long, and when he faded away it was as if he'd never been there at all.

And now, here he was, putting his shoes in a dance bag at a Y in a Long Island suburb.

He started for the door, grumbling about the woman at the desk. "I get to have another go at that battle-ax who controls the lockers. What an attitude she has!"

I've never had a problem with the woman myself but could understand why John did. If I'd been less enthralled with this rediscovered star, his smugness would have annoyed me, too.

"She's okay. I'll help you."

It only took a minute to get John's locker problems straightened out.

"Here's your locker number and the combination."

The woman handed him a slip of paper with a series of numbers written on it.

"Locker number eight. Combination eight, sixteen, twenty-four," he read. "That's going to be tough to remember."

I waited while John went off to stow his gear. He'd let it drop that he was going to walk to the train station, so I'd offered him a ride. The station was on my way, but I would have gone out of my way, too.

When John saw my car in the parking lot he gave a long, low whistle. His breath froze in the air.

"It's not mine, really," I said. "It's my fiancé's." As mentioned, the Chrysler had been Eileen's, and is one of the ghost-haunted items I've taken over. Eileen was a tall woman—about five nine—and this is a tall woman's car. Sam bought it for her when her breast cancer was first diagnosed. It was a way of saying "We're going to lick this," a grand gesture. Grand gestures touch me. I hope that Eileen enjoyed this big white beauty. My feelings about it are mixed. I use it gladly but if I ever get a car just for me it will be smaller, faster on the take-off, and cheaper to operate.

"Did I hear Max say you were going to work in the office at The Dancing Fool?" John asked when we were in the car.

I shook my head. "That was an idea of Eddie's. I've already got a job." Before starting the ignition, I slipped one of my business cards from my tote bag and handed it to John.

He smiled when he read it, then tucked the card into a leather wallet. "If I ever have a corporation to move, I'll call you."

"Thanks."

"You're probably smart not getting involved with the club. It seems to be doing all right, but why get mixed up with those jerks who run it? I don't know what Dawn's doing with them. She's got a lot going for her."

I'd already heard enough about the lovely Dawn Starr to hold me for a while. I was more interested in John. Where had he been between *Dance Fever* and The Dancing Fool? I was as curious about those missing twenty years as Mrs. Mintz, but not quite as rude.

Between the Y and the train station there is a quiet stretch of road bordered on one side by a golf course and on the other by trees. This road curves, and at the bottom of a slight decline there's a bridge that turns icy even when the rest of the road is dry. I braked to let an oncoming yellow school bus lumber across, and then steered slowly over the treacherous stretch.

"What about you?" I asked. "Why are you at the club?"

John had leaned back into the cushioned headrest.

"It's temporary, I hope. Ballroom dancing has never been my thing, and lately I've been concentrating more on acting than dancing. But the club's only a couple of blocks from my apartment and I like the scene." He chuckled. "Bright clothes, bright lights, shiny faces. The whole bit. Do you understand?"

"Of course."

"I pick up a few dollars there, too," he added, "and

get a look at the new dances. Sometimes I go back to my place and work them out for myself.''

"Why not work them out at the club?"

"I've thought about 'going public,' " he admitted, "but . . . eh . . ."

Whatever he'd been about to say was lost in the whistle of an approaching Manhattan-bound train. Stepping on the gas, I coaxed some more speed from the Chrysler and pulled into the station a couple of minutes ahead of the train.

"Thank you, and I'll see you same time, same place, next week," John said.

"Okay."

When he'd gotten out, he paused with his hand on the open door, and I wondered if he'd forgotten something.

"Maybe it *is* time for me to go public," he said after a second. "Why don't you show up at the club for Ballroom Night tomorrow? You can help me make a spectacle of myself."

It was a heady feeling, being invited to dance in public by one of Broadway's shining stars, even though this star had shone twenty-some years earlier. At the same time, I couldn't believe I was the best partner he could find. Was it my too-large car he was after? Or perhaps my too-large body?

John must have sensed my unease. "I'm not coming on to you. It's just that we dance pretty well together, and if I'm going to do this, it should be with a partner I trust."

I considered his offer for a moment, but finally shook my head. The club scene wasn't for me. I was a little too old, a little too settled. I wished John good luck and drove away, thinking that I'd be seeing him only on Wednesday afternoons, and that I'd seen the last of The Dancing Fool.

That evening I had dinner with my plump neighbors. After stuffing myself with breaded pork chops and scalloped potatoes, followed by chocolate cake, I made my swollen way across the snow-covered lawn that divides

Sam's house from theirs. The phone was ringing as I unlocked the kitchen door, and I fumbled with the key hurrying to get inside.

The call was from Buffalo, as I'd expected, but before Sam got on the line I talked to Billy for a few minutes.

"Hey, Bonnie. Crisis has a gig in Manhattan the end of the month. Okay if I spend a couple of nights in your apartment?"

There was a question guaranteed to raise my anxiety level. So far there hadn't been any trouble about my lease, but my ever-complaining Washington Heights neighbors, the Codwallader sisters, griped to the landlord every time Billy showed his face in the building. My story was that Billy was my younger brother. My landlord's no fool, though. Surely he didn't believe that the tall, red-haired kid and I were related.

"Sure," I said. "Just don't . . ."

"I know. Don't do anything you wouldn't do."

"And don't do some of the things I *would* do, either."

"Yeah. Right."

When Sam came on the line his first words were, "Do you miss me?"

"Desperately."

"Would you like it if I flew down Saturday night?"

"I'd love it."

We made plans for me to meet his plane, then talked for a few minutes more. He didn't mention Panama, so neither did I. Maybe there was still hope for Paris. It came time to say goodbye, and I found myself wishing I could keep the phone line open, and Sam on it, all night. Yup, I missed him.

When I'd cradled the phone, the house felt especially empty. Sure, I've been lonely in my apartment, but somehow it was different there. Even in the middle of the night I could hear other lives going on. Pipes rumbled in the walls; voices came from across the courtyard. Sometimes the pipes were annoying, sometimes the voices were angry and disturbing, but in their own strange way they were comforting.

My hand strayed, unconsciously, to the refrigerator door. The next thing I knew, it was open and my fingers were prying the lid off that shiny heart-shaped box. Three lone chocolates remained on the top layer: a jelly, a caramel, and . . . was that another buttercream? The king of chocolates? Oh, it was!

The little beauty was in my hand when I realized what was happening. "No way, tub tub." I got out of the kitchen fast.

I worked off my dinner by finishing the bedroom ceiling and wall. That should have finished me off, but when I'd taken my shower, shoved Moses onto Sam's half of the bed, and settled myself on my half, instead of falling asleep right away I reached for the phone on the night table.

When I started spending most of my time at Sam's I'd tapped into the answering machine in my Washington Heights apartment every night, as religiously as someone else might say their prayers. By now, though, everyone knew where to find me. The messages—at least the messages I was interested in getting—had all but stopped. Still, you never know. There could be an old friend, or Publishers' Clearing House telling me I was a final, absolute first-prize winner.

I punched in the code and listened. A beep a second later indicated that there were calls.

"Miss Indermill. This is Lee again. I called earlier today. It's most important that we speak. Please call me back as soon as you get this message."

The caller, who sounded cranky, had left a Manhattan number.

Lee? Did I know this man? I reeled back to his earlier message.

"Miss Indermill. This is Captain Lee, New York Police Department Organized Crime Control unit. We met several years ago. I need to speak to you.'' There was a momentary pause, and then Lee added, ''This is a police matter. Do not tell Eddie Fong or his partner Maxwell Breen that I've contacted you.''

7

THE NEXT MORNING I DROVE THE Chrysler to the Huntington station and took the train into Manhattan.

The brick building that houses One Police Plaza is in lower Manhattan a couple of blocks south of Chinatown. I'd been there once before a few years earlier. Coincidentally, that earlier visit had been on a bitter cold winter day like this one. Not so coincidentally, I'd been there because of Eddie Fong.

Memories of that first visit ran through my mind as I made my way to the plaza that abuts Organized Crime Control headquarters. Then, as now, the wind was blowing. If the almost $40,000 I'd carried on the earlier trip had fallen out of my shopping bag, the air would have been thick with Andy Jackson's portrait.

As I passed between the neat rows of trees that line the plaza a branch, heavy with ice, cracked like a gunshot. That, and the extra dusting of snow on my face, brought me back to the present.

Captain Lee had been evasive when we'd spoken that morning, so I was still in the dark about what he wanted. I kept trying to convince myself there was nothing to worry about, but self-delusion wasn't working. This involved Eddie, and that meant trouble. When I walked into the building, anxiety was already gnawing at me, and by the time a patrolman had logged me in and shown me into Lee's office, I had worked myself into a state of dread that, as it turned out, wasn't an overreaction.

I don't know how long ago Captain John Lee's family arrived from China, but he is pure New York City: gruff and cynical. To me he looks as sturdy as his name. He's built sort of like a concrete block standing on end. Although there must be a neck in there somewhere, his large head seems to sit directly atop this block. Lee's face is round and his features so flat, they seem to have been punched into it. His gray-flecked black hair is cut short enough for a Marine recruit, and his ears hug the sides of his head so closely they might have been painted on like the ears on a porcelain doll.

By NYPD standards, Lee's second-floor office is posh, and the upholstered chair facing him across the wood desk proved surprisingly comfortable. The windows to my left overlooked the street, and while Lee reached into a drawer for a file I glimpsed office workers pouring from a nearby building. It was lunchtime, and they huddled together against the bitter wind as they made their way down the building's steps.

The pleasantries—an odd word for a handshake with someone you're scared of—were dispensed with quickly. Lee didn't waste any time on small talk or even smile. There was a thick file in the center of his desk. After studying me carefully for a moment, he opened it slowly, with such deliberation that he might have been pondering the pros and cons of sharing the contents with me. This was part of his act, I imagine. He wanted me to understand that this was a *weighty* matter.

''Would you mind taking a look at this, Miss Indermill, and tell me if you recognize the subjects?''

He slid a photograph from the top of the file and placed it on the desk facing me. It was a 5-by-7 black and white, slightly out of focus and grainy, as if it had been taken in poor light or perhaps from a moving vehicle. Never-

theless, I recognized the subjects immediately. Every time
I look in the mirror one of those subjects looks back at
me. If I'd looked in the mirror right then, however, the
face that stared back probably would have looked more
confused than the one in the photo. It's not every day that
my picture is taken without my knowledge and ends up
on the desk of someone like Captain Lee.

This didn't strike me as funny, but for some reason I
smiled. "Of course I recognize the subjects. That's me,
and Eddie Fong beside me. We'd just had lunch."

The oversized palm print painted on Jaguida's window
was visible in the photo, but the name of the restaurant
wasn't. "At Jaguida's Restaurant, on Tenth Avenue. I was
trying to flag a cab. It was really cold, and the walk to
Penn Station . . ."

I once heard an IRS agent say that the more a taxpayer
babbles, the guiltier of deception that taxpayer usually is.
I wasn't guilty of anything, but I babbled anyway. The
thing was, staring down at that photo, I began to wonder
if my expression hadn't been a bit . . . desperate. Sure, the
only thing I'd been even slightly desperate for was a cab,
but wasn't there a hint of trapped-animal wildness in my
eyes? And Eddie was smiling in the photo. That's all it
was: a smile. But was there something a little too slick,
too cajoling in his face? And his gloved hand on my
shoulder, what did that mean? In my imagination, which
was starting to run amok, I envisioned Eddie as one of
those hideous seducers who picks up teenage runaways at
the Port Authority, and myself as his nervous, gullible
victim.

"He was trying to talk me into stopping by his club."

While Lee slowly nodded, he lifted another photo from
the file. "And he did talk you into stopping by The Dancing Fool. You went there that afternoon, and again the
following night."

The second grainy 5-by-7 print showed the front of the
club. The fact that it was a night shot, and in sharp focus,
made it seem spookier than the first picture. It had the

strange, clandestine quality of a still photo from an old
spy movie, one of those films where murderers lurk in the
deep shadows and any light is jarring and suspect. The
photographer, who must have been hidden just up the
block from the club on the same side of the street, had
caught only a bit of Eddie's pride and joy, the flashing
neon sign. The one word that showed up in the photo was
elongated, probably photographed at an angle. That word
was *Fool*. It glowed against the murky background, and
the way it appeared to sprout from the side of my head
was quite odd. My paranoia flashed me a signal that this
was a message from the great beyond, or at least from a
photographer who knew things no ordinary photographer
knew, but as I studied the picture, I knew it was not a
signal at all. It was clear that the photographer hadn't
focused on me. Amanda was the one he'd wanted.

We were shown walking between the velvet ropes toward the driveway that led to the club's open door. The
camera's shutter must have clicked at the instant Amanda
had looked at me and said, "I hope Tony never finds out
about this," because, to put it bluntly, she looked guilty
as hell, like a wife sneaking into a no-tell motel to meet
her lover. On top of that, the snaking mass of her hair
made her appear—and I feel bad saying this—rather
trashy. Looking at that picture made me wish I'd never
mentioned Eddie's invitation to her.

If there was an oily seducer in the shot, it was me. The
tilt of my head, the turn of my lips, and—God!—the way
I'd tucked my chin into my shoulder, all seemed to say,
"Come with me into the devil's playground." "Come
with me," I'd said to my best friend. "You can't very
well work on your marriage when Tony's not home."

Lee cleared his throat. "This woman is your friend, and
also Eddie Fong's."

"Yes. Her name's Amanda Paradise."

That hasn't been her name for some time, and I don't
know what gave me the silly notion that I could get away
with it. Lee glanced at a piece of paper in the file, though

I'm sure he didn't have to. "Paradise was her maiden name. Her married name is . . ."

Here, for effect, Lee squinted and pretended to study the paper. ". . . LaMarca. I understand that her husband is a lieutenant on the force. Midtown." He looked over the top of the page. "I believe Amanda LaMarca is the same woman who was involved with Fong several years ago."

I felt like such a traitor that I had trouble making my lips move. "Um-hum."

Lee returned an "Um-hum," flipped to another page in the file and scanned it for a few seconds, which gave me a chance to pull myself together. Whatever Eddie was up to, common sense told me that Amanda and I didn't have anything to be concerned about. The only thing I might be guilty of was naiveté. As for Amanda's lie, what possible motivation could Lee have to expose it to her husband?

"But why are you interested in who Eddie has lunch with or who goes to his club?" I asked. "Eddie told me there are no charges against him."

Turning his chair, Lee stared contemplatively into the plaza. After a moment he turned back toward me and sighed as if a difficult decision had been reached. In a low, somber tone that suggested this was going to be something momentous, he said, "What I am going to tell you about your friend Eddie Fong, and The Dancing Fool, is not be to repeated. Do I have your word on that?"

I nodded and braced myself.

"You know that Fong left the U.S. in a hurry, pursued not only by the authorities, but by an illegal organization working out of Hong Kong that was involved in gambling and money laundering, and possibly . . ."

Lee's glance flickered to me, and then quickly moved away. ". . . drug smuggling and prostitution."

I'd heard that the gang had been broken up and the leaders either jailed or deported, which I told Lee.

"You are correct, but by the time that happened Eddie

Fong had run off to the Philippines. He found a job tending bar in Manila, in a part of town that attracts sailors from the U.S. naval base at Subic Bay. Not a nice part of town," Lee added before scanning the sheet of paper again.

"That job lasted several months, until the wife of one of the sailors who frequented the bar complained to her husband's commanding officer. It seems that on two consecutive paydays, her husband cashed his paycheck, stopped into that bar for a drink, and proceeded to lose most of his cash in an illegal card game."

"Oh, no," I said softly.

"Oh, yes. The bar was made off-limits to the sailors, and your friend Eddie ended up spending a few days in jail. He got out on bail, jumped bail, and left the Philippines one step ahead of the police. His next stop was Singapore."

Lee turned to a new page. He was hardly a quivering mass of emotions, but something he read, or pretended to read, made him shake his head and utter a disapproving "tsk tsk."

"I will not go into everything that happened in Singapore, but again Fong became involved in an illegal gambling operation. This time the wife of a high-ranking politician was involved," Lee added ominously. "Once again, the gods smiled on Fong and he got out of the country in time. A good thing, too. Justice in Singapore can be harsh.

"U.S. Immigration authorities think Fong got to Vancouver, British Columbia, by freighter, and then slipped over the border into the States. It is believed he was in San Francisco for about three months before he contacted Immigration and told them he wanted to make a deal. Your friend Fong said he would tell them all he knew about the Hong Kong organization if, in turn, charges against him could be dropped."

Why did Lee keep referring to Eddie as my friend? I was starting to feel like I was involved in this, though I didn't even know what "this" was.

Lee had closed his eyes, and I waited quietly while he slowly shook his head as if pondering the harebrained ways of Eddie Fong. "Understand, Miss Indermill: we had all the information we needed about the Hong Kong people. After some time and consideration, though, we decided to give Fong his 'deal.' You see, by then Fong had relocated to Los Angeles and become involved in still another venture, and it occurred to us that if we gave your friend enough rope, he might hang not only himself but several other people."

That jolly thought brought a sly smile to Lee's face. Thumbing through the folder again, he pulled out a few more photographs, examined them, and then carefully placed one of them alongside the first two. "This was taken in New Orleans several months ago."

"That's Max and Steve," I said. The photo showed them at a restaurant table. They both looked innocent enough, but I wasn't surprised to see them pop up in the rogues' gallery Lee was creating. A man in a dark suit sat across from them, his back to the photographer. His hair was thin and the skin of his neck criss-crossed with lines.

Lee put one of his blunt-tipped fingers next to Max's image. "Maxwell Breen was manager of a club in the Westwood section of Los Angeles. He was also part-owner. The money he put into the club had been a loan from his father.

"It was a very trendy place, I am told. Eddie went to work there, first as a bartender, then as Max's assistant." Lee raised his eyes to mine. "Your friend learns everything quickly, except how to stay away from trouble. Steven Breen, Max's younger brother, tended bar and worked as a bouncer. Unlike Eddie Fong, Steven is not too bright."

That was something I'd figured out for myself, though I hadn't realized that he and Max were brothers.

"But like Eddie," Lee continued, "Steven is known to the police. He has a juvenile record of burglary, and an adult cocaine possession arrest.''

"What about Max?''

Lee shook his head. ''Nothing. The L.A. club appears to have been clean, too, or as clean as any place of that type ever is. One or two reports of drugs, of minors drinking . . . but nothing unusual. I gather that such places have a limited time in the spotlight, and this club ultimately went broke. Max lost his father's money.

''Eddie and Max both have roots in New York, and they decided to open their own club here. Once again, Max was forced to borrow from his father.''

A fourth picture took its place on the desk. It was another shot of the three men at the table, but taken from a different perspective. In this photo, Max and Steve had their backs to the camera and the other, older man, faced it. The photo wasn't terribly clear, but I got the impression that this had been a large man who had, with age, shrunken. His shirt collar was too big for his neck, the wrists protruding from his shirt sleeves too thin.

''This gentlemen is Max and Steve's father. He lives in New Orleans, but he has . . . friends, shall we say? in New York City. One of those friends had a warehouse standing vacant, another one had some helpful connections with the liquor licensing board . . .''

Since walking into Lee's office I'd been waiting to hear something terrible. So far, that hadn't happened, and I was growing impatient. So the authorities hadn't gotten Eddie in either the Philippines or Singapore. So the U.S. hadn't pressed charges. So the club in L.A. hadn't been involved in anything unusually awful. So what *had* happened? Why was I sitting there when I had walls left to paint?

''. . . and so our boys Eddie and Max got their liquor license and opened up shop.'' Lee moved his finger from the picture of Max, and placed it beside the image of the old man. The contrast of the blunt, thick finger and the old man's shrunken frame was grotesque. ''Their benefactor's name is Salvatore Napoli. His connections and his money greased the way for The Dancing Fool. Does his name mean anything to you?''

I shook my head.

Lee repeated the name slowly, as if he liked the sound of it. "Salvatore Napoli. As a kid, Salvatore had a quick temper. He went to work for a New Orleans organization with suspected gangland ties. By the time he was nineteen he was known by his alias, Sally the Shotgun. Later on, he worked his way up and bought into a couple of clubs.''

The next thing Lee took from his folder was a copy of an article from a New Orleans newspaper. The date in the corner of the page was October 12, 1963.

"Charges Against Reputed Racketeer Dropped,'' read the headline. "The District Attorney's case against Salvatore Napoli, New Orleans club owner who had been accused of transporting minors over the state line for purposes of prostitution, and also of being a link in the smuggling of illegal firearms, disintegrated yesterday when a Federal Court judge ruled that evidence gathered by the District Attorney's office was inadmissible. . . .''

The article went on to quote Salvatore Napoli's lawyer on his client's future plans. "Mr. Napoli is an honest businessman whose reputation has been damaged by the D.A.'s spurious charges. He may decide to seek damages against the D.A., but right now all he wants to do is get back to his business and to spend time with his family.''

"He never sought damages,'' Lee said laconically.

I handed the article back to him. "Where did the name Breen come from?''

"Salvatore Napoli was much older than his wife. When Max and Steven were youngsters she divorced him and married a Mr. Breen, who adopted the boys. The family moved to New Jersey, where they still live. Nevertheless, as you can see from that photo, Salvatore Napoli and his sons have kept up their relationship. He might have been a tyrant, or maybe he was a loving father, but one way or another, Salvatore has inspired loyalty in his sons.

"The old man doesn't have long to live,'' Lee went on. "Lung cancer. The word is that Sally has gone soft trying to make up for his past. As for Max, we hear that the loss of the club in Westwood was a blow to his ego. He perceives himself as a disappointment to his father, and is determined to make a go of this new club as much for his father's sake as for his own.

"My colleagues and I find it fascinating," Lee said, "that your friend Fong, who has been involved with Chinese organized crime, has managed to hook up with the sons of Salvatore Napoli. Quite the coincidence, don't you think, Miss Indermill?"

I wouldn't have minded blurting, "He's not that close a friend," but controlled the impulse. "I don't know what to think."

Lee took a moment to gather the article and three of the four photos, stack them neatly, and put them back in the folder. When he had finished, only the photo of Amanda and me remained on the desk.

"Yesterday morning," said Lee, "Eddie Fong walked into the office of the Property Clerk of the City of New York and attempted to claim approximately forty thousand dollars that you turned in several years ago. He used the fact that you would be working for his club to support his claim."

I'm slow, but not so slow that I didn't get an inkling of what was coming. Even as I was shaking my head, Lee let me in on his scheme. It confirmed my worst fears.

"Based on that information, and the fact that in the past you've been a public-spirited citizen and a good friend to the NYPD, we decided to give Fong the money. With you working at The Dancing Fool, who knows how many necks we might catch in our noose? You will be the eyes and ears of the NYPD's Organized Crime Control unit, and of the District Attorney's office."

"I will be the fool of the century," I sputtered, aghast.

Lee drew back slightly. "Think of the good you could accomplish."

"Think of the awfulness of the job. I'd have to be the dumbest dodo in New York City to work at The Dancing

Fool. I mean—'' The situation brought out the Barrymore in me and I flung my arms wide. ''Eddie Fong's bad enough, but those other . . . criminals, mobsters . . .''

Lee held out a hand as if to calm me. ''Please, Miss Indermill. We don't know that any criminal activity is taking place, or will take place. We merely want to keep on top of things.''

''I'm sorry, but you'll have to keep on top of things without my help.''

It was time for me to finish with this and get out of there. As I pushed back my chair, though, my gaze followed Lee's to the desktop, to that one remaining photo.

''I'm sorry, too, Miss Indermill. I don't look forward to asking your friend, Mrs. Amanda LaMarca, to resume a relationship of some kind with Mr. Fong. Her marriage has experienced some difficulties, I hear, but''—it was Lee's turn to be dramatic. Looking up from the picture, he raised his hands helplessly—''What else can I do? You give me no choice.''

My head reeling, I sank back into the chair. Poor Amanda. What was this going to do to couples therapy? Can a woman work on her marriage while she's involved in some weird, illicit relationship with an ex-boyfriend?

''You wouldn't. That would be blackmail.'' I tried to sound confident, even belligerent, but my stomach was churning.

Lee folded his hands on the desk as if in prayer, though from my perspective he was an unlikely holy man, and nodded almost imperceptibly. ''It would not be a pleasant thing for me, or for Mrs. LaMarca, but the things that these organizations do to people are much less pleasant.'' Picking up the remaining photo, Lee slipped it back in the file and then, after a pause, withdrew yet another one. ''Allow me to show you one more picture.''

This one was in color, but I had trouble getting it into focus. It looked like an abstract painting done by an angry art student, all red slashes and yellow blobs. It was a moment before what I was staring at took shape as a man's body. The face, or what would have been the face, was a misshapen black splotch.

"A shotgun, at close range, does terrible damage," Lee said. "When Sally the Shotgun was young, this man made the fatal mistake of trying to cheat one of Sally's bosses in a deal involving illegal drugs. I have several pictures of this type, each with a different corpse, Miss Indermill. A number of them are women."

He glanced through the folder again, and for a horrible moment I thought he intended to show me the whole grisly collection. When he simply slipped the photo into the file and put the file in the drawer, I let out a deep breath.

"If you think that's going to tempt me, you're wrong."

Lee shook his head. "I'm not trying to tempt you, Miss Indermill. I'm trying to make you understand why I would prefer to have you, rather than Amanda LaMarca, involved with The Dancing Fool. In the past you've shown yourself to be resourceful and cool in emergencies. I don't think you'd have difficulty with anything you'd be asked to do. Mrs. LaMarca, on the other hand . . ."

He didn't have to finish the sentence. Amanda is my superior in many ways, but in an emergency her tendency is to scream and reach for the Valium bottle.

"If I go to work at the club, what would you expect me to do?"

Lee's broad features spread into a smile. "Absolutely no cloak-and-dagger stuff, Miss Indermill. Nothing involving carrying a weapon or a miniature camera, or wearing a wire . . ."

I felt a little better until he added, ". . . unless you actually uncover something. Then we'll see. What you will do, initially, is nothing more than you would do on any other job: go to the office and keep your eyes and ears open. You will use public phones—*avoid using* your home phone *and never use* the phone at the club—to contact me at a number I give you. You will do this whenever you have something to report. The main thing you will look for is evidence of contractors who are charging too much, or too little. You will make copies of contracts or other documents that might be even remotely suspect."

"I don't think there's a copy machine at the club."

Lee nodded at the tote bag I'd draped over the arm of my chair. "You can carry papers in and out of the club in that. Take them to a copy shop."

"That could be . . ."

I was going to say "dangerous," but Lee interrupted. "Save the receipts. You'll be reimbursed. You should also look for evidence of contact with people who might be connected with the Sicilian or Hong Kong organizations. Look for Italian and Chinese surnames, for signs of drug dealing . . ."

"Drugs?" My mind took a leap. "Maybe there's already something."

How pleased he looked! I was already a star pupil. "And what is that?"

"You know that actor who committed suicide a few days ago? Brad Gannett?"

From the way Lee put his hand to his chest you'd have thought he was grief-stricken. "A great actor, and a great one for the ladies, too. My wife and I never missed that show. Never."

"Well, Gannett visited the club twice, and apparently the second time . . ."

I repeated Steve's story about Gannett's second visit, and mentioned my experience with Max in the room with the monitor and safe.

When I finished, Lee nodded slowly. I thought he might have second thoughts about sending me into this den of goons, but no such luck.

"That's interesting. You see what I mean, Miss Indermill? You're a natural for this work. I'll have someone check on Gannett's autopsy results. You should keep your eyes open for anything else that suggests there might be drug deals at the club. Also, look for large amounts of cash being funneled through the place, for evidence of gambling, prostitution, firearms. . . . ''

As Lee recited this charming list of items on my job description, the queasy feeling in my stomach turned into a full-out ache. Talk about your glamor jobs. This one scraped the bottom of the employment barrel. I would be spying for this Machiavelli across the desk, and at the same time working for Eddie, whose lifestyle gave me the willies, and for Max, whose personality had the same effect. And for minimum wage, yet.

Minimum wage? Those two words suddenly beat a little rhythm in my head. Would James Bond have worked for minimum wage? Not likely. This wasn't Her Majesty's Secret Service I was getting involved with, but . . .

''And my pay for doing this?''

Lee's smile faded. ''I was wondering when you would get around to that. The Department is prepared to be generous—relatively generous. . . . ''

When he translated ''relatively generous'' into real numbers, the figure might have caused James Bond to defect to the other side. For me, though, it wasn't bad. I wouldn't be buying an 007-type Astin Martin to maneuver through traffic on the Long Island Expressway, but something a little sportier than that Chrysler didn't seem so far out of reach.

''And what about the woman who works at the club?'' I asked. ''Her name's Dawn Starr.''

Lee had obviously seen a picture of Dawn, because the mention of her name brought the smile back to his face. ''What about the woman? I don't know. We haven't checked her background. But where you've got a woman like that, you've probably got trouble.'' Pleased with himself for this bit of reasoning, he chuckled.

Ho, ho, ho. Now that this spider had trapped me in his web, he was developing a sense of humor.

''Should I spy on her too?''

Still smiling, Lee repeated the word ''spy,'' as if it were alien on his tongue. ''Who said anything about spying?

You're keeping your eyes open. That's all. So you keep them on the woman too. If you find anything interesting about her, you tell me. What you're going to do is get me everything you can.''

''And if I haven't found anything within a couple of weeks . . . ?''

''Then we'll re-evaluate the situation.''

And so I became a spy. During the train ride back to Huntington I tried out all the other words. *Undercover cop* wasn't accurate. *Informant*? Sounded sleazy, like an addict selling his soul for a fix. *Mole* was too . . . fuzzy, and *secret agent* too glamorous. As for *spook*, it scared me. *Spy* was the word I liked. And—though I'm embarrassed about this—as I approached the Chrysler in the parking lot, I felt a tingle of anticipation. Sure, corporate moves are exciting, but when you stack them up against 007's exploits—sky-diving, skiing off mountains, swimming with sharks—they pale.

I called Eddie Fong that evening and told him he was right. Boredom had set in. The Y wasn't enough. I wanted a temp job—about two weeks, I told him, maybe longer—and not just any job but a specific job, organizing the office at The Dancing Fool.

Eddie was ecstatic. ''You don't know how much this means to me, Bonnie. Max is a great guy and all that. Smart, hard-working. But I'll sleep better knowing I have a real friend like you looking out for my interests. Steve—'' He hesitated. ''Steve's Max's brother, but I don't . . . umm . . .'' His voice dropped to a whisper. ''I don't quite trust him, if you know what I mean.''

On that issue Eddie had company that he didn't know a thing about.

I was in the shower later that evening when Amanda called and left the first of several messages on our answering machine.

''Bonnie, it's Amanda. I need to talk to you about . . .

personal things. Please call me.''

I knew what personal things she wanted to talk about, and I was in no mood to hear them. She had a marriage counselor for that. I didn't return her call.

8

You could die working for Eddie Fong, but not from overwork. At eleven the next morning, the time Eddie and I had agreed on, I pounded on The Dancing Fool's door. In response there was silence. Just as I was about to head for Jaguida's for a cup of coffee my new boss trotted across the street, unshaven and blinking his eyes against the daylight. He peeled off his leather gloves, then opened the two locks that let us into the club. Inside, he demonstrated how a third key turned off the club's security alarm.

"Once you're inside you have fifteen seconds to do this. Otherwise you'll wake up the world." Inserting the key into an inconspicuous outlet near the coat-check, he quickly twisted it. "Remember, one turn clockwise."

Then, while he covered a yawn with one hand, he handed me the ring of keys with the other.

"These are yours. From now on you let yourself in. This early-bird stuff isn't for me."

The keys weighed a ton. I hoisted my tote. "Maybe I should clean this out. I'm carrying house keys, apartment keys, car keys . . ."

I followed Eddie up the stairs to the office, already thinking like a spy. There were eight keys on the ring in

my hand. Two for the front door, one for the security
alarm. A fourth key unlocked the hall leading to the office.
One was for the Celebrity Lounge. That left three keys
unaccounted for. The club's back door probably would
take two of those.

"So," he said once we were in the office. "It's all
yours." He waved at the mess. "In this room, you are
queen."

"That's like being the Queen of Nothing."

As I threw my parka on a chair, there was a loud
thump, almost a shudder, from somewhere below us.
Eddie noticed my alarmed expression.

"That's the furnace. Perfectly safe."

"I'll bet."

I proceeded to examine my shabby kingdom. A pile of
unopened envelopes spilled across the desk that was intended for me, and the world's oldest Dictaphone—a gray
metal instrument of torture—had taken its place alongside
the ancient adding machine and typewriter.

"I found that down in the storage room," said Eddie.
"Figured I'd do some dictating at night. Then you can
type it up the next day and put it in the IN box."

He nodded officiously at two scratched wooden trays,
one labeled IN and the other OUT, that had been added to
the rubble on the second desk.

"In your dreams, Eddie."

"What kind of attitude is that, Bonnie? You just walked
into the place and you're already a disgruntled employee."

"I don't do Dictaphone."

"We'll see. Anyhow, you can start looking through
things. I'm going to go get some breakfast. Want me to
bring you anything? Jaguida has the best doughnuts
you've ever tasted. Any kind you want."

"Jelly, and a black coffee."

Yawning again, he mumbled, "I'll lock the door behind
me."

The phone rang as he was leaving.

"You can handle it," Eddie said, but then, like a typical boss, he stood in the doorway to make sure I did it right.

For a second I mulled over how to answer: "The Dancing Fool" was a mouthful.

"Hello," I said.

"Is this The Fool?"

It was a man, youngish from the sound of his voice, and a little hesitant, as if he was unsure of himself. I grinned at Eddie. "No. This is the fool's secretary. Can I help you?"

"Is Max there? Or Steve?"

"No, not right now."

"Tell them Terry called. Okay?"

He reeled off a number which I jotted on the back of an empty envelope.

"Will they know what you're calling about?" I asked, but Terry had already hung up.

"You can answer 'The Dancing Fool' from now on," Eddie said. "I'll be back in a few minutes."

As he clopped down the stairs, I transferred the message to a clean piece of paper and put it on the other desk, like a good secretary. And then, because a man named Terry had come to the club twice with Brad Gannett, I put the envelope with Terry's number on it in my tote, like a good spy.

The moment the club's front door slammed shut I headed like a shot for the room across the hall with the locked door. A little fumbling with a couple of keys and the next thing I knew, a big key with a six-sided top had turned the tumbler in the lock.

Wow! Thinking that this spying business was a piece of cake, I twisted the doorknob. As I pushed at the door, though, something caused me to hesitate. A sound from downstairs? Yes! Someone had unlocked the front door!

Heart pounding, I quickly closed the door, relocked it, and trotted quietly back into the office. As footsteps pounded on the stairs, I grabbed a handful of unopened mail from my desk. I had just plopped myself into the chair behind my desk when Max walked in.

"Good morning, Bonnie. I ran into Eddie outside and he told me you'd already started. That's terrific. We need someone with some discipline around this place."

"It's just for a couple of weeks," I said.

"That will help. Eddie told me he gave you keys."

Max read the phone message and then slipped the piece of paper into his shirt pocket. "Bills and more bills," he said as he looked through the IN box. "That's the story of my life. What are you working on there, anyway?"

I hadn't had time to glance at the mail, much less work on it. It was crumpled in my two fists. So was the key ring.

"I'm not quite sure. Looks like some . . . bills. Some of them are past due."

I showed Max a phone bill with a nasty reminder stamped in red ink on it. He raised an eyebrow.

"This time they're threatening to turn off the service." Walking around the desk, Max opened a drawer and took out a checkbook. "It's been touch and go around here. When you're able to make sense of this account, and if it turns out we're not broke, you can write out checks for some of the older bills."

"You'll sign them?"

"Either Eddie or I can sign. If you decide you're going to stick around here longer than a couple of weeks, we'll put your name on the account," he added casually.

Max then explained how they handled the cash that came through the club. At night, after closing, he and Eddie counted up together. "That way, we keep each other honest." He grinned as if he was joking, but if he knew Eddie as well as I did, he meant this. "We try to vary what we do with the money. Sometimes we take a cab to a bank with a night deposit box. Other times we drive there. And other times we lock the money in the safe—that's in the secure room across the hall—and take it to the bank the next day. Again, if you decide to make this your life's work you'll get the combination. Then you can experience the thrill of waiting to feel a gun in your ribs.''

"I'll look forward to it."

All this was disappointingly ordinary. For a man who was suspected of being a gangland henchman of some sort, Max was pretty open about the club's finances. Moreover, he seemed to be as nervous as any normal person would have been carrying a large amount of cash around New York City.

"I guess there's always a risk."

He nodded. "We have a handgun in the safe. When we make a night deposit one of us rides shotgun. It's still nerve-racking, though. Neither one of us are exactly Wyatt Earp types. And whenever we leave the cash in the safe, I'm always scared it won't be there in the morning. In fact," he added with a grimace, "I'm going to have an anxiety attack if I don't look in the safe right now. I'd let you watch, but I'm sort of a nut about the combination."

"That's okay. I don't want to risk another . . ." Instead of finishing the sentence, I rubbed my upper arm.

Max's gaze dropped to the floor. "Oh, Bonnie. What a goon you must think I am."

A goon. That was exactly how I'd thought of Max. But as I looked at him standing there so obviously contrite, I wondered if maybe he wasn't a goon at all. If he wasn't feeling guilty, he sure was putting on a good act. When he added, "I wish I could take that scene back," I really started to waver. There was a very good chance that Lee was wrong. Max might be simply be a victim of his father's reputation. Fraternally incorrect.

"Forget it. There was no harm done. Not even a bruise. I'll never mention it again."

"Just the same, I wish it hadn't happened."

I heard Max unlock the secure room, and the squeak of the door, but I stayed put and started opening the rest of the mail. When Max returned, there was a fat brown envelope in his hand.

"You want to come along on this trip? I'll show you where the bank is."

He slipped the envelope inside his shirt, and I glimpsed a shoulder holster and the shiny butt of a pistol.

"As long as you promise there won't be a shootout."

He chuckled. Big joke.

I was reaching for my parka when the keys Eddie had given me slid to the floor. I bent for them, but Max was faster. Scooping them up, he held the keys out to me. Before I could take them back, though, he focused on them and his eyes narrowed.

"You don't have to worry about lugging all these around."

Max fiddled with the key ring. When he handed it back to me a moment later, there was one less key for me to lug around: the one with the six-sided top that opened the secure room. That one he slipped into his front pants pocket.

I did an about-face. Lee was right. Something was going on, and it was going on in the room with the safe, the security monitor, and those video cassettes stacked on the shelves.

It looked like the spying game wasn't going to be quite as easy as I'd thought. As long as Max had those pants on, that key was safe from my prying fingers. For that matter, when he took the pants off I didn't want to be anywhere within prying distance either, so it was safe then, too. But Eddie was careless. I'd get a chance at his keys sooner or later.

Down, but far from out, I pushed the key ring into my pocket.

We ran into the still bleary-eyed Eddie on the sidewalk outside. He made a joke about the dangers of letting me handle the club's money, but I could tell he was tickled that his new partner and his old friend were getting along.

Max had a dark green four-wheel-drive Bronco, and I

rode shotgun beside him to the bank. I wasn't much concerned about robbers, though. As a spy, I thought about getting my hands on that six-sided key. And as a hedonist, I was totally taken with the jelly doughnut Eddie had brought me from Jaguida's.

It was four P.M., and about time for me to leave. I'd managed to balance the checkbook, write checks for some of the older bills, and start a rudimentary file system for them. I'd also glanced through some of the other papers scattered around the room. The lease Max had signed with his father's friend had been mixed in with a stack of agreements with contractors. The only suspicious thing I noticed about the lease was the very low rent, but friends are friends. As for the dealings with contractors, it looked like the club was getting decent prices from a plumber with an Italian surname, and a Sing Yee had supplied what seemed to be some awfully expensive bar equipment, but what did I know about the club business?

These were the kinds of papers that Lee wanted me to copy. Max was downstairs doing something in the storage room, and Eddie had gone out to try to "force himself"— his words—on an entertainment columnist from one of the daily newspapers, a woman who could make or break a career or, for that matter, a club, or so Eddie claimed. I had the whole second floor to myself, but after my secure-room scare earlier that day, I was nervous about smuggling papers out.

On the other hand, chances were almost nonexistent that Max or Eddie would start looking for a specific contractor agreement on a Friday night. Latin Dance Night. Even if they did, the office was such a mess that the logical assumption would be that the agreement was buried somewhere in the chaos.

After mulling this over, I folded two of the contractor agreements and opened my tote bag. A couple a day shouldn't be a problem. . . .

"You do turn up in the strangest places."

I jumped to my feet, in the process dropping the agreements and banging my leg into the desk.

"Jesus! Did I catch you dipping into the petty cash already?"

John Daly was at the office door, a black plastic trash bag swinging from his hand. Unable to think of an answer, I shook my head.

"I'd never tell," he said. "I'm just surprised you took them up on their job offer. Or are they paying you more than they're paying me?"

"I was bored," I said.

"Yeah. Me too. That's why I do this."

Retrieving the agreements from the floor, I put them in a neat stack on the desk. Tomorrow was another day.

John gave the plastic bag in his hand a shake. "Any recyclable containers?"

"No. Everything I ate today came out of a greasy paper bag."

He was emptying the trash can under the other desk when it occurred to me that some more spying might be possible.

"Hey, John? You must have heard about Brad Gannett."

Straightening, he gave me a curious look. "What about him?"

I shrugged. "That he committed suicide. Were you here either of the times he visited the club?"

"The first night I was here until I found out he was here. Then I beat it out the back door."

Eddie had forgotten his gloves. They were lying on the desk. Picking them up, John fingered the leather covetously. "Wouldn't mind having a pair like these. Probably cost a fortune," He peeled back the cuff and looked at the label. "Saks."

Eddie's wardrobe was indeed splendid, but it wasn't something Captain Lee wanted to hear about. I changed the subject back to where I wanted it to be.

"You didn't want to see Brad Gannett?"

John shook his head. "I didn't want Brad to see me. I knew him professionally. The idea of him catching my janitor routine bothered me."

"And the second time Gannett dropped by?"

"I wasn't here," John said. "Steve told me about it, though."

"Oh. Well, it's sad. Gannett's suicide, I mean. He must have been terribly depressed."

John tossed the gloves back onto the desk. "If he was, I didn't notice. If anything, he'd been elated."

"I guess you can't ever tell what's going on in someone's head."

"You mean in the dark corners of his mind Brad was in agony? That's bull. He had some problems, but he wasn't suicidal. And I never saw any drugs, either," John added, "despite what Steve thinks."

"Gannett *did* commit suicide."

"That's what they're calling it."

According to everything I'd heard, they were calling it suicide because that's what it was.

"What would you call it?" I asked John.

" 'Murder' might be as good a word as any," he said.

"Are you serious?"

John considered me quietly, then shook his head. "No. I'm kidding. I guess you're going back to the wilds of Long Island now," he added, deftly changing the subject once again. "Tonight's Latin Night here, you know. Fancy. Everybody dresses to the teeth. Eddie's out trying to get a reporter to show up, maybe with a photographer. If I can talk you into sticking around, we can make our 'debut.' "

"Sorry, but look at my outfit." I'd dressed for the job: jeans, a sweat shirt, and sneakers. "Besides, I'm really not all that great a dancer."

He grinned. "I know, but you're all I've got."

I smiled back. "Thanks a lot, but—"

I was interrupted by the sound of boots thumping up the stairs. A second later Dawn raced into the office. What a Kewpie doll she was in her blue parka and blue wool beret. Most of her hair was hidden by the beret, and just a curly red fringe surrounded her face. Her skin was flushed from the winter air, but looking at Dawn, the word that came to mind wasn't "cold" but "healthy."

She barely acknowledged John—a careless nod did for him—but she gave me a warm smile.

"Bonnie! I was so happy when Eddie said you were going to be working here. It will be nice having another woman around."

"Thanks. It's only temporary."

"All my jobs are temporary. I have about half-a-dozen of them."

I started to clear some things from a chair for her, but Dawn shook her head.

"Can't stay." Opening the closet, she began digging frantically through a jumble of shoes on the floor. "I never have the clothes I need where I need them. Right now I've got to go to my waitress job." She found a pair of loafers that would do the trick and tucked them into a black tote bag she had over her shoulder.

"See you in a couple of hours. You're going to be here tonight, aren't you? It's a great scene."

"So I hear, but I . . ."

"Got to run," she said. "Let's get together for lunch one of these days. I want to hear all about your dance career. Did you sing, too?"

I hardly got "When they'd let me" out of my mouth before she was out the door and trotting back down the stairs.

"Does she sing?" I asked John.

He'd been staring out the dirty window, his expression as chilly as the air outside. He grabbed the bag of empties from the floor. "Dawn has a fancy voice coach, and Dawn is taking acting lessons from one of the best teachers in the business. Dawn is a budding star."

"So maybe you could make your debut with her. She seems pretty nice. If you ask . . ."

John laughed bitterly. "You noticed how nicely she treats me. The Prom Queen isn't about to be seen in public with the janitor. And I don't suppose you know someone in the area you could borrow some clothes from?"

It was a simple question, but there was a caustic quality to it. He might not believe me if I said *No*. He might think I was one more Prom Queen.

I felt sorry for John. A lot of his trouble was his own doing, but he'd been young when money and celebrity had been thrust at him. Who knows? If I had gotten rich and famous at that age, I might have fallen apart, too.

"I can't think of anyone my size, but I've got a closet full of dance-type things up in Washington Heights. I'm warning you, though, I can only stay for an hour or so tonight."

His sour look disappeared, and I saw a hint of the smile that had melted my adolescent heart.

"Wait until those ponytailed bozos get a look at us tonight!"

Ponytailed bozos. Funny, but that was the same phrase Brad Gannett had used. Maybe it was some sort of "in" expression that hadn't yet reached the wilds of Long Island.

Billy had used my apartment last. For some reason he'd left the radiators off, and the place was cold as a tomb. Dark, too. The overhead light in the bedroom had burned out, and the fluorescent light in the kitchen flickered as if it was about to blow. While I waited for the radiators to clang to life so that I could change clothes, I retrieved the envelope with Terry's phone number from my bag and tried some more spying.

A man answered. "Lincoln," he growled.

"Oh, hi. This is Greenleaf Florists."

"Oh, hi." He oozed sarcasm.

"I have a delivery for Terry, but I can't read your address."

"Are you puttin' me on? Somebody's giving Terry flowers?"

"A flowering plant."

The man broke into laughter. Between guffaws he called to someone else, "You won't believe this one. Someone's sending Terry something from a florist." When the man caught his breath, he sputtered out an address: "Lincoln Motel. West Forty-first between Tenth and Eleventh. Bring your bodyguard."

He was still laughing when he slammed down the phone.

The Lincoln Motel was in the Yellow Pages. Other motels and hotels in the directory pushed their convenient locations and health spas. The Lincoln's ad read simply, "Inexpensive rooms by the month, week, day, or hour."

Not exactly the Waldorf.

Neither, for that matter, was my apartment. It never had been, but it seemed to have hit a new low. The water in the sink ran too hot and then too cold, and putting on makeup in front of the mirror over the sink gave me problems. There was a spot where the mirror's backing had worn off, and if I didn't position my head just right, it looked as if a five o'clock shadow was growing on my chin. The spot had always been there, but over the years I'd gotten used to not seeing it or seeing through it or something.

Eleven years.

As I slipped into my dress, the opera singer downstairs began running her voice up and down the scales, torturing her vocal cords and her neighbors. The wail of a police car siren joined her in a mercifully brief duet. In the courtyard behind the building the super, George, yelled to the kid who helps him. The kid, no slouch in the yelling department, answered with a stream of Spanish. I'm not sure how much Spanish George understands, but the kid was considerate enough to end his sentence with a couple of universally understood obscenities.

Dressed, I examined myself by lamplight in the full-length mirror on my bedroom door. The Dancing Fool was the kind of place where you could wear the things you can't wear anywhere else. I'd decided on a red dress I'd worn ten years before in a short-lived Off-Broadway revival of *On the Town*. The reviews had been scathing, but the dress was good on me: flared skirt for dancing and for hiding my extra ten pounds, tight, sexy, sequined bodice for who knows what.

I had started feeling some of John Daly's excitement. This butterflies-in-the-stomach often happens to me before I go on stage. Sure, The Dancing Fool wasn't Radio City. On the professional dance scene it was nowhere. You couldn't put it on a resume, and dropping the name in dance circles would get you a blank. None of that mattered. I was going to dance and, if I was good enough, people were going to watch me. That's what mattered.

I had turned to check the view from the back, when a tiny flicker of movement in a shadowy corner of the bedroom caught my eye. My gasp frightened my intruder and he, or maybe she, quickly disappeared under the radiator. I tried to tell myself that my vision was at fault and that the little intruder hadn't really been there, but that didn't work. A mouse had moved into my apartment. Mouse? Mice, probably. They get lonely, too.

Before leaving for the club I knocked on George's door and reported this mouse situation to his teenage daughter.

"You have to tell the landlord if you want a mouse exterminator," she told me. "We're only authorized for roaches."

Terrific. From the way my landlord talked, this building was the crowning glory of his slum empire, but from the way he maintained it, he probably wouldn't care if there were bull elephants running loose in the halls. As I walked to the A train, I was having second thoughts about hanging on to my Manhattan *pied à terre*.

9

I ARRIVED BACK AT THE DANCING
Fool before John did. The club was already full, and on the bandstand the
members of a four-piece combo, who
looked as if they were straight out of
Havana, circa 1952, were tuning their
instruments. The crowd was a little
older than the line dancers, and decidedly more elegant. It was quite a scene,
with every conceivable type dress, from
slinky with thigh-high slits for dancing,
to yards of chiffon and a retro-fifties
flared poodle skirt. Men leaned toward dark suits and
white shirts, some with pleats or ruffles, and there were
several tuxedos in evidence.

Seeing me, Eddie, a sartorial dream in a tux that didn't
look rented, whistled. "Well, well! Nice dress. Couldn't
stay away, could you?"

"Thanks. Once a hoofer, always a hoofer. Besides," I
said airily, "a Broadway celebrity made me an offer I
couldn't refuse."

He blinked and asked, "For real?" and glanced toward
the table Amanda and I had shared with him a few nights
before. There, a pudgy, pale woman with short brown hair
was chatting with Dawn, or better put, chatting *at* Dawn.
Dawn, dazzling in a low-cut black dress, was leaning back

in her chair examining her fingernails, and looking—Was it possible?—bored. Where was that sweet smile? The pudgy woman, whose lips were moving rapidly, stretched across the table toward her.

I nodded. "A for-real Broadway celebrity. Is that woman from the newspaper?"

"Yes. Don't stare. She's not exactly what I had in mind, and she didn't bring a photographer. Not even a camera."

"She's not what I expected either." Being in the midst of so many trendettes, I'd formed a mental image of an entertainment columnist as someone thinner, better dressed, and more "of the moment." The woman at the table with Dawn may have been about my age, but I think—hope—that we were stylistically eons apart. I'm several rungs removed from the top of the trendiness ladder, but surely her pink crocheted vest and lank, do-it-yourself haircut placed her even farther down.

Eddie turned his back so that the woman couldn't see the disgusted look on his face. "She's the columnist's assistant. Said she 'just loves the dance scene.' I couldn't get near the real thing, but that creature stuck to me like glue! In a weak moment I let her talk me into a free pass."

"So maybe she'll carry a glowing report back to her boss. What's her name?"

"She's such an idiot I doubt if she could carry a cup of coffee back to her boss. Her name is Elsie, and it fits her," he said nastily. "Elsie the Cow. Who's your celebrity, anyway? He can't be any worse than my 'columnist.'"

Eddie was so disappointed by Elsie that mentioning T'Bird might have sent him into a major snit. Shaking my head, I said, "I was kidding. Forget . . ."

A drumroll came from the bandstand.

"Oh, well," said Eddie. "The show must go on."

Leaping to the platform, he beamed out at the crowd. "Ladies and gentlemen, thank you all for coming tonight. I'm Eddie Fong, your host, and over here is . . ."

He gestured toward Dawn. She had gotten up from the table and exchanged her bored expression for one of her spunky smiles. ". . . Dawn Starr. We'll be happy to help you with any steps you find tricky. No step is too tricky for Dawn," he added, smiling.

The first swooping notes of an old standard, "Cherry Pink and Apple Blossom White," came from the band, and couples moved onto the floor. And at that moment, John Daly appeared at my side.

He'd finally gotten a decent haircut, and being one of those fortunate men whose hairline was holding its own against time, seemed younger than he had earlier that day. Realizing that I was staring, he shrugged.

"I decided to buck the ponytail trend."

"It does get tiresome, doesn't it? You look good."

So good, in fact, that it was hard to believe this was the same man who had been emptying trash cans earlier that day. His white shirt with ruffles down the front and the cummerbund around his waist may have come out of mothballs, or out of a Salvation Army bin for all I knew, but they fit the scene and him perfectly. On his feet were spiffy black oxfords with a soft shine.

"New shoes?"

"Yup. This comeback better work out because it's costing me a fortune. If it doesn't, I better win the Lottery."

Eddie was stepping off the bandstand when he caught sight of John. Eddie is a master at putting on a good front, but the expression that crossed his face was one of utter disbelief. One of utter disgust quickly followed. Dawn had walked over to him, and I thought they would dance. Instead he propelled her across the floor and stopped at my side. Leaning close, he whispered, "Great day I've had. We have airhead Elsie instead of a columnist, and a wino instead of a celebrity. If he causes any trouble, he's dead. And so are you."

With that, he gathered Dawn into his arms.

The tango is danced with the man and woman close

together, but Eddie overdid the closeness. He looked a little rough, too, but it's hard to glide smoothly and keep your knees soft when you're annoyed at the world.

"So? Did Number One Son corral a reporter?" asked John. "I don't see anyone with a camera."

He fidgeted with his bow tie as he spoke. If I had butterflies, John must have had eagles batting their wings in his stomach. I glanced at the plump woman in the pink vest. "She's some columnist's assistant."

John rolled his eyes. "Kind of a strange-looking bird, at least for this place. Looks like the world won't find out about my debut, but, as the man said, shall we dance?"

His arm went around my waist, our hands clasped, and we joined the crowd on the floor.

Some strange form of Darwinian natural selection often takes place on a dance floor. The less accomplished dancers move to the sides, yielding the spotlight, and all the room they need, to those with more skill. At least I hope it's natural selection and not a case of bullying the others off the floor. John and I were in the center in no time, sharing it with Dawn and her not-so-accomplished partner. And then, as I'd expected we would, John and I had the spotlight to ourselves. I felt the eyes of the spectators on us, and actually saw one couple stop dancing to watch. The tacky bar, the cheap lamps and plastic chairs, passed through my field of vision in a hallucinatory blur, and for those few minutes The Dancing Fool took on a lovely impressionistic quality. For all I knew or cared, we could have been floating across the floor at The Rainbow Room.

The trumpet wailed, the saxophone put out sounds that dipped and rose, and then the number ended with a long, trailing note.

The applause from the people at the tables and standing around the floor wasn't just for us. There were other very good dancers out there. And the applause wasn't deafening, either. The Dancing Fool wasn't a Broadway theater or Lincoln Center. It was a seedy club on a seedy street. But I ate that applause up. It had been a long time.

The loudest clapping came from the woman in the pink crocheted vest. She was pounding her hands together so hard that you might have expected sparks to fly from them, and a huge smile bisected her face. It's wonderful to cause that kind of reaction, but I wasn't the one who had occasioned it. The woman's eyes were locked on my partner.

I glanced at John to catch his reaction. This was the time when, after a performance, the performers exchange looks that say, Wow! We did it! But John's eyes were focused across the floor. They were dead serious, and the tilt of his head and turn of his lips appeared to hold a challenge. I followed his gaze.

Dawn Starr! And she was staring back.

I'm often wrong about things. Sometimes I jump to conclusions that have more to do with an overactive imagination than reality, but never for a second did I doubt my instinct on this one thing: John was eyeing Dawn as a prospective partner. He and I had just scored a victory. I was half of the team, and half the victory was mine, but for him I was bush-league. John was already planning his move into the majors, and from the look on Dawn's face—astonishment showed in the open mouth, curiosity in the rapt eyes—she would greet John with more than a curt nod from now on.

Suddenly, and irrationally—Dawn hadn't done anything except be there—I agreed with everything Amanda had said about her. She was a phony, and no doubt a lot older than she looked. As for John, even now it's hard to put what I felt into words, but the one word that comes closest is "rejection," and this, at least briefly, was as painful as being rejected by a lover.

Understand, I hadn't responded to John sexually, or at least I don't think that was part of it. Some of you who know me may say, sarcastically, "Oh, sure," and yes, I have occasionally responded to an attractive man in ways that my mother will never hear about from me. That doesn't usually happen with dance partners, though. Ballroom dancing is a sensual experience for me, but in a different way than sex. I want to look and feel as good as possible when I'm on the dance floor, and the better the partner, the better I look and feel. Put simply, John Daly was the best social-dance partner I've ever had, and I'd already lost him.

The next number was that old war horse "Tea-for-Two Cha Cha." A samba followed, and as Eddie had said, the show must go on. John and I were fine, but something, some spark, had gone from my step. It felt a little leaden, a little less confident. I wasn't sure John noticed until we'd finished the samba and the musicians were taking a short break.

"Getting tired? You seemed kind of rocky on that last turn."

"This isn't a performance, John," I snapped. "It's social dancing. It's supposed to be fun."

"For me it's a performance," he said.

I glanced at my watch. "Well, I'm afraid the show's about over for me."

"Oh, yes. The trains and all that." As he spoke, he was looking over my shoulder.

It's disconcerting to stand in a crowded room talking to someone whose sight is set on bigger game. Their eyes flicker past you, scanning the crowd for Ms. or Mr. or something Wonderful. John's Ms. Wonderful made her appearance, conveniently, at that moment. To her credit she did acknowledge that John, at least temporarily, had a partner.

"You two are unbelievable! I can see why Eddie wanted you here, Bonnie. And you, T'Bird . . ."

"My name's John."

From nearby came a high-pitched squeal. "I knew it! I knew it!"

The woman from the newspaper pushed herself into our group, shoving Dawn to the side in the process, which didn't upset me terribly.

The assistant columnist was several inches shorter than

I, but no lightweight, and when she hurled herself at John Daly and buried her face in the ruffles of his white shirt, he tottered from the impact. He and I exchanged astonished glances until the woman had backed away.

"I'm Elsie Scott," she said breathlessly. "You probably don't remember."

As he straightened his shirt, John shook his head slowly, and it occurred to me that there might be any number of things in John's past that he didn't remember, or would just as soon forget. Had this woman and John shared a bottle of cheap wine? Had she been a one-night stand in a fleabag hotel? Or maybe a fellow guest at a rehab center? I waited for her revelation, anxious that she might embarrass John, but still curious.

"Elsie Scott," she repeated. "I was founder and president of the Brooklyn chapter of your fan club!"

John slapped his forehead "Oh, of course. How could I have forgotten you, Elsie? And all your terrific friends . . ."

If he was being sarcastic, and I suspect he was, Elsie didn't notice. She blushed so that her almost eerily white skin turned pink. "I saw *Isadora* three times, and *Dance Fever* five. All of us were just . . . crazy about you. Because of you I took dance lessons. Of course, I was never very good."

How weird. This odd, pale person was reciting my own history. I had a doppelganger!

As the musicians returned to the bandstand, Elsie glanced at me. "You two make such a great couple, but I wonder . . ."

Anticipating the woman, John took her hand. "You rumba?"

"Oh, my God!" she squeaked, and from her worshipful expression as she trailed John onto the floor you'd have thought she was about to be swept into the arms of a divine being.

"What's that all about?"

Dawn was following the couple with her eyes.

"John was in a couple of shows on Broadway a while back."

"I had no idea."

We watched as John led Elsie through a not-too-bad arch turn. When they did their solo turns, Elsie clockwise and John counterclockwise, you could tell who the expert was. Elsie's steps were too slow and her hip movement exaggerated. John maintained that quick-quick-slow rhythm and the easy hip movement that comes from the knees. Cuban Motion, dancers call it.

"He's fantastic. Even better with a good partner like you," Dawn added kindly. "How did you get to know him?"

"We teach a dance class together at the Y in Huntington."

Eddie, who had joined us, snorted derisively. "T'Bird was in Broadway shows? It must have been a long time ago. From what I hear, he's spent most of his life drunk."

Eddie might as well not have opened his mouth for all the attention Dawn paid him. She nodded toward the dancing couple with a glint in her eye. "Elsie asked me to have lunch with her tomorrow. I was dreading it, but now there's something interesting to talk about. Want to join us, Bonnie? It might be fun."

To be honest, the prospect of lunch with an old fan of John's, and a new one, didn't sound like that much fun. I almost said no, but when Dawn mentioned something about meeting at her apartment, and said we could get something delivered and have lunch there, I changed my mind. Beyond being a dancer, beyond being an office worker, I was a spy, and here was a chance to do one of the things Lee wanted me to do: find out more about the woman.

It turned out that John and I left the club at the same time. The rumba with his adoring fan finished, John collected his coat, changed from his new shoes to his heavy boots, and followed me into the bitter night air. I thought for a moment that this was a touch of gallantry, but John set me straight. The last thing he said to me that night was, "You should always leave the fans wanting more."

I turned in the direction of Tenth Avenue, but I hadn't gone more than a step or two when a young woman passed me on the sidewalk. Like everyone else in New York City she was wrapped in a big coat, but she was wearing earmuffs instead of a hat, and as she passed under the flickering neon sign her short, punkish black hair caught my attention.

"Hey, John," she called. "Is that you?"

"Yeah. Katharine? Are you headed home?"

John paused until the young woman trotted up to him. I paused, too, and watched as they crossed the street together. John said something I didn't hear, and the woman's high-pitched laughter floated through the chilly air.

I thought I was alone out there, but when the woman's laughter faded and the couple disappeared into the night, I was surprised to hear a man say the woman's name softly—"Katharine"—and add, "How interesting."

Max was standing at the edge of the driveway, all but hidden in the building's shadow.

"I didn't realize you were there," I said.

"Yeah. Needed some fresh air. That T'Bird's an interesting guy. One surprise after another tonight. Dawn just told me that you teach a class with him. You must know him pretty well."

"Not really."

"Oh. Well, do you need a ride to Penn Station? My car's just up the block."

I would have loved a ride, actually, but not with Max. On one level I was concerned that he might become interested in me. Sexually, I mean. On another level, I was scared.

On the train ride to Huntington I mulled over those few moments outside the club. John was, indeed, full of surprises. The woman he'd walked into the night with, the one called Katharine, was the woman who, according to the news, had been romantically involved with Brad Gannett.

How does someone whose boyfriend has killed himself on Tuesday behave on Friday? Laughter? Heading home with another man?

Interesting, as Max had said.

But probably not interesting enough for Captain Lee. My tote bag, bare of the smuggled papers that might have fascinated Lee, weighed heavily on my mind. My first day as a spy and I had nothing more than a six-sided key removed from my key ring, an address for a man named Terry who had left a message for Max and Steve, and the sound of a girl's laughter on a dark street.

10

THE LINCOLN MOTEL. IF EDDIE WANTED to find the people who smell sweet, this wasn't the place to look. The smallish, three-sided structure shared a back wall with an older brick building, but the motel itself was 1970's modern-tacky. The faded turquoise and coral panels that covered it were rusting and peeling. There were two floors of rooms, and a count of doors showed six rooms on each floor, all opening onto an outside walkway. Each room had a picture window, though the picture—Forty-first Street—was dismal in the gray late-morning light.

Beneath the first floor there was an open parking area where, in addition to a couple of cars, there were overflowing garbage cans, broken bottles, a pile of dried-up Christmas trees, and something that looked suspiciously like a makeshift tent. As I walked toward the stairs that led to the office, a rat almost as big as Moses darted from behind a trash can and scurried into the trees' dead branches.

Ah, wilderness.

I darted, fast as that rat, up the steps.

The sign suspended by a string over the office door read

"Open" but the door was locked. I pushed a buzzer and a moment later the sign swung to one side. A man's face appeared.

"Yeah."

"I'm looking for one of your guests."

The sign swung back and the door opened.

"Guests?"

He hadn't shaved in a while, but it looked as if he was on the brink of taking the blade to his face. He had a cruddy razor in his hand, and an equally cruddy towel over his shoulder.

"Which of my 'guests' do you want?"

"Terry. A young guy with dark, shaggy hair down on his forehead. Sound familiar?"

The man lifted his shoulders lazily. "Sounds like our boy, but he comes and goes like the wind blows. You might catch him in now, though." He jerked the razor toward the ceiling. "Room seven. On the end over me. And you better knock real hard."

Puzzled, I asked what he meant.

"Terry had company up there last night. They had a grand old time."

The top floor of the motel was less protected from the elements than the lower floor, and as a result was in even worse shape. The rubberized treads on the walkway curled under my feet, and the plywood door to Room seven—and plywood outside in Manhattan stands about the same chance as plywood in hell—was warped and peeling.

I knocked, and called softly, "Terry?"

No answer. I knocked harder. Again, no answer.

Top 40's–type music was coming from inside the room. I pressed my ear to the door. Bruce Springsteen. "Dancing in the Dark."

Taking the advice of the man in the office, I pounded and called again, "Terry!"—but got no response.

There was no window in the door and the knob held fast when I tried it, so I shifted my attention to the picture window. The curtains had apparently started out as a beige

and gold print—autumn leaves or something of that
sort—but now the color was as murky as the forest floor
after a hard winter. The curtains were shut tight at the
center, but the one on the left, farthest from the door, had
lifted slightly at the bottom. Stepping to the edge of the
window, I crouched and squinted.

The bottom of a human foot showed through the glass.
An involuntary "Oh" escaped from me.

The arch was turned down toward the floor and the
little toe up, toward the ceiling. It was a filthy foot. The
big toe, resting on a nest of gold shag carpet, was dark
brown. But the little toe was pale pink. Why . . . ?

I leaned closer, until my face was almost touching the
glass. The Springsteen song had ended. ". . . And guess
what Mother Nature's got in store for us," a smooth-toned
announcer was saying. "Clear today, but by tomorrow
afternoon . . ."

I tottered back on my heels and clamped my hand over
my mouth to smother a full-out scream. The muffled
screech that came from me was lost in the noise of the
city. When it faded I had a hard time getting my breath.

"Someone's dead in there," I gasped into the phone.
"Blood has settled in the lower part of the foot."

"I don't understand this, Miss Indermill," Lee said.
"You were on your way to lunch with the girls but you
stopped at this motel because this Terry person might
have been Brad Gannett's friend?"

"Yes. And because he—Terry—called the club and
wanted to talk to Max or Steve. And now he's probably
dead up in his room."

The room was easily visible from the phone booth, but
now I couldn't make myself look at it. I stared west toward the Hudson.

"All right, Miss Indermill. What I want you to do is
leave. Forget the motel and forget the foot. Go to your
luncheon. I'll notify the people who need to know."

"But . . ."

Lee exploded. "Miss Indermill! You are on the payroll because I need a dependable person inside The Dancing Fool who can make copies of documents and keep her eyes and ears open. I do not need or want a female civilian at Tenth Avenue and Forty-first Street. You seem to be trying to turn your assignment into something it isn't. A glamor job. I suspect you've seen too many movies and TV shows. There is nothing glamorous about real under-cover work, Miss Indermill."

As if there was something glamorous about the foot in the window.

"If I'm not mistaken," Lee went on, "the Lincoln is a well-known hot-bed motel. Do you understand what that means?"

"I can guess."

"Not long ago a female prostitute was murdered and then mutilated in one of those rooms. I hope I do not have to describe the extent of the mutilation to get you out of there now. Go meet the girls for a nice lunch. Have a wine spritzer. My wife sometimes enjoys a spritzer with lunch."

Spritzer? After that foot, a few double martinis would have been more like it.

When I saw the luxurious apartment complex where Dawn lived my first thought was, This looks odd here. Considering what I'd discovered half an hour earlier, my perceptions may have been skewed, but the pink granite buildings around the landscaped plaza—complete with pristine snowman—belonged on the East Side, maybe in the seventies, with pricey boutiques for neighbors and mink-coated matrons for tenants. Among the old Irish bars and boarded-up storefronts along Eighth Avenue the com-plex stood out like a well-groomed, snooty poodle at the dog pound.

My second thought about all this, as I waited for the Puerto Rican doorman to announce me, was, How can Dawn, with her handful of part-time jobs, afford this?

"Hey, Dawn. Beautiful lady name of Bonnie's coming up," the doorman said sloppily into the speaker.

Okay, he wouldn't have gotten away with that class act in the East Eighties, and as I crossed the lobby, signs of neglect showed in the dusty corners and smudged wallpaper, but they still weren't giving these apartments away.

The elevator had just arrived when I was assaulted by an already too-familiar voice.

"Wait for me, Bonnie! Wait! Let's ride up together."

Here came Elsie trotting across the lobby, arms draped with shopping bags, and what a sight she was. With her fluffy white goosedown coat, white boots, white cheeks, and white crocheted hat with a little red pompon, and her crimson nose, she bore an amazing resemblance to that snowman in the plaza outside.

"I got off the subway at the wrong stop," she panted. "I thought it was Eighth Avenue but it turned out to be Broadway. . . ."

She had an annoying way of thrusting her head forward when she spoke, as if getting her mouth close to your face would somehow help you understand her. It didn't work for me. The only place I'm able to tolerate a stranger's face inches from mine is on public transportation when there's no choice, and even then I don't like it. Blanking out the rest of the subway saga, I stepped away from Elsie and held the door so that she could maneuver her unwieldy load of shopping bags onto the tiny elevator.

"This is so sweet of Dawn," she said once she was settled. "She's such a darling little thing, isn't she?"

Dawn may have been darling, but by no stretch, or shrinking, of the imagination was she a little thing. As I pushed the button for the eleventh floor, I responded with a nod. That wasn't effusive enough for my companion. Shuffling the shopping bags around, she edged closer, aggravating the elevator phobia that I usually keep under control, and latched her dark brown eyes onto mine in the strangest way.

"You do like Dawn, don't you? I know it's rare for a girl to be as pretty and talented as Dawn, but she's so nice at the same time. I try never to let envy get the best of me."

"Of course I like her."

Elsie reached toward my face and I flinched. The episode with the foot had left me squeamish, and when she tweaked my cheek with her finger, I almost gagged.

"I'm so glad, Bonnie. Some girls our age might be jealous of Dawn, but she's such a sweetie. And so generous. I wanted to interview her, but she suggested I try for John Daly first. Comebacks make such great copy."

"You're a writer?" I asked once that detestable finger was out of my sight.

"Oh, yes. I've been trying to get my own byline at the paper, but my boss is such an old witch. I can't tell you how many times she's put her name on my work. I hate her."

"Why do you stay?" I naively asked.

"Why? Because celebrities are my life. Ever since I was a little girl. My very first memory is watching the Mouseketeers march out in their darling outfits and count off their names: 'Rickie, Annette' . . ."

Shit! No wonder Eddie had been about to tear his hair out. Thirty seconds with this lunatic and I was ready to slap her silly. Would a scream be inappropriate? Probably. I broke through Elsie's gusher of nonsense by looking at the shopping bags and asking, in a voice so aggressively blaring that it would have disturbed any normal person, "What have you got there?" *Anything sharp? Because before our lunch is over I may either have to kill you or cut my own wrists to keep from listening to you.*

"Oooh, just some little goodies that Dawn, and you especially, might enjoy. They'll take you all the way back to your youth," she tittered as an afterthought.

"My youth isn't all that far . . ."

"They certainly take me back. All those years just disappear and I might as well be seventeen and all full of hope, instead of"—a profoundly sad sigh filled the tiny space—"thirty-eight."

Thirty-eight? As the elevator stopped and the door opened, I fumed over that tidbit. Life can be a bitch.

"And full of . . . ?" I asked, knowing full well what I thought Elsie was full of.

"Memories."

As I followed this creature and her bundles of goodies from the elevator, it wouldn't have taken much urging to get me to plant one of my booted feet on her white quilted backside.

The carpeted hallway spidered out in several directions, which was enough to elicit a big moment from Elsie.

"Now, which way do you suppose we should go?"

You would have had to be blind not to see the series of numbers and corresponding arrows stenciled on the wall directly in front of us.

"To the far left," I barked.

Confused, Elsie turned on her heels, causing one of the shopping bags to swing wide, hit a corner, and rip. Its contents—books and magazines—tumbled onto the carpet.

"Oh, I'm such a silly," Elsie said while I helped her collect the fallen goodies. "Don't you dare leave here without me today, Bonnie, or I'll wander around this building forever. Okay?"

"Um."

The close spacing of the doors along the hall indicated that these apartments were small. When Elsie had gotten her bags together, I kind of herded her along in front of me, using the books now stacked against my chest as a prod. At every door she insisted on pausing and reading the name of the tenant in the little slot under the peephole.

"Nope. The Piesmans live there," she squeaked, and "Whoops. Wrong one. That's the Meyers' apartment."

"Fuck you, Elsie," I said under my breath as we finally got to the door that caused her to squeak, "Here's our star, at last. Dawn Starr."

Any doubts I may have had about Dawn's acting ability disappeared when she welcomed us into the box she called home with a squeal of delight that was every bit as giddy as Elsie's.

The foyer that Dawn waved us into would have been a tight squeeze even without our fat coats and shopping bags, and the three of us tumbled into the combination living and bedroom in a breathless rush of apologies for pushing, poking, and bumping elbows.

"What a cozy little nest! I already feel snug as a bug in a rug," said Elsie as she looked around.

I tried to push my vile mood aside and get into the chirpy spirit of the occasion by peeping and cooing about our hostess's microscopic apartment, but "cozy" and "snug," when used to describe Manhattan living spaces, are euphemisms for "You can lob a spitball from one end of the place to the other without taking a deep breath." Dawn's studio apartment was no exception. It was a tiny square, with four even tinier squares protruding from it like warts: bathroom, kitchen, closet, and terrace warts.

What struck me most strongly, though, had nothing to do with the apartment's size. To me, the place didn't look . . . lived in. I don't mean that I doubted Dawn lived there, but rather that the apartment didn't feel as if it had a past, or a future. For that matter, there didn't appear to be much present around, either. The painted white dinette set and coffee table, as well as the daybed and chair with their flower-print upholstery, had the sterile, no-character look of the furniture in a model apartment.

I don't have such terrific furniture myself, but there's a discernible difference between stuff that you choose, even if you choose it because it's cheap, and stuff that you just fall into. I had a strong suspicion that Dawn had rented the place furnished. Suspicion is an odd word to use, I suppose. There's nothing suspect, much less criminal, about renting furniture. But I was looking for clues, and for me, rented furniture was one. It suggested money to burn.

"And look at the dear, dear terrace," Elsie gushed. "You must enjoy it so in the summer. And the view! Have you ever seen an apartment with such a beautiful view, Bonnie?"

The apartment faced west, and the tiny terrace, which was coated with a sheet of ice that afternoon, would offer all the charm of a toaster oven in the summer. I couldn't imagine Dawn baking her peaches-and-cream pelt out there on an August afternoon. To be fair, the view of the Hudson wasn't half bad, but if I'm going to be honest as well as fair, the one from my ghetto apartment is better. I don't have to look across the tops of four blocks of tenements to see water. This wasn't a time for honesty, though.

"Never. It's gorgeous."

Dawn relieved Elsie of the snowman outfit, but after frowning into the crammed closet for a second, she tossed the white coat across a chair.

I put my load of magazines and books on the coffee table and handed Dawn my coat. That went, without ceremony, on top of Elsie's.

"I've made a salad and ordered a pizza," Dawn said as she moved into the kitchen. "I hope you both like mushrooms."

The table was set with a roll of paper towels, three forks, three glasses, one salt shaker, and a cardboard container of grated cheese. To these, Dawn added a two-liter bottle of diet soda. No chance of a wine spritzer at Saint Dawn's place.

"The pizza should be here soon. We'll have to go downstairs and get it, though. They don't allow delivery people to come up."

Elsie shivered theatrically. "That's very smart. Just think about the awful people you might find at your door otherwise."

"Yes. Think about that." Dawn's back was to Elsie,

but I had a clear view of her profile and caught the malicious twinkle in her eye. "Have you brought the things you mentioned?" she asked as she took a big plastic container from the refrigerator.

"Of course. After you said you were interested, I spent hours gathering all my keepsakes. Oh, don't imagine it was work, though. There's nothing I enjoy more than a trip down memory lane. Now—" Elsie plopped the two remaining shopping bags onto the coffee table. "—I just hope you and Bonnie have as much fun as I did this morning."

The conversation had momentarily lost me. Regardless, the prospect of looking through Elsie's keepsakes was frightful. I figured Dawn would have the same reaction, but to my surprise, when she brought the plastic bowl of salad from the kitchen and said, "I can't wait," she looked as if she meant it.

In no time, Elsie had shoved Dawn's forks and paper towels to the side and dumped the contents of one of the shopping bags onto the table. I stared in speechless dread at the jumble of Broadway *Playbill*s and movie magazines, all of them yellowing and dog-eared.

"Bet you thought *Isadora* was John's first Broadway show, didn't you, Dawn?" the little rascal teased. "You were wrong. And Bonnie, you've probably never seen most of these, even though I'm sure you know much more about John than I do, considering your special relationship. And before I forget," she added, "I want to thank you for letting me take him away from you for those few minutes last night. Frankly, I can't wait to pick-pick-pick at your brain."

Huh? Everything I knew about John Daly could have been condensed into a fifteen-second speech.

With a self-satisfied smirk, Elsie picked up a *Playbill* the years had turned almost brown, and cleared her throat. "John Daly's first Broadway show was *Hair*." She trumpeted this as if she'd come up with the winning answer on a TV game show, and then looked from Dawn to me, and back to Dawn again. Neither of us opened our mouths.

"Here. You see." Opening the *Playbill*, Elsie read: " 'John Daly is honored to be making his Broadway debut in *Hair*. John recently toured England in *West Side Story*, and starred in *Bye Bye Birdie* at the Baltimore Playhouse. He is a graduate of New York City's High School of Performing Arts.' "

After carefully closing the *Playbill* and putting it aside, Elsie opened a photo album.

"Here's an early picture of John when he first went to Hollywood. It's from *Photoplay*, and here's . . ."

Early on during this absurd lunch date I'd mentally positioned myself with Dawn. We were two rational women keeping the door shut against a certifiable crazy. We would listen to Elsie, and look at her "goodies," but there would always be a snicker threatening to burst loose from one or the other of us. If I'd kept some perspective on this whole business, though, the fact that I didn't know Dawn any better than I knew Elsie might have occurred to me. As Elsie bent supplicant-like over a yellowing head shot of a younger John Daly, I eyed Dawn across Elsie's back. I expected to catch her eyeing me back sardonically, but she was gazing at the photo with an expression of mute, drop-jawed admiration.

So there I was, stuck in a confined space with the entire two-person membership of the newly revived John Daly fan club. Waiting for the pizza to show up, we thumbed through old movie magazines I'd never known existed, examined publicity photos, and read press clippings from over twenty years earlier. In that tiny studio, for that short time, the whole world revolved around a song-and-dance man who in reality was so washed up that if he had dropped dead as we poured over his old *Playbill*s, there wouldn't have been a hiccup on *The New York Times* obituary page.

It was easy enough for me to enthuse over Elsie's mementos, and at the same time pull back mentally and put this luncheon in perspective. We were three women who hardly knew each other, huddling together like old friends. The reality was, we all wanted something we thought that one, or both, of the others could provide.

What I wanted had nothing to do with John Daly or with dancing. I was there to find out what I could about Dawn's life. I knew what Dawn wanted, too. There had been that avid curiosity in her eyes the night before at The Dancing Fool. Now, as she looked through Elsie's mementos, soaking up John Daly's past like a sponge, I could almost feel her curiosity changing to . . . want. She wanted my dance partner. Elsie and I were there to feed her information about John.

And why was Elsie there? Because she was nuts, I thought. She was a hero-worshiping fan, an unattractive, not-very-smart woman who had created a world for herself that could be toted around in shopping bags. She lived through the celebrity of people who would hardly give her the time of day. Being with Dawn, a potential celebrity, must have fed her ego. Being with me . . . well, I knew John.

"There's something you could do for me. It would be really wonderful," Elsie said. "I'd be in your debt forever."

Since she and Dawn had been bent over an ancient clipping from *Variety*, I thought that whatever she wanted she wanted from Dawn, which was fine with me. Having Elsie forever in my debt didn't sound like a desirable state of affairs. I was kind of surprised to find that Elsie was looking at me.

"I'd be your friend for life."

I didn't even want her as my friend for lunch, but flat-out rudeness would have been out of place and probably wouldn't have fazed her anyway.

"Oh?"

Her eyes flickered to my left hand. "I'd like an exclusive interview with your fiancé. You see, Bonnie . . ."

She scooted toward me, holding a magazine and looking thoroughly demented.

"I told you how hard I've been trying to get something published with my byline. I have to edit everything the old witch writes, and I never get any credit."

She didn't want to make money, she babbled. She was doing it for love. "Celebrity gossip," she said reverently and with a messianic gleam in her eyes, "is my life."

It was a moment before I grasped what was going on. When I said, quite forcefully, "I'm not engaged to John Daly," you would have thought I'd socked Elsie in her solar plexus. She seemed to deflate like a balloon, but at least she backed away from me.

I glanced at Dawn, who shrugged. "I knew John wasn't your fiancé, but you did leave together last night, so I was wondering about your relationship, too."

"John and I got as far as the sidewalk together. I'm engaged to Sam Finkelstein. He works for a moving company."

Dawn's response was a big smile.

"I'm such a silly. But you do know John better than the rest of us, don't you?" Elsie asked hopefully. "If you were to tell him what I'm interested in . . ."

Recalling John's reaction to this woman the evening before, I quickly shook my head. "I couldn't approach him with that."

Crushed, Elsie looked down at her feet.

"He's a private person," I lied.

She stood silently, and without her babbling the apartment seemed so uncomfortably quiet that for a moment I almost wished for the sound of her voice. Then, thank goodness, an awful static noise filled the room.

"Pizza's here." Dawn bounded into the kitchen, spoke into an intercom for a second, then announced, "That will be about five dollars each."

Excited at the prospect of getting away from Elsie, even for a couple of minutes, I dug out my money and volunteered to go down for the pie. Dawn, equally eager, all but snatched the money from my hand.

"I'll go."

"We'll all go," Elsie offered, her blue funk apparently over.

Here was my opportunity! "You two go. I have to use the bathroom."

"We can wait for you." That, of course, was Elsie.

I gripped my stomach. "I'll be in there a while." I was prepared to double over at the waist and start moaning if that's what it took to get five minutes alone, but things didn't quite come to that. My two lunchmates took me at my word and left.

The second they were gone I was into Dawn's closet. A horror. If the living room had too little of Dawn, the closet had too much. Clothes—and she had a lot of clothes for a struggling type—were stuffed in until they bulged. The floor was thick with shoes, and when I reached toward a box on the shelf, the hats and sweaters all round it threatened to fall on me.

Giving up on the closet, I headed for a small white desk. It was so tacky that it almost fell over when I yanked the top drawer open. Steadying the piece of junk, I searched quickly through the drawer. There was a clutter of stationery, envelopes, rubber bands . . .

Ah! A checkbook. I glanced over the register. It was a bigger mess than mine. Dawn's handwriting was atrocious and she didn't keep a running balance. From what I could tell, over the last couple of weeks she'd written a number of small checks, but no big ones that might cover the rent on this apartment. As for deposits, there had been a number of small ones, the kind you get when you have several small jobs. I put the checkbook back where I'd found it.

Dawn's bank statements were at the back of this drawer. Leaving the most recent ones alone, I took two from several months earlier and slipped them into my tote.

In the next drawer, Dawn kept the things associated with getting a job: resumes, press clippings, telephone numbers. I took a few resumes—on paper, Dawn's life, like mine, appeared in several forms—and shoved them in with the bank statements.

At the back of this drawer I found her charge cards, held together by a rubber band. And what was this, rattling in the corner? A key ring, with—I counted quickly—eight keys, one of them six-sided. Bingo! I struggled to separate that one from the others, but soon gave up and pocketed the entire ring.

On to the credit cards. I thumbed through the top few. Visa, MasterCard, and a California department store. Her bills were stacked here too: phone, cable TV. There was nothing unusual about any of this, except perhaps that there wasn't more. Where were letters from her family? What about birthday cards? Old photos?

But reconsidering, I knew there was nothing suspicious or even unusual about this. The size of Dawn's apartment would have forced her to live . . . light. Keepsakes she wanted to hold on to could have been stored with her family. Anything superfluous was probably tossed.

No, I decided. Dawn is probably just what she appears to be: an aspiring Broadway star.

I had started to put the credit cards back in the drawer, when the rubber band that held them together snapped. My heart jumped as the cards spilled onto the rug. I took a deep breath. Calm down, Bonnie. Just stack the cards and put them back in the drawer with the loose rubber band. Dawn will think it broke in the drawer.

I had gathered the cards into my lap and was trying to rearrange them in a logical order, when my eye was drawn to one in particular. It wasn't a credit card at all. It was a Louisiana driver's license, issued to a Dawnella Starkey. I couldn't help smiling as I studied the photo on the license. It was Dawn, all right, but a rounder-faced Dawn, with bigger hair. Huge hair.

Dawnella Starkey. Hardly a natural for a theater marquee. I didn't blame Dawn for changing it. But why Louisiana? Had she gone to school there?

The license showed her date of birth. Wow! Could she really be that old?

I was calculating Dawn's age when the apartment door burst open.

I slammed the drawer violently, but unfortunately I didn't manage to get all the cards into it. What did get into it was a good bit of my hand, and I was forced to grapple not only with the ghastly embarrassment of being caught with some of my hostess's credit cards in my lap, but searing pain. As I squeezed my fingers, every filthy word I've ever heard ran through my mind.

Elsie spent a couple of seconds with her jaw hanging—a sight I hoped never to see again—and then sized up the situation.

"Shame on you, Bonnie! Stealing. And from someone as sweet as Dawn."

Rubbing my throbbing fingers, I said from between clenched teeth, "It's not what it looks like."

"Humph. Dawn sent me back to make sure you were all right. There she is, worried about you, and here you are . . ."

. . . caught with my fingers in the damned till again. This was a nightmare! I was the world's worst spy. How on earth was I going to deal with this? Elsie's cow eyes had narrowed into beady slits and her lips were gathered into a pious little knot. She was going to squeal for sure.

Shaking her head, she spat, "You're a thief! Wait until Dawn finds out. She trusts you alone in her apartment, and you try to rob her."

My mind was racing around in circles. Should I explain to Elsie that I was a spy? Lee would kill me, and Elsie wouldn't believe me, anyway. She was weird, possibly crazy, but she wasn't necessarily stupid, and right then she seemed to be a lot less stupid than I was. What a damned mess! I stared at the jumble of cards in my lap, frantically trying to think of a way out of this.

"You should be ashamed of yourself."

Shame. That seemed to be a big thing with Elsie. I

screwed my face into an unhappy pout, which, considering the way I felt, wasn't difficult. With Elsie watching me closely, I returned the credit cards to their place at the back of the drawer.

"I am ashamed but I can't help myself. It's a disease. Sometimes, when I admire someone tremendously, I want something of theirs, some memento . . ."

A credit card is some memento, all right. I sounded like an imbecile. Elsie stared at me hard, as if she were looking at a specimen in a bottle.

"Like kleptomania?"

"Yes. Something like that. Thank you for stopping me. Please don't tell Dawn."

"Don't tell?"

But wouldn't that make her disloyal to Dawn? Elsie paced the little room, forehead creased as if this were a matter of national security she was mulling over. I promised her, and literally—God help me—crossed my heart that I'd control my thieving urges. Dawn was going to be back with the pizza soon, and I hoped fervently that Elsie was satisfied with this. You can't imagine how unnerved I became when she stopped pacing, put her hands on her hips, and gave me a calculating stare I wouldn't have thought she was capable of.

"I won't tell Dawn, but you have to do something for me."

There were definite limits to the things I was willing to do for Elsie. If what she wanted was too disgusting, I was going to call Lee and tell him he could start blackmailing Amanda.

"Get me that interview with John Daly."

Behind that cow façade beat the heart of a weasel. At that instant Dawn pushed through the door, the pizza box in her hands. If she noticed that there was a tense standoff taking place in her apartment, she didn't mention it.

"Anybody hungry?"

Looking at Elsie, I nodded. "Okay."

• • •

Dawn—"I'm always watching my weight"—picked at one slice. I—"My appetite's disappeared"—picked at another. Elsie—"Gee I wish I had a cute figure like you girls"—polished off the rest of the pizza, and finally the worst, most interminable lunch of my life, was over.

When the woman—the person—I hated most in the world had trundled herself and her bundles down the subway steps and out of our sight, Dawn and I walked the few blocks to The Dancing Fool.

Dawn had mentioned that she was teaching an aerobics class somewhere in the neighborhood later that afternoon, and before we left her apartment she had put on a leotard and tights. I figured she was going to the club because she wanted to dig another pair of shoes out of the closet. As for me, with Sam due back that evening, I didn't want to put in any more time at the office, but my spying had been so abysmal that I felt I should take another stab at sneaking out with some contracts.

When we walked into The Dancing Fool, John Daly was standing on a chair polishing the mirror behind the bar. He greeted us with a nod and kept working. I hadn't had time to think about the best way to approach John, but I wanted to get it over with. I walked to the bar, expecting Dawn to head straight upstairs. She stayed right with me, though.

"I need a favor, John," I said.

Nodding, he looked at me. "For you, partner, anything."

I didn't believe that for a second, but what the heck. "I sort of promised Elsie Scott an interview with you. She wants to submit it to her paper."

"Elsie? That strange fan-type person who was here last night?"

Shrugging, I said, "I felt sorry for her."

"You ought to know that pity is an emotion that gets you nothing but trouble, but I'll do it for you. Tell her to give me a call. My number's in the book. Maybe I can get the interview done with by phone."

I had my doubts about that, but kept quiet.

Dawn had been keeping quiet too, but when I started to walk away, she said, "I really enjoyed you last night. You are so impressive."

Her tone was flirtatious, making the most of the double entendre, and I knew she wasn't talking to me.

"Thank you, Ms. Starr," John said.

Looking properly chastised, Dawn took a step nearer the bar. "Please call me Dawn. I'm sorry if I've seemed kind of abrupt. I'm always so busy and frantic and   "

"That's okay," he said lightly. "Old T'Bird's gotten used to people being abrupt."

She extended her hands palms up, a gesture of helplessness. "Come on, John. I've apologized. Can't we be friends?"

Stepping off the chair, John leaned over the bar and smiled at Dawn in the most superior way imaginable. His ego might have taken a beating over the years but there was a core of toughness in there.

"Am I hearing you right? You want to be friends with T'Bird, the drunk who sweeps up around here? Or do you want to be friends with John Daly, the Tony Award winner?"

Dawn slipped off her coat and threw it across the back of a bar stool. She was wearing a bulky pink sweater over her leotard, which had the effect of making her look a lot more frail than she was. "I'd like to be friends with both."

"Sorry, but T'Bird's not around anymore. You'll have to settle for me."

"That would be all right."

The aloof quality disappeared from John's smile, leaving just a smile. They had forgotten about me, and when I tromped up the stairs neither of them glanced my way.

There was no one on the second floor, and for all the interest the pair downstairs had in me I could have walked out with everything in the place. I gathered some papers to copy, acutely conscious of the mating dance that was

going on below me. The feelings I'd had the evening before—rejection, resentment—were gone. These were two
determined, talented people with their eyes focused on the
prize. I wished them both luck. He'd had a hard time, and
who knew what Dawnella Starkey had gone through before she became Dawn Starr.

After looking up John's number and leaving it on Elsie's answering machine, and calling my landlord's secretary to report my mice, I went back downstairs.

Dawn and John were in the middle of the dance floor,
side by side, hands clasped. He was counting: ". . . two,
three, slide, close." It wasn't a ballroom step they were
working on. I think it might have been a bit from *Chorus
Line*'s great finale, "One Singular Sensation."

They didn't notice that I was leaving until I waved and
called, "See you next week."

"Bye, Bonnie . . . four, five, six."

Dawn's bulky sweater lay in a heap on the floor, and
looking at her, I knew that she was the reason God had
invented Spandex.

As I walked out into the gray afternoon Eddie was
walking in. When he saw the couple on the floor, his
expression was murderous.

11

"THE CONDITION YOU DETECTED ON the foot in the Lincoln Motel—the blood pooling at the lower portion of the body—is called *livor mortis*, Miss Indermill."

"But was it Terry?"

"I will tell you more when I know more, *if* the information is relevant to your job."

"But was he shot? Max has a pistol. . . ."

"For which Max has a license. And no, the person who died in the Lincoln Motel had not been shot. Go on about Miss Starr, please. You tell me she has a Louisiana driver's license and she's changed her name. If my name was Dawnella Starkey and I was in show business, I'd change it too."

Lee sounded cranky and impatient, as if I was keeping him from more important things. Was he like James Bond's control, managing a huge network of spies? Maybe I was only a minor player in his network, the equivalent of a secret agent from Bermuda.

"But she said she'd lived in California since she was a teenager. This Louisiana driver's license was issued ten years ago. And she's lying about her age. Her resume says she's twenty-four but she's almost thirty."

Lee snorted into the phone. "My wife lies about her age by more than that. What else have you got for me?"

That dead body I'd found for Lee apparently amounted to no more than a tiny blip in his busy day. "I've taken some papers from the office and had them copied."

"Can you speak up? I can't hear you."

It's tough being a spy in a city where private phone booths have become obsolete. The pay phone at La-Guardia had a tiny tin bonnet around it to offer privacy from the rest of the world. The bonnet was a joke. In the background there was the ceaseless drone of engines, and every few seconds the airport public address system announced arriving and departing flights. While hoards of people surged past, some of them so close that they buffeted me with their luggage, I called out names of some of The Dancing Fool's contractors.

"What was that last one?"

"DeJulio Plumbing," I shouted. "But I've got to tell you something else important. I got caught going through Dawn's . . ."

"What?"

"Someone caught me . . ."

A man at the phone next to mine was involved in his own shouting match and glared around the bonnet. The roar of an arriving plane drowned out my words.

"Announcing USAir Flight 231 from Buffalo, arriving at Gate . . ."

"Forget it," I yelled. "It's no big deal. I've taken care of it."

Disgusted, I hung up. Elsie had blackmailed me and I couldn't even get the message through to Lee. But what did it matter? Lee was blackmailing me, too. He'd probably admire her.

Through the big window overlooking the runway I saw the plane taxiing toward the ramp. There were still a few minutes to wait so I called Information and got the number of the management office at Dawn's apartment complex.

"Twelve hundred and eighty dollars a month," the

woman who answered the phone told me when I asked the price of a studio.

"For one of those little places? That's ridiculous."

"The rent includes electricity, gas, and water," she assured me. "If you would like to see . . ."

"Thank you, but I can't afford it." At that price, the rent would have to include food, clothing, and transportation, too.

Sam's plane had stopped moving, but the doors to the ramp were still closed. I glanced hurriedly through the two bank statements I'd filched from Dawn's desk. There was no check for $1280, and there was no check payable to the management company. This meant that someone else was paying Dawn's rent. Maybe a wealthy relative, or a boyfriend, or even an ex-husband.

On the surface, Dawn seemed open and ready to tell all, but in reality she had told almost nothing, and a lot of what she'd told had been a lie. If I dug deeper—maybe into the fertile Louisiana soil that big-haired Dawnella Starkey had sprouted from—there was no telling what might turn up.

The passengers from Sam's flight were finally streaming into the airport. I joined the clot of people waiting by the gate, and when Sam walked through lugging his old duffle bag, I realized, suddenly, how much I'd missed him. Sam wasn't only my lover and my fiancé. He was my best friend and my feet on the ground. I hugged him so hard that Dawn's key ring pressed into my hipbone, and while we were together I didn't have much trouble keeping my mind off the cast of characters at The Dancing Fool.

One A.M., in bed. We'd been there for some time. Don't believe anyone who tells you that men over forty-five are on a downhill slope. Or that their minds are slipping, either. Panama was still very much on Sam's.

"So, what about it?" he asked.

"I'm not sure I understand about Panama."

"What's to understand? We go, we relax, we have a good time. This trip is something that . . ."

He shifted his body away from mine, a sign of trouble.

". . . that I've wanted to do for years, but there were always problems. Money, or time. And then, when I finally had the money and the time . . ."

Sam grew silent, and I understood about Panama.

Eileen had been more of an outdoor type than I am. Water skiing, fishing, boating. She'd loved those things. This Panama trip was probably one she and Sam had talked about for years. They'd probably gotten brochures, maybe even planned itineraries. . . .

Sam shifted close again, and when I peered through the dark I made out the strong contours of his face.

"So what do you say?" he asked.

"It sounds fine to me."

Was that a cop-out? Probably. But that's what I said, and what the hell! I've never been to Panama.

While Sam and I were together those two days, I told him about one of my new jobs. At first he didn't understand it. Why, he wondered, was I wasting my time working in The Dancing Fool's office? Friendship, I told him, and since Sam values friendship, he accepted that.

I can't imagine what he would have thought if I'd told him I was a spy.

Nine P.M. Monday. I'd just dropped Sam at LaGuardia. The car's headlights made bright funnels against the dark asphalt. Otherwise, except for the glittering patches of ice at the side of the road, the moonless winter night seemed pitch-black. At the end of the access road from the airport I tapped the brakes, slowing. Left to Long Island, or right to Manhattan?

The Dancing Fool was closed on Mondays. If there was any business or any cleaning to be done, it would have been done during the day. Nobody would be there now.

The driver behind me blasted his horn, goading me to make a decision. Hitting the accelerator, I turned right and merged into the Manhattan-bound traffic.

I left the Chrysler in a lot on Ninth Avenue and walked the rest of the way. It was almost ten by the time I got to West Forty-fifth Street. It wasn't one of Manhattan's bright spots even when the lighting was at its best. With The Dancing Fool's neon sign off and no moon above, the block had an eerie quality. Even the best of the tenements, which in the light of day took on a jaunty, defiant air, looked ravaged. It was too cold for all but the most determined walkers, and the Broadway theaters were closed on Monday nights, so vehicle traffic was light.

As I got closer to the club my heartbeat quickened. It wasn't fear, though. It was excitement. An adrenalin rush. The two days with Sam had been a pleasure, but this spying business offered its own kind of kick. Sure, the fact that my spying was authorized by a police captain took some edge off the danger—if worse came to worst I could always scream for the cops—but as I hurried up the street I imagined myself dressed in black from head to toe, with camouflage paint on my face. As it was, I was wearing my bright green parka and a tan hat. Only my shoes were appropriate for breaking and entering. I'd driven to the airport in sneakers, wearing an extra pair of socks to help keep out the cold.

At the walkway leading to the club's entrance I paused and glanced around. There was no one on the sidewalk in either direction and, though lights shone from the tenements on the other side of the street, it was much too cold for anyone to be hanging out on the steps.

I'd taken a flashlight from the Chrysler's glove compartment, but enough light came from a street lamp so that I didn't need it. Both locks turned easily when I inserted the keys. Slipping through the door, I hurriedly relocked it from the inside. Fifteen seconds to get to the alarm and turn it off. I didn't dare turn on the club's lights, but I'd rehearsed this move in my head. Holding the key for the alarm in my fingers, I rushed on the tips of my toes to the alarm switch next to the coat-check. A second hand inside me was counting: four-and-a-five-and . . .

One turn clockwise, Eddie had said. And I'd watched him turn off the alarm with just that: one turn clockwise. But the damned key wouldn't move clockwise. Sweat broke out across my forehead. Could it be counterclockwise? My fingers started shaking and I couldn't keep the key in the lock. It slipped free and tumbled among the others on the ring.

No time to grab for my flashlight. My inner second hand was ticking as I groped for the alarm key and tried to get it back into the lock: thirteen-and-fourteen-and—

Fifteen. Too frightened to think any further than the next second, I braced myself for the scream of the alarm. Sixteen-and-seventeen . . . No time even to run.

When my count reached twenty, I let myself take in a shallow breath of air. At about thirty, that breath came out in an involuntary, almost silent gasp. The alarm wasn't set. The last person out of the club had forgotten to activate it. Eddie was probably the guilty party, and I gave mute thanks for his carelessness.

My earlier exhilaration was gone, replaced by anxiety. I wanted to get the job done with and get out of there fast.

The only light in the club came from the skylight far overhead. In full daylight the big window was caked with dirt, and light barely penetrated it. On that moonless night only a soft gray light made its way through the glass.

The club was surely empty, but obeying the furtive part of my nature I left my flashlight in my pocket and tiptoed almost soundlessly up the stairs.

As virtues go, furtiveness may not be in a league with chastity or patience, but it has its moments. Sometimes it can save your spying neck. I had crept to the top of the stairs, when I saw the muted glow of a light down the hall. For a moment it shone so steadily that it might have been a weak bulb left burning. Then it moved, sweeping the area in an arc before fading.

I froze, terrified. There was another person in the club

with me. When my breathing steadied I peered around the corner toward the office and saw the vague outline of the open door. And then a muffled sound caused me to glance toward the other side of the hall. The faint light glimmered again. It was coming from the security room. Someone was in there with a flashlight.

That paranoid nut Max, messing with his equipment. That was my first thought. He'd be furious if he found me there. I had to think of some story. The next thing that flashed through my mind was even worse. Max didn't need to sneak around in his own club. There was a thief in the club, a man—and I immediately assumed it was a man—who wouldn't give a rat's ass what kind of story I concocted.

I crept down the steps on tiptoes that were even softer than the ones that had climbed up. No sooner had I reached the first floor when there was the unmistakable squeak of the security room's door. The almost unbearable sound of footsteps in the hall above followed.

The thief was heading for the stairs. Where could I go? The front door was too far away and too hard to unlock. Edging silently into the coat-check, I crouched behind the partly open half-door.

He came down the stairs on feet as quiet as mine had been, but a metallic clank followed each of his steps. He was carrying something. When he reached the bottom floor I held my breath. The flashlight's beam swept the wall behind me and was gone again. His steps took him toward the bar. I recognized the sound of the cash register opening, of fingers scraping through whatever bills and coins it held. When he'd finished with that he moved toward the coat-check again, and then past it. With every step, whatever he carried clanked.

He was at the outside door now, unlocking one lock and then the other.

And finally a quick beam of light was followed by darkness as the door closed behind him. The tumblers moved in both locks, but I didn't budge until the sound of the thief's footsteps and the faint clang of metal that accompanied them had disappeared.

My knees were shaking so hard I had trouble getting to my feet. As I steadied myself on the counter of the coat-check, I fought the urge to leave. I'd gone through too much to give up, though, so after a moment I climbed the stairs.

The security room's door was shut, but it swung open when I pushed it with my shoulder. The videotaping device wasn't running and the room was completely dark. I scanned it quickly with my flashlight. Everything looked the same. Figuring that when Max discovered the break-in he might have the place fingerprinted, I slipped on my gloves before touching anything.

I tried the safe first. Locked. The videotape cassettes were lined up neatly on the shelves above the safe. When I'd been in the room before there had been no time to study them. Now I focused the light on the first shelf, where the cassettes were in easy reach. They had red-rimmed labels and had been numbered by hand. The first read "1." Shifting the light to the end of the shelf, I saw "31." Thirty-one possible days in a month. These were the tapes Max used in the video recorder. If he worked in a logical way, and Max was nothing if not logical, he would reuse them month after month. That way he would always have a four-week history of what had gone on at the cash register and in the restrooms. Efficient and simple.

Some of the tapes on the second shelf appeared to be back-of-the-video-store stuff. *Naughty, Bawdy Nurses*, and the like. A few of these had hand-printed labels but most were typeset, indicating they had been purchased from a supplier. Maybe these tapes were the reason Max spent so much time in this room. I was tempted by *Tempestuous Temps*, but moved on with my flashlight.

If anything in the room looked different it was the cardboard cartons stacked along the wall. There seemed to be fewer of them than before. Crouching, I dug my gloved fingers under a flap of cardboard and pried it loose.

My flashlight's beam caught a dozen quart bottles nested inside. Taking one out, I saw that it was filled with an amber liquid. What on earth . . . ? I twisted the cap free and was almost overcome by a smell so strong it made my eyes water. Cheap whiskey, in unlabeled bottles.

Was this it? The big crime Lee's bad boys were involved in? I almost laughed out loud. Max and Eddie were pouring cheap liquor into the bar's fancy-label bottles. Illegal, sure, and they could lose their liquor license if the authorities found out, but it was a long way from drug smuggling and prostitution. If this was the extent of their crime, Max and Eddie were on the Milquetoast end of "bad."

Before leaving the secure room I dropped one of the bottles into my tote. Lee wanted evidence; he'd get a bottle of cheap booze.

I shone my light briefly around the office. From my quick examination, the room was unchanged. It had been a dump on Saturday and it was a dump now. A burglar would have to be damned desperate to take anything from it.

Down in the cellar the furnace shuddered to life. It was a familiar sound, but not one I'd heard while sneaking around the building in the dark. It spooked me, and my heart jumped.

Furtiveness didn't play much of a part in my exit from The Dancing Fool. Trotting down the stairs, I unlocked the door and got out fast.

I was already at the corner of Tenth Avenue when I remembered that the thief—the first thief, if the bottle of cheap liquor in my tote made me a thief, too—had locked both locks in the front door. I almost retraced my steps but changed my mind. The thief wasn't likely to come back and insist, "I did *too* double lock the door."

There were a couple of blue and white police cars in front of the club when I got there Tuesday morning. I hurried in, all set to act just as shocked and huffy about the robbery as anybody else. The mob of cops inside indicated that my bosses had raised a serious fuss. In a perverse way it was fun watching Eddie in the role of the injured party rather than the guilty one. He stormed around, first flinging open the cabinets behind the bar, then jumping to the bandstand to glare at the DJ's mixing board and say, angrily, "At least they didn't touch this. It's the most valuable thing in the place."

Amazing. At the tax shelter firm where we'd met, Eddie's indifference to his job had been an inspiration to the entire staff. Goes to show you what happens when your own money is involved.

A second later Max followed a couple more cops down the stairs. Having seen his temper at work, I expected him to be in a fury that equaled Eddie's, but he was strangely subdued.

"They didn't get into the safe," he told Eddie.

Eddie sniffed. "It was empty anyway."

"We had a break-in?" I asked, all innocence. "What did they take?"

Max glanced over. "Twenty-some dollars out of the register, and the adding machine and Dictaphone from the desk. At least that's what we've noticed so far."

Why don't you tell the cops about the bottle of cheap booze, Max? "Maybe Steve just borrowed the money from the register," I said.

"No way," said Eddie. "Steve knows better."

"And you say the security system was activated when you left here yesterday?"

That was one of the cops, anticipating a question I'd wanted to ask.

"Yes," Eddie answered. "We have this guy who comes in to clean but he doesn't have keys. After he left yesterday I turned on the alarm myself."

"You're sure of that? A couple of times you've forgotten about it." Max's voice rose as he added, "This is *my* investment we're playing with here, you know."

Eddie responded hotly. "I've got money coming if that's what's bothering you. And I *did* set the alarm and lock the door behind me, so don't try to blame me."

Max, no longer subdued, snapped back at his partner. "What's bothering me isn't just being robbed. It's being robbed by someone who had keys and knew how to turn off the alarm system."

"Okay, guys. Cool it. There's no real damage done," the cop said.

When he asked Max who had keys, I learned that there were quite a few sets floating around. Max, Eddie, Steve, Eddie's aunt, Max's father.

"And Dawn. She lost hers, so I gave her a second set just this weekend."

All innocence again, I said, "Someone might have found the keys she lost."

Max shook his head. "She thinks they're somewhere in her apartment, but even if they're not, there was nothing on the key ring to identify the club."

The cops left a few minutes later, and the moment they were gone Eddie and Max were at each other's throats. Max didn't know his ass from his elbow when it came to security, Eddie said. They should have hired a professional. Max countered that Eddie was a careless jerk with a thirty-second attention span who couldn't be trusted to do anything right.

Lee was wasting his time with this pair. Their partnership wasn't going to last long enough for them to get into too much mischief.

Leaving them squabbling, I went upstairs. The floor was deserted and the security room door wide open. I wasn't about to risk going into the room while Max was around, but I took a moment to examine the door frame. Like the door, it was metal. It didn't appear that a tool had been used to pry the door, and when I ran my fingers over it I found the metal smooth. There was no sign of scraping or picking around the lock, either.

That meant that the thief who had beat me to the club

had carried a full set of keys. But most of the people who had keys also knew that the club was closed on Mondays, and there was little chance of finding a big stash in the register or even in the safe. Of the key-holders who might not be aware of that, I immediately scratched Eddie's aunt. I've met her. A smart woman in her fifties, she'd no more consider robbing a dance club than she'd consider hijacking an airplane.

What about someone connected with Max's father? Suspected criminals, but just the same, would they sneak into a club to steal what amounted to pocket change? Hardly.

As for the others, I couldn't come up with any reason why either Max or Eddie would have faked this, and despite Dawn's secret past, she didn't strike me as a sneak thief.

That left Steve, and though with my leather pants phobia I can't be trusted to objectively judge people who wear them, he was my best bet. I figured he'd stopped by to pick up *Dirty Debutantes* or one of the other classics from the film archive in the little room. He'd needed some cash, so he emptied the register. But his reason for taking the old adding machine and Dictaphone eluded me, and why he'd done all this in the dark was another mystery.

Eddie and Max stayed downstairs long enough for me to return the smuggled documents to their proper stacks on the floor. Both my bosses had left letters on the desk to be typed. Max's, to a company that supplied commercial restaurant equipment, asked for prices. Eddie's, to a law firm that had recently moved to the area, described the club's facilities and suggested that the firm might want to rent the space for special events.

How ordinary this all was. Here was a new business trying to keep afloat and grow, and doing all the things a business in that situation would do. Not only that, but Max and Eddie, whom Lee suspected of being involved in God-knows-what nasty business, apparently hadn't had any reservations about calling the police when the place was robbed, and letting those police wander all over the club.

Their spat seemingly over, Eddie and Max came up to the office as I was typing the letters.

"You know what we need?" That was Eddie.

"A computer," I responded.

"Forget it," Max said.

"We need stationery with a club logo."

"Okay, but what's the club's logo?"

"Hmm."

Pulling a finished letter from the typewriter, I said, "The dancing feet, like on the neon sign."

Both men nodded, and Eddie gave me a thumbs-up. "Look into getting some printed."

"Get prices," Max put in, "but don't order anything. We're twenty dollars poorer than we were last night."

What a low-rent operation this was. If this pair was laundering money or selling drugs, they weren't doing it very well.

"Maybe I can find a printer who wants to learn to dance," I said.

My bosses were discussing what a fine idea that was when someone pounded on the front door. Max trotted down the stairs, and a second later I heard him shouting.

"You've lost your second set of keys? The ones I just gave you Sunday? What's wrong with you, Dawn? We've been robbed and it's probably because you're leaving keys all over the city."

"Not all over the city, Max," Dawn yelled back. "Both sets are somewhere in my apartment. I just can't find either of them."

Dawn was in her usual rush when she came upstairs to dig some clothes out of the office closet. "Someone broke in last night?"

She was looking at Eddie, but he made a point of ignoring her. His gaze seemed frozen on one of the letters I'd typed.

"They took the cash out of the register and also the

adding machine and Dictaphone,'' I told Dawn.

''How strange. Why would anyone want that junk?''

It *was* strange. So was the fact that Dawn was missing not just the keys that I'd taken from her drawer, but a second set as well.

By late afternoon Max had changed all the club's locks, including the one on the secure room. He was real parsimonious in handing out the new keys. When he handed me a set for the front door and the alarm, I nodded toward the locked door of the Celebrity Lounge.

''What about the ladies' room?''

''Why can't you use the one in the office?''

''Because it's disgusting.''

Max pressed the Celebrity Lounge key into my hand almost as if it hurt him to let go of it.

''What about the room with the safe?'' I knew what the answer would be, but I wanted to see his reaction.

''You've got all the keys you need for now.''

Max tried to temper the hostile edge in his voice by forcing a smile, but it didn't work. Funny how every time I started thinking that Max was just one of the guys, he did something to change my mind.

I spent the afternoon typing, filing, and looking for clues that might make Captain Lee happy. The first two I did pretty well, but as for the clues . . . *nada*! Eddie and Max were in and out of the office constantly, but that wasn't the problem The problem was that, other than the cheap booze, I couldn't find anything going on that shouldn't be going on.

I was finishing up late that day when I discovered that Elsie had come through for John. Actually it was Eddie who discovered it. He was sitting behind the other desk reading the newspaper when he blurted, ''She screwed us! Can you believe it?''

''Who?''

''That Elsie . . . person.'' He read out loud: '' 'Ever wonder whatever happened to John Daly, the dreamboat

Tony Award winner we all adored in *Isadora* and *Dance Fever*? After some lean years, which he admits had a lot to do with wine and women and not enough to do with song, John is back and he's better than ever. He's a member of the Hell's Kitchen Actors' Workshop, and will soon appear in their production of William Inge's *Picnic*. Good luck, John. We're rootin' for you.' ''

Stepping around the desk, I looked over Eddie's shoulder. I wouldn't have believed it possible, but there was Elsie's byline at the top of the article. It was really more of a blurb than an article, I suppose, amounting to about two inches at the bottom of a page in the entertainment section, but she had managed to say a lot.

Looking up at me, Eddie raised his eyebrows. "Dreamboat? Better than ever? T'Bird's a lush. He just managed to drag his sorry ass to the dentist and the barber in the same week."

John was a member of the same actors' workshop that Brad Gannett had belonged to, but I didn't mention that to Eddie. "I don't think John is drinking these days, and he is really talented."

"You're part of his fan club, too? Interested in the 'dreamboat' yourself? What would Sam say?"

"Come on, Eddie. You're overreacting." I nodded at the paper. "Maybe the article will get John some work. How did Elsie screw you, anyway?"

"How? By not mentioning the club; that's how. I'm working like a coolie here. Killing myself. And for what? So my janitor can get his name in the paper."

Eddie circled the article with a red felt-tip marker and threw the paper into the IN box. "I'll leave this for Max. Reading it should do a lot for his disposition."

He swiveled his chair so that it faced the window. "I hate this weather! And they're predicting more snow."

Eddie sat lost in his thoughts as I put on my jacket.

"Well, I'll see you tomorrow."

"Before you go, Bonnie, there's something I want your opinion about." He swiveled the chair back toward me.

"Sure."

"Do you think Dawn's interested in T'Bird? I saw them practicing Saturday afternoon, and then Sunday they were here for Ballroom Dancing."

Ordinarily Eddie can put on a happy face in situations that would send most of us into therapy, so this hangdog look surprised me.

"I mean," he continued, "they showed up separately but left together. I'm sure she'd never sleep with that bum or anything like that, but . . ."

Judging from Eddie's expression, he wasn't sure of that at all. As for me, I wouldn't have been shocked to learn that Dawn and John were doing the tango on her flower-print daybed at that very instant.

"Dawn and John are in the same field, and they're both ambitious. It's not surprising that they're . . ."

I was trying to be kind and at the same time reasonably honest. There was no point in keeping Eddie's hopes up. But Eddie looked so miserable that I couldn't quite bring myself to say *interested in each other*. A phrase Billy uses that covers a multitude of sins is what I ultimately came up with.

". . . hanging out."

"Hanging out?" Eddie rubbed his fingers over his fore-head, thinking. "Yeah. That's probably all it is. They both like to dance, and so they're hanging out. It's probably not anything heavy. Like . . . Bonnie?"

"What?"

"When you were trying to make it on Broadway you didn't sleep with all the guys you danced with, did you?"

The question was so ridiculous that I couldn't keep a straight face. "No. I sure tried, but some of them were gay, and some of them were married, and some of them just didn't want me."

A small smile crossed Eddie's face. When I left the office, he was on the phone with a woman who was in-terested in having her wedding reception at the club. He was doing a real selling job on her, and seemed like his old self.

12

IN THE SUMMER YOU SEE STREET PED-
dlers everywhere, but in February—
especially a February like the one New
York City was struggling through—it's
a desperate peddler who takes to the
street. The one I got involved with that
afternoon—and when I say involved it's
not the same kind of involved I suspected Dawn and John of—was desperate.

Lee's directive—"Get me everything
you can"—had caused me to stuff my
tote with a pile of bills from the Fong Yee Laundry and
a bill from Santini Wholesale Liquors. From what I could
tell, Eddie and Max got their unlabeled booze from Santini. Was this information likely to light up Lee's life?
Probably not. It was relatively warm—low-30's—and
fading daylight or not, I had decided to walk to Penn
Station. I didn't want the exercise so much as the air.

I was on Tenth Avenue just past Jaguida's when I spotted the peddler. Before I spotted him, he spotted me; that's
for certain. They seem to know that I'm an easy mark.
Maybe it's my weakness for those five-dollar earrings in
little Saks and Lord & Taylor boxes that they hawk.
Everyone knows that in their tawdry little lives these ear-

rings have never seen the inside a decent department store, but I can't resist.

He was a short, light-skinned black man with a ragged, patchy beard and a bad case of the jitters. A Yankees jacket peeked from under the mountain of ponchos wrapped around him, and on his feet were green rubber boots with some serious rips in them. As street peddlers go, he was strictly low end. He'd set up shop inside the vestibule of a tenement that happened to house a print shop. The shop was closed, but I had paused by the window. I was wondering what they'd charge to print up some Dancing Fool stationery, when the peddler called from the vestibule's open door.

"Lady! I got great stuff in here."

It's one thing to be a sucker for junk jewelry, but quite another to have a death wish. I stepped away from the building to put some distance between myself and this man.

He darted onto the sidewalk and danced nervously in front of me.

"Check it out, check it out," he kept saying.

His eyes were wild, the jumpy eyes of a speed freak. As I tried passing around him I glanced into the entryway, where the man's wares were displayed in all their seedy glory on a sheet that looked as if it had done hard time in the Lincoln Motel. I wouldn't have touched the sheet, or most of his wares, with a ski pole. Among the things he was trying to entice me with were chipped plates, broken glasses, and warped records. And, at the edge of the sheet nearest the door, caught by a shaft of fading daylight, one antiquated adding machine and one obsolete Dictaphone.

The peddler, realizing he had a live sucker in his hands, jumped back into the dimly lit vestibule. "Anything you want. You tell me what you want to pay."

I pointed from the safety of the sidewalk. "How long have you had that adding machine and Dictaphone?"

"I picked them up this morning. Brand-new. Boxes got

damaged. That's why I'm sellin' them cheap. Three dollars each.''

He might have just gotten the machines that morning, but they hadn't been brand-new for two or three decades.

"Where did you get them?"

Perhaps I sounded more fierce than I felt, because he became very indignant. "I didn't steal them! You saying I stole them?"

"No. I just want to know where they came from."

The peddler fidgeted his way back onto the sidewalk. "Did you buy them from somebody?"

I suspect he was weighing his options. Was I a cop? Or the real owner of the machines? Or did I just want to know their pedigrees before I plunked down my six bucks?

"I found them. You want them or not? Don't be wasting my time."

Opening my purse, I took out a ten-dollar bill. "I want them, but only if you show me where you found them."

The man's jumpy eyes steadied briefly at the sight of the money. "Sure I show you."

He handed me the adding machine and Dictaphone, one at a time, and then stretched out his mittened hand, palm up. I dropped the merchandise into my tote and shook my head. "After you show me."

When the peddler had stacked his remaining merchandise behind the tenement's door, he draped the sheet over it. Considering the condition of that sheet, it probably amounted to some of the most formidable burglar-proofing in the city.

The old office equipment weighed a ton. They don't make them like they used to. I could hardly keep up with the peddler as he jittered his way to the corner and turned east on Forty-fourth. He kept glancing back over his shoulder at me, afraid I might take off without paying. We might have looked like an unlikely couple—a reasonably together woman trotting after this jived-up mess— but no one in the heart of Hell's Kitchen gave us a glance.

He stopped in front of an alley between two five-story tenements. "There. That's where I got them."

One of the buildings was in decent shape. Lights shone from behind new windows, and the fire escape snaking up the building's side had been painted recently. The thump thump of salsa music blared from one of the apartments.

The other building was boarded up. There was a Dumpster in the alley, and a big tube—it must have been twenty inches in diameter—ran up from it into a third-floor window of that deserted building. The top of the Dumpster stood open, propped against the wall, and the trash in it had overflowed into the alley. There was a lopsided pile of tires back there, too, and a discarded stove.

I glanced at the peddler. "You found these things in the Dumpster this morning?"

"Right on top. I swear on the Bible."

He was bouncing back and forth on the balls of his feet as if he were dodging bullets, but his eyes kept aim on the fist where I clutched the ten-dollar bill. When I stretched my hand toward him, he snatched the money, said "Thank you thank you," and was gone in a flash.

It was twilight now and the shadows of steel window guards from the occupied tenement cast ornate patterns on the ground. At the alleyway's far end an ailanthus tree, bare of leaves, poked through a chain-link fence topped with a tangle of razor wire. The passage looked deserted, but I decided against taking a stroll into its depths. It wasn't likely, but a very quiet bogeyman could have been hidden in the shadows behind the Dumpster. After my experience in the club the night before, I'd had my fill of bogeymen.

As I walked to Penn Station, the old office machines were heavy on my shoulders and on my mind. There was no reason for the peddler to lie, so the first question was: How had these pieces of junk from the club ended up in the Dumpster? Answer: The person who robbed the club had looked for an out-of-the-way place to get rid of them. Next question: Why? Answer: Obvious. Because he hadn't wanted them. Last question: Then why take them in the first place? Answer: Because the thief thought on first glance that they were valuable? No way. A thief sophisticated enough to get into the club without setting off the alarm system wouldn't be so stupid. Wasn't it more likely that the thief had taken the adding machine and Dictaphone to make it look as if he were only after valuables?

"Five-thirty-five to Jamaica, Hicksville, Huntington," was being announced when I got into Penn Station. I hurried down the steps to the platform, the equipment in my tote banging into my hip. When I'd settled into a window seat and the train's wheels were rumbling, I asked myself what the thief might have been after if it wasn't valuables. And that led to still another question: Had he found it?

"Bonnie? Why haven't you called me? I've got to discuss something with you. I'm absolutely sick with worry. You're not working tomorrow morning, are you? Please come for brunch. Tony will be gone, so we can talk."

Sick with worry. That was a new one. I couldn't ignore Amanda after hearing it.

She answered the phone immediately, but I could tell by her too-light voice that Tony was nearby.

"See you at eleven tomorrow. I have a new omelet pan and a recipe that uses aged goat cheese. What do you say?"

Whoopee!

Amanda and Tony have squeezed it all into their kitchen: juicer, blender, dicer, slicer, cappuccino machine. The biggest cooktop this side of a four-star restaurant, and a refrigerator that does everything but hover nervously and ask, "Is everything all right," while you eat. In their kitchen, if you're so inclined, you can make carrots look like confetti and radishes look like rosebuds.

They're not rich by any means. Amanda blew every

nickel of a small inheritance from a great-aunt on this
stainless-steel wonderland. From what Amanda has told
me, that little old Southern lady cooked on a wood stove
most of her life. I wonder what she'd make of nuking a
turkey in a microwave? Probably not much.

The last time Amanda had a secret she "just had to
tell" me, she confessed that she was in love with—in fact,
engaged to—Tony. That wouldn't have been a big deal
for me except that her involvement with Tony kind of
overlapped my involvement with Tony. That's okay, I'd
thought at the time, and I'd wished her well. Magnani-
mous of me? It really wasn't. By the time Amanda confessed, the ponytailed man I mentioned earlier—and he
was *not* a bozo—was a big part of my life.

Now the most important part of my life was Sam. I
never for a second seriously thought that Amanda was
going to tell me she was playing around with my fiancé.
Still, as I sat at the sparkling counter waiting while she
ground the beans for our coffee and then pressed them
through an infuser, a cloud of melancholy settled over me.

For the most part, I'd managed to stay out of my
friends' marital troubles. It's not that I don't enjoy sticking my nose into other people's business, but half of this
troubled marriage was my best woman friend, and the
other half and I had once carried on a simmering, though
not scalding, affair.

"Black, right?"

Amanda was talking about the cup of coffee she put in
front of me, but the word suited my mood as well. Nodding, I laced a finger through the impossibly dainty handle
of an almost translucent porcelain cup. Sam and I drink
our coffee from big mugs with "Five Finkelstein Boys"
printed on them. Not so genteel, but they do the trick.

"I know you don't like your eggs runny, but the runny
part isn't egg," Amanda explained as she slid omelets
onto our plates. "It's goat cheese. And there's basil from
the hanging basket. . . . "

She was saying something about a pepper grinder when

I kicked the stool across from me from under the counter. "I'm fine, Amanda. Sit down and eat while it's hot."

"I've just got to pour the orange juice. It's fresh."

Of course. These days Amanda always fusses in her kitchen, but that morning she was twitching almost as much as my street peddler. The bomb she was going to drop, whatever it was, was going to be a biggie. She was going to announce an impending divorce, maybe. Or a pregnancy. As I watched my friend pour orange juice into long-stemmed goblets, I stared hard at her stomach. Flat as an ironing board.

I stabbed my omelet and watched some white goo ooze out of it. "So? What is it?"

Amanda sat down. "Goat cheese, like I told you."

I only half-believed her, but I started eating it anyway. "What's the thing you've just got to tell me?"

She chewed quietly for a second. "I haven't always been like this."

That much I knew. When I met Amanda, her lifestyle wouldn't have fit even the broadest definition of the word "domestic." Nodding, I continued to eat.

"I mean, in my life, before you met me, I did some things that weren't . . . nice."

Was this about before we met? If that was the case, I already knew some of it. Like many young women, myself included, Amanda had come to New York with big ideas. She'd wanted to be a fashion model. That hadn't worked out. She was a little too short, and just not lucky. From what I understand, though, she made quite a splash at the Art Students' League.

"Nice? If you're talking about nude modeling, you've already told me. There was nothing wrong with that, Amanda. Haven't you told Tony? I don't think he'll be upset. Figure modeling is perfectly . . . nice."

She was playing with her omelet, running her fork through the goo and studying its tracks. "Of course I told Tony about that. He just said he didn't want me to do it anymore." She looked up. "Not that I would."

"Then what is this 'not nice' thing we're talking about?"

"Before I moved to New York. Bonnie"—she stretched across the counter—"not one person in New York knows I did this. Not even our marriage counselor. You've got to promise you won't tell a soul, because if this gets back to Tony he'll leave me."

What on earth had she done? "You weren't a call girl, were you?"

I meant it as a question, but it must have sounded like an accusation because Amanda's eyes blazed and she came back fighting.

"No! I never did it for money! I might have done some other things for money, but not . . . it."

That said, a flood doused the fire in her eyes. Before I could put my fork on my plate, tears were spilling down her cheeks.

I shoved back my stool, hurried around the counter, and put my arm around her. "Let's go sit on the sofa and talk."

Amanda is one of those rare creatures who can cry and look good at the same time, but this was no ordinary cry. By the time we got to the living room and settled on the sofa she was a ruin. Her nose looked like a radish, pre-rosebud condition.

"I've been worried sick, scared you'd find out," my friend wept.

"Find out what?"

"That I wasn't always so . . . nice."

" 'Nice' is relative, Amanda. I haven't always been so nice either."

She swiped her fist at one of her eyes, smearing the mascara she is never without. "What's the worst thing you've ever done?"

Trying to cheer my friend, I smiled and told her I'd have to think about that. "But there are definitely things I wouldn't want to see on a billboard."

"Like, have you ever dated an old, fat tourist for money?"

What? That wasn't anything close to an atomic bomb, but it was weird enough to cause a small boom. "Well, no. I haven't done that. But no old, fat tourist has offered me money yet."

I was still trying to joke, but Amanda would have none of it.

"Or, did you ever go to a hotel suite and take off your dress and dance to a Donna Summers record in front of a drunk Canadian executive with horrible breath? And then, when you wouldn't do some . . . special, gross stuff he wanted you to do, end up running out of the room almost in the altogether with a bed sheet wrapped around you?"

Her words were coming in a breathless rush now, so fast I couldn't have interrupted even if I'd had anything to say.

"And then the hotel security guard calls the police, and they put you in the back of a police van? Has that happened to you?"

Again, not a nuclear attack, but the rumbles were sure getting louder.

"Have you ever been booked for prostitution and fingerprinted and locked up in a jail cell? Did that ever happen to you?"

Boom!

We've all heard the expression "The silence was deafening," but I never fully experienced it until then. After a moment Amanda continued talking. Her voice had dropped, and she spoke in a monotone as she described what the Canadian with bad breath had wanted, and why she'd run. When she was finished she sat still as a stone, quietly staring at her hands.

I wanted to say something, but Amanda's embarrassment and my own seemed to fill the room so completely that there was no space for any words. For a few seconds the most I could manage was a shake of my head. Finally, unable to stand the quiet, I squeaked out a noise, something between an "Oh" and a "Wow."

Having gotten through the humiliation of her confession, Amanda became defensive and angry.

"Your expression says it all, Bonnie. You think what I did was disgusting."

"No, no. Not disgusting," I quickly assured her. "Different. Not what I expected."

"Well it *was* disgusting, and I wasn't even good at it! The owner of the escort service I was working for—this horrible old man with a cigar sticking out of his mouth—said my attitude was poor. I got fired after two nights."

An inappropriate quip is as much a part of defensive behavior as is inappropriate anger, but mine spilled out before I could stop it. "Probably just as well. That way you don't have to include it on your resume."

Amanda's tears were drying. I thought there was a slight twitch at the corner of her mouth, so I risked a grin. "It does sound like the pits. Worse than the steno pool."

She started giggling about a second before I did. "It was unbelievably gross, and I wouldn't dream of doing most of the special stuff."

The two of us collapsed in an uncontrollable fit of laughing. We were both wheezing by the time it was out of our systems. When she could, Amanda took a deep breath. "I'm going to tell you everything. I better."

In some cases ignorance is bliss, and as far as I could tell, this was one of those cases.

"Are you sure you want me to hear this?"

"You have to hear it," she insisted.

Amanda's living room isn't as "done" as her kitchen. It's a mixture of dark-ugly rococo hand-me-downs from Tony's parents and a few tacky leftovers from his marriage, his ex having made off with the best pieces. Usually, I'm quite comfortable in this room, but now I was as jumpy as my hostess. Leaping to my feet, I said, "First let me get our orange juice. It really is good."

Amanda called after me. "It will be much better with

champagne. There's a bottle in the refrigerator. If you'll get it, I'll open it out here."

Oh, boy. I was in for an earful!

"I was in my second year of secretarial school, still living at home with my parents. We lived in Mississippi, you know, on a soybean farm. I couldn't wait to get away. Everything was just so impossibly . . . small town.

"One of my cousins went to New Orleans when she graduated from high school. She was younger than I was, but when she came back to visit a few months later, the way she'd changed just"—there was a big, theatrical sweep of Amanda's arms here—"blew me away. Her clothes, her hair, everything."

Which came out, "everthang." Sometimes when Amanda gets a little overwrought the Southern accent pokes through.

"Even the way she walked. She said she was a hostess for an escort service.

"The courses I was taking—shorthand, bookkeeping—bored me silly and I wasn't very good at them, anyway. My cousin told me she could get me a job where she worked."

Amanda downed a sip of the juice-champagne mixture. "I wasn't a complete fool. I was no angel myself, but my cousin had always been the wild one in the family. I asked her right out if she was doing anything she shouldn't be, and she said absolutely not. She said being a hostess was a perfectly respectable occupation, like being a tour guide. That's what she compared it to. She admitted that sometimes her date might ask her to do something special, and if it didn't disgust her she might do it but that was entirely up to her. When she did those things, though, the tips were huge.

"I might have forgotten all about New Orleans, except that she—my cousin—was wearing this gorgeous peach-colored silk suit. I thought I recognized the style, and sure enough when she threw the jacket across the back of a chair, I saw the label. It was a . . .''

From the hushed way Amanda said the designer's name, she might have been whispering it in prayer.

''Bonnie, I'd been subscribing to fashion magazines for years. I knew the kind of things I liked, and I knew you don't get them by taking dictation. Oh, when I graduated I got a job at an insurance company, and then after a year or so I got a better one in a bank, but it still wasn't very good and the guys I was meeting were so . . . country. Finally''—Amanda flicked her hand, splattering fizzy dots of champagne across the back of the sofa—''I went to visit my cousin in New Orleans.''

She noticed my grin. ''What?''

''You were seduced by a suit.''

''I've always appreciated quality clothing. Anyway, she took me to see her boss and he . . . interviewed me.'' Amanda rolled her eyes. ''That meant I went in his office and took my dress off and walked around in my underwear in front of him. It wasn't as awful as you might think. He was at least fifty. To me that seemed ancient. And besides, his 'secretary'—she looked about sixteen—was in the room too, and he was so busy squeezing her fanny that he hardly paid any attention to me.'' Amanda rolled her eyes derisively. '' 'Ella baby,' he called her. Anyway, he put me on the payroll right away.

''I sort of knew what I was getting into, except I really didn't. My first night I went out with this older man. He said he was a physician. He was really fat and he didn't look so healthy, but maybe he was a doctor. He took me to a jazz club, and then asked me to go back to his hotel for a drink. I was nervous, but he seemed to be harmless enough, so I thought, Go for it! Well, Bonnie, he made a pass but when I said no, he was a perfect gentleman. And he gave me a tip, anyway. Not enough for a designer suit but more than I made at the bank in a whole day. So I thought, This isn't bad.

''The next night they fixed me up with the business executive from Canada. He was staying in a fancy corporate suite, but if you ask me he was"—she paused to finish her drink, and then refilled the glass to the brim, mostly with champagne—"a piss-poor executive."

That made me laugh, which started Amanda giggling again. "I'm serious. Anyway, we went to a couple of clubs and he seemed nice enough too, except for his breath. Then he asked me back to his hotel for a drink. I thought I knew the routine by then, so I said yes.

"Well, he was a lot younger and healthier than my first date, and a lot more"—she bit into her lower lip—"persistent. The drink he gave me was stronger than anything I'd ever had before, and I started getting woozy. I'm not clear how it happened, but I just remember that when this guy lunged at me, Donna Summers was singing 'Last Dance' on the hi-fi and my dress was on the floor." She looked at me from under lowered lids. "I put up a fight, ran out of the room with a sheet wrapped around me, and the next thing I knew, a policewoman was rolling my fingers over a pad of black ink down at the city jail.

"The escort service's owner sent a lawyer to get me out, and that was it. The charge against me was reduced from prostitution to disturbing the peace—that old escort service owner had connections—and the following Monday morning I was back at my desk at the bank."

"And that was it?"

She nodded. "Oh, I thought about it for a while, but then I stopped feeling bad. Nothing actually happened. I wasn't a loose woman, just a dumb twenty-two-year-old who wanted designer clothes. Do you agree, Bonnie?"

"Of course I agree."

"And you know what? I found out from my cousin later that she bought that peach-colored suit at a resale shop. It was secondhand."

We got another giggle out of that. I was puzzled, though. Why was Amanda coming clean now? If she'd put the experience behind her, what was she doing confessing it years later?

"Amanda, you're thirty-three years old. This happened

more than ten years ago in another state. Why are you worried about it now?''

Her moan sounded as if it came from the depths of her soul. ''I saw that girl the other night, Bonnie, and it all came back to me.''

''What girl?''

'' 'Ella, baby.' I'm sure she didn't recognize me, with all the years and this hairdo, but I know it was her. I'm good with faces.''

I stared at my friend, still not understanding.

''Dawn Starr. That's what she calls herself now.''

Amanda, who by now was feeling no pain, emotional or otherwise, slapped her hand on her thigh. ''You should see your expression, Bonnie.''

''Dawnella Starkey. I think that's her real name.''

Amanda hooted. ''She's probably had more names than she can keep track of.''

''And her boyfriend? Boss? Whatever he was. Do you remember his name.?''

''I never knew his name. He was just a tacky man in a tacky business, smoking a huge cigar and squeezing Ella baby's rear.''

''What was the name of the service?''

''French Quarter Escorts, or something like that,'' she said with a shrug before collapsing into the sofa cushions. ''I'm so glad I got this off my chest, Bonnie. You've got to vow that you won't tell a soul. Okay?''

Vow. That meant I couldn't tell Lee, but if I couldn't tell Lee, I'd be leading a triple life instead of a double one. For a weak person who likes to dish the dirt, a double life is more than enough.

''I will never tell anyone that I heard about French Quarter Escorts from you,'' I promised.

That seemed to be good enough for Amanda. In any event, she was too potted to argue. I left her dozing on the sofa, went to a pay phone on the street, and called Captain Lee.

''About ten years ago Dawnella Starkey was working

for an escort service, maybe called French Quarter Escorts, in New Orleans. The guy that owned it was about fifty, then, and smoked cigars.''

There was silence on the other end, for so long that I started wondering if Lee had heard me.

''Captain . . .''

''That's interesting. I'm not sure what we can make out of it, but I'll add it to the file.''

''Maybe you should check into who is paying Dawn's rent,'' I put in, ''because she's not.''

''Will do. And I have some news for you. I got the results of Brad Gannett's autopsy.''

''And?''

''He died just like we heard, from a single gunshot wound to his head. He was in a locked room, the gun was in his hand, and only his prints were on it. A small amount of marijuana was found in his apartment, but the autopsy did not pick up any in his bloodstream.''

''And what about Terry? I assume the body in the Lincoln Motel was Terry's.''

''Ah, yes,'' Lee said. ''Terrence Doyle. Twenty-one-year-old male with a history of drug abuse. Drugs and drug paraphernalia were found in Doyle's room, and the autopsy turned up a considerable amount of cocaine in his system.''

''But what killed him?''

''Asphyxiation. When the police discovered the body, there was a plastic bag over Doyle's head and a canister of nitrous oxide—laughing gas—on the floor beside him. Apparently Doyle was releasing the gas into the bag, then placing the bag over his head. The cocaine in his system may have caused him to misjudge the amount of nitrous oxide. He got careless.''

''But why was he doing it at all?'' I asked.

A long breath escaped from Lee. ''It is a form of autoerotic stimulation not unknown in young men, Miss Indermill, but it is not something you need to concern yourself with.''

"The motel manager told me there had been a lot of noise from his room the night before."

"There may have been someone in Doyle's room, but we don't know. Apparently he entertained guests . . . male guests . . . with some frequency."

"You mean he was gay?"

"It would seem so. The police are calling Doyle's death an accident. The fact is, his lifestyle almost guaranteed he wouldn't be around to collect Social Security."

A light snow had started falling. As I brushed some flakes from my hair, an idea was rattling around in my head. What if Gannett's raised highball glass in that photo over The Dancing Fool's bar hadn't been an accident? What if Gannett had wanted Doyle's face concealed? Considering Gannett's macho reputation, what I was thinking amounted to blasphemy, but I had to ask.

"Captain Lee? You don't think that Brad Gannett might have liked"—the word stuck in my throat—"men? He had a girlfriend, but maybe you should have someone talk to her. She's an actress. Her name's . . ."

"Miss Indermill! I want—I *insist* that you get over this obsession with show business personalities. You are going off on tangents that have nothing to do with the job you were hired for. Forget show business and concentrate on contractors!"

His words were clipped and his exasperation hammered into my ear. I walked away from that phone feeling like a rogue spy who had better clean up her act or else.

Or else what, though? The Gannett-Doyle connection intrigued me. Doyle's call to Max and Steve intrigued me. The Dancing Fool's contractors didn't. And, anyway, what's wrong with occasionally being a rogue?

13

THE U.S. WEATHER SERVICE WAS PRE-
dicting even colder weather, but my senior citizens were hot stuff. They had never
looked so elegant. Surely they hadn't
spent last evening on the phone, compar-
ing outfits like kids getting ready for the
junior prom, but they had all dressed with
the same thing in mind: look good for the
new teacher. The polyester double knits
that had been good enough for Monte and
me were gone, replaced by a wondrous
array of silk and satin. Mrs. Bottie was
stunning in a black velvet sheath, and her husband wore
a bow tie and a too-tight shiny jacket with every button
fastened. Mr. Alonzo had replaced the gray in his hair
with a tint—I think it was the comb-in type—that was so
glossy it shimmered like a moonlit lake when the light
caught it, and over her blinding pink chiffon dress his wife
wore a white fur cape.

They had never tried harder to dance well, either. Mrs.
Mintz, who looked sweet in her blue flowered skirt and
jacket, followed every move John made, and though her
lips moved as she counted off the steps, there was hardly
a peep from her.

Finally, when the last box step had been stepped and
the class was over, Mrs. Mintz approached John so hesi-

tantly you would have thought she was going to ask him for a date. As she came closer, his shoulders stiffened and a more perceptive person than Mrs. Mintz might have been intimidated. Reaching into her jacket pocket, she withdrew a little blue autograph book and offered it shyly to him, along with a ballpoint pen.

"I wonder if you would mind signing this. It's for my niece."

With its worn cover and yellowing pages, the book looked about fifty years old. Taking it from Mrs. Mintz, John thumbed through the pages until he found a blank one, and signed with a flourish. "With great affection, John Daly."

When she saw what he'd written, Mrs. Mintz drew herself as tall as she could. Blood rose in her cheeks, and it almost seemed as if she dropped thirty years. "I loved you in *Dance Fever*," she said; then suddenly afraid, perhaps, that she might be making a fool of herself, she giggled behind her hand and fled the studio.

I was really tickled by all this, but when the last of the class had followed Mrs. Mintz through the door, John, who had started stacking the records, muttered, "This is the professional rung beneath which I never again want to step."

Annoyed, I snapped at him. "The class adores you. They may be the most appreciative audience you've ever had."

John winced. "Sorry. With all the other problems I'm trying to work out, sometimes I forget to be human."

"You're forgiven. Do you want a ride to the station?"

"Of course."

It took me a few minutes to stow my gear in my impossibly small basement locker. I got back to the first floor reception area, and found John talking to the woman who worked behind the counter. They were getting along better this time.

"I must have lived in Manhattan too long," he said to her.

"That's possible. We don't have break-ins. I promise that the things in your locker are safe. See you next week," she added, smiling.

When John fell into step beside me, I brought up Elsie's article. "I was surprised she pulled it off."

"Me too. I'll have to thank her somehow, though I hope it doesn't mean getting too involved with her."

"She mentioned that you're in the Hell's Kitchen Actors' Workshop. You must have known Brad Gannett pretty well."

"Not really. We've got this production coming up. *Picnic.* Gannett had the lead and I'd been helping him with the dance scene. Have you ever been to any of our productions?"

I shook my head. "The other night I saw you with Gannett's girlfriend."

It was such a graceless attempt to keep the subject on the dead actor that John glanced at me and raised an eyebrow.

"Katharine's a neighbor of mine," he said as we walked out into the frigid afternoon, "and she's also a member of the Workshop. She's the one who got me involved. Sometimes there are as many actors on the stage as there are people in the audience, but the experience is valuable. There aren't a lot of parts around for a man who's strictly song-and-dance."

He was being chatty to the point of rambling. Funny, but every time I steered the conversation to Brad Gannett, John steered it away.

We got into the car and the doors closed with a soft, expensive whoosh. I started the engine, and John leaned back in the seat.

"I do like my creature comforts. Got used to them once before. It's a shame I was too foolish to hang on to them."

Temporarily giving up on Brad Gannett, I asked John what he had done during those foolish lost years.

"What did I do? It's common knowledge. I drank."

"You couldn't have done that sixteen hours a day."

"I certainly tried," he said. "I also got married and divorced a couple of times, appeared on *The Love Boat* and some other TV shows, and did a few pilots. That sort of work, along with residuals and savings, kept me afloat. I wasn't living like royalty, but I wasn't in the gutter, either.

"Then, about four years ago, in a rare moment of clear thinking, I realized that Broadway was the best place for me. I moved back to New York, kicked my subtenant out, and managed to get myself a second-rate agent. Showed up drunk for my first audition. That took care of that comeback. I tried again, and again, went in and out of AA, and then one day last summer . . ."

John peeled off his thick wool gloves, loosened the top buttons of his black overcoat, and reached into his shirt. "You see this quarter I wear around my neck?"

After pulling into traffic, I glanced over. A hole had been drilled in the quarter and a silver chain threaded through the hole.

"Yes?"

"Last summer I was asleep—passed out—on a bench in Bryant Park. Something hit my chest and woke me up. There were two quarters lying on my T-shirt. I looked around and saw a woman leading a little boy away. The kid was about six. He looked back, and I heard him say, 'He found them, Mommy.' That night I went to AA and I've stuck with it ever since."

"Good for you. You have guts."

John fingered the quarter. "Pride's more like it. I had a jeweler drill this hole for me, and during the first couple of months I was sober, every time I wanted a drink I thought about being a charity case for that little boy. It's been eight months now."

At the train station I edged the Chrysler to the curb. John was rebuttoning his coat when I noticed what at first glance might have been a couple of bright copper threads on his sleeve. A closer look and I recognized them as wavy red hairs.

"Can I ask you something else?"

"My life's an open book."

Reaching across the seat, I picked one of the hairs from the black wool. "Where do you suppose this came from?"

I half expected the open book to slam shut, but instead a sheepish look crossed John's face. Love or lust, or whatever it was, had softened him up.

"When I first saw Dawn I couldn't imagine her letting me get within touching distance. Now," he said, grinning, "things have changed."

Now John was within touching distance of Dawn, which meant that he was within touching distance of Dawn's keys. We had a few minutes to wait for the train, and he'd been so forthcoming for the last few minutes that I felt like asking him straight out if he was the one who had broken into the club. Instead, I sidled up to the subject. Furtive.

"You heard about the robbery at the club?"

He leaned back into the seat again. "Yeah. Dawn told me that the thief left the front door unlocked. Is that true?"

I shrugged. "As far as I know."

"Hmm. And stole a little money, some office equipment, *and* a bottle of cheap booze?"

"So I'm told. Curious, isn't it?"

"Curiouser and curiouser." He gave me a sidelong glance across the car seat. "Is it my imagination, Bonnie, or are you kind of curious yourself? I mean about various things going on at the club."

"Kind of," I admitted.

"So am I." For a moment he sat quietly. "I wonder if we're curious about the same things," he finally said. A high-pitched whistle announced the arriving train. John opened the car door. "Got to go. Thanks for the ride."

"See you at the club tomorrow?"

"Sure. Maybe we should talk some more about . . . curious things."

"Tomorrow?" I quickly asked, but the car door slammed. If John had heard me, he didn't respond. Still, watching his long-legged stride to the platform, I experienced a heady surge of elation. John had broken into The Dancing Fool just ahead of me. I would have bet the Chrysler on it. Not only that, but something about the club, and about Brad Gannett's death, was bothering him.

I wasn't such a bad spy, after all.

The woman I glimpsed through Jaguida's grimy window didn't look as if she belonged there. I walked inside for a cup of coffee to go and to satisfy my curiosity. The woman was East Side–thin, with a good haircut and a stylish, very uptown suit. Her makeup didn't conceal her years, but it had been applied with a careful, tasteful hand. It was her dark brown mink coat that really gave her away, though. She'd draped it carelessly over the back of her chair so that part of the glossy fur and silky lining rested on the floor. Anyone walking into Jaguida's would have known that though this woman was in Hell's Kitchen, she was not *of* it.

John, who was sitting at the window table with this woman, looked up briefly and nodded when he saw me, but any ideas I might have entertained about his saying, "Hey, Bonnie, come on over and meet my friend," quickly vanished. As for the woman, her eyes flickered at me, expressionless, and flickered away.

A little put out, I wandered to the counter. Strange, my relationship with John. Sometimes, like the afternoon before, we seemed at the point of a real friendship, but at other times, like now, I felt I hardly knew him.

The doughnuts in the cardboard carton looked nice and fresh. Bright red jelly oozed from one of them, and another one had shiny vanilla frosting. Trying to distract myself from these temptations, I watched John and this strange woman from the corner of my eye, and entertained a pleasant thought: Wouldn't it be fun if a fat brown cockroach found a nest for itself in that plush fur coat?

Where had I seen the woman? She looked vaguely familiar. My back was to the window, but I kept taking sneaky looks at their table. John was speaking softly and looking down at his hands. The woman was nodding.

I paid for my coffee, but as Jaguida handed me the bag I pointed at the doughnuts. "A doughnut. No. The one with vanilla frosting."

Jaguida snatched the bag back. "Make up your mind."

It wasn't until I was leaving the restaurant that I got a good look at the woman. It happened to be at a moment when she flashed a smile at John. I'd seen that smile before, a couple of times a week on the entertainment pages of one of the newspapers. She was a gossip columnist, a woman who knew everything there was to know about everyone on Broadway, a woman who could make or break a career. She was Elsie's boss, the "old witch." Before stepping out into the cold, I glimpsed a tiny tape recorder on the table between John and the columnist. Even that looked expensive.

At the corner of Tenth and Forty-fifth a large white blur, crowned by a smaller, pointed one with a red pompon atop it, caught my eye. It looked like Elsie in her winter finery, but when I tried to focus, she disappeared through the door of a health food store. I was almost sure she had seen me, and under normal circumstances I would have run the other way. However, this un-Elsie-like behavior aroused my curiosity. Crossing the street, I walked into the store.

The red pompon showed above a counter of herbal teas. A peek through a display of salt-free soup revealed the white blur moving quickly down the next aisle. I called "Elsie?" but she went the other way and disappeared around a wire rack of vitamin pills.

It took a minute or two of this ridiculous hide-and-seek through the aisles for me to trap my prey in a dead end of snack foods. On one side of us was a shelf stocked with low-fat potato chips, on the other sugarless candy, and behind us those inescapable rice cakes.

"Elsie! I thought that was you." Surprise.

Glaring defiantly, she snatched a sack of potato chips from the shelf. "I've gone on a cleansing diet."

She sounded as if she expected a fight from me about that. I lifted the bag from Jaguida's. "I should do the same thing. But why are you shopping here? I thought your office was on the East Side."

Her mouth remained in a defiant set, but her eyes clouded. The next thing I knew, a lone tear was making a slow trail down her face. The tear was alone for only a moment before it had company.

"I discovered John. Because of my article, he's got some directors and producers interested in him. When he's famous again, it will be because of me."

John was a long way from fame, and when and if he did make it, it would be due mostly to his own drive, but I had serious doubts about Elsie's sanity and didn't want to argue. She could, after all, still turn me in to Dawn as a thief.

"Is that your boss with John now?"

She nodded. "He gave me six minutes on the phone. I timed it. And the old witch is getting a breakfast interview. You can bet your life I'll have to type it up and edit it, too. She's almost illiterate. I'm too nice, you know. Too nice."

Nice. I was really starting to hate that word. "What do you mean?"

"Before I left yesterday, the old witch had me get John on the phone for her. I heard her say something about breakfast. And so this morning when she went out, I followed her and caught them in the act."

From the way Elsie's jaw quivered you'd never have thought that the act she'd caught them in was a breakfast interview. Still, much as I disliked Elsie and as strange as I found her, I sympathized. I know what it's like to do the work and have someone else take the credit.

"It seems unfair. Maybe you should talk to her."

"Unfair?" Blood rushed to Elsie's face and settled in a strange, butterfly-shaped blotch across her nose and cheeks. "It's rotten. I hate her. And him! After what I did, look how he's repaid me. Well, let me tell you something: I'm going to get even with everyone. Everyone!"

Elsie swiped at her damp cheek. Her eyes almost crossed as they focused on the bag of chips she still clutched. When she raised her free hand, it was balled into a fist so tight that her knuckles showed white. That scared me. This woman wasn't operating with a full deck, and if she decided to let loose among the rice cakes and carob crisps I didn't want to be within striking distance. I stepped back, but not quickly enough. Elsie smashed her fist into the plastic bag. The airtight wrapping popped and we both got a shower of salt-free, fat-free and, if the pieces I picked from my jacket were representative, taste-free potato chips.

Before I left the store I stepped on a scale and dropped a dime into the slot. When the numbers finally stopped bouncing around, the number left for me to consider was shattering, but not shattering enough to make me throw away that doughnut.

Several of us witnessed the fight that afternoon.

I was in the office when it started, typing labels for my new filing system. Max and Steve were in the secure room, maybe pouring cheap liquor into fancy-label bottles. John had finished cleaning, and he and Dawn were downstairs on the dance floor running through a routine for that evening. The music was turned low. A jitterbug, as I remember. Ballroom Night, and maybe their blood was already running hot when Eddie got to the club.

The street door opened and slammed shut, and I heard the familiar sound of boots crossing the floor below. And then Eddie's shout: "What the hell do you think you're doing to her?"

I'm sure that whatever John had been doing, he had been doing it *with* Dawn and not *to* her. But whatever Eddie saw tapped into some strong feelings—infatuation, jealousy, resentment. Dawn's voice came next, but I couldn't make out what she said. And then I heard John, loud and clear:

"... so mind your own business, Charlie."

I was out of the office by then, heading down the hall. "The name's Eddie, and this is my business you're trespassing in right now."

Max and Steve beat me to the stairs and we all took them two at a time. We found Eddie and John facing each other on the white and black tiles, fists and jaws clenched. I was close enough to Eddie to see a vein pounding in the side of his forehead.

Dawn had backed to the side of the floor and was saying something feeble, like, "Come on, guys. Let's talk." The guys weren't interested in talking. They were rutting male animals ready to go at each other. John was a little taller, Eddie a little younger. They might have been evenly matched but the match had barely started before it ended.

Eddie had shoved John's shoulder with his hand. "I want you out of here, and I don't want you coming ..."

John threw a right-arm punch, but Eddie turned his head in time and the blow just grazed his eye. It didn't look as if there had been a lot of power behind the punch, but Eddie rocked back, maybe as much from the surprise of being slugged by John as from the impact itself.

By then Steve and Max were on the floor. Steve grabbed John's arm while Max stepped between the fighters.

Eddie looked shaken. He put his hand to his eye and then examined his fingers as if expecting to see blood. There was none, but from the way the color drained from his face he might have been mortally wounded. Max steered him to the bar.

Dawn hurried to John's side. "Let him go, Steve. Eddie started it."

Steve, after glancing at Max and seeing his nod, released John's arm. "Looks like round one goes to you, T'Bird."

John was still glaring at Eddie, but he didn't look eager to start round two. Steve's remark added fuel to the fire that had been burning in Eddie, though. Chest heaving, he said to John, "Out, now! And don't come back. You either, Dawn."

Max looked at John and Dawn.

"He's right. You two are going to have to find somewhere else to get exposure. We're trying to run a business. Having you around isn't working."

John's reaction was surprising. He stepped a little closer to Max and stared the other man right in the eye.

"I'm leaving now, but I'll be back this evening with Dawn. Do you feel like arguing about that, Max, or do you feel like letting it slide?"

I flashed back to another confrontation between John and Max, when Max had found me in the room with the safe. John had stood up to Max but his fear had been obvious. Now he showed no fear at all.

Max's response was even more of a surprise. He, the thug, the son of a gangster, took a step back. After staring at the other man for a moment, he walked over to Eddie.

Leading his partner away from the couple, Max spoke quietly to him.

"Listen, Eddie. John was interviewed this morning. Because of him we're getting a nice mention in tomorrow's paper. And there's a big-time director coming by here tonight to meet him. You've heard of—" Max mentioned a name that was familiar to all of us. "He's got a couple of shows running on Broadway right now."

Eddie nodded almost imperceptibly.

"So do you think you can cool it? Dawn's a grown woman. She can go with any guy she wants, and it looks like for now she wants John."

"John!" The name shot from Eddie's lips in a gust of hot air, but at least he was composed enough by then to keep his voice down. "Suddenly you're on his side, too?"

"I'm on the club's side. Are you?"

Eddie squirmed his shoulders free of Max's hold and sank onto a bar stool. "Yeah. Of course. How can you ask me that?"

Lowering his hands to his side, Max said loudly, for everyone's benefit, "Then let's all calm down. Okay? We're in this together."

He looked at John, who shrugged. "It's over for me."

Dawn left John's side and walked to the bar, her heels beating into the tiles of the suddenly silent room. "Want to go get some coffee, Eddie? Maybe we can talk things over."

Eddie spun the barstool and slipped off it without looking at her. His eye was red and starting to swell. "Not right now. I'm fine." Glancing at Max, he said, "See you tonight."

When the door had shut quietly behind Eddie, Max turned to Dawn. "You and John, try to stick to dancing when you're here. Okay? Please?"

Please? Wasn't Max being . . . nice?

Dawn and John left together a few minutes later and I went back upstairs and continued typing labels. I was pounding on the keys of the old typewriter when I got the uncomfortable feeling that someone was watching me.

Steve was in the office doorway. In one of his hands he had a small tin box.

"Max decided we should keep petty cash in the office."

He handed me the box and I peeked inside. Two twenties and a ten. For The Dancing Fool this was high finance.

"Max said you should keep it in your drawer, and lock your desk when you leave at night."

"Sure." Max was the law.

Under Steve's watchful eye I put the box in my bottom drawer. When I'd closed the drawer I expected him to disappear, but he stayed put, slouched against the door frame.

"So what do you think of that scene downstairs? Looks like we've got ourselves another fool letting his dick lead him into trouble."

Funny how when I'd first seen Steve his leer had seemed like a smile. If there was one fool at the club who seemed likely to follow his dick into trouble, he was it.

With the coldest night in years predicted, I'd dressed in a thick tunic that went from my neck almost to my knees. Nevertheless, I automatically checked my front to make sure there was nothing protruding that might interest Steve.

"Eddie will get over her," I said.

Steve's eyes slid across my chest before rising, disappointed at the lack of scenery, I expect, to meet mine.

"I meant the other fool. T'Bird. John. Whatever his name is."

"What do you mean? Dawn seems to really like him."

Steve rolled his shoulders. "Right. True love. You can take my word, Bonnie. This comeback of T'Bird's better be successful. Otherwise she's going to use him and lose him the same way she did Eddie."

Steve had moved behind me, and when I turned he was so close that I found myself staring at his crotch. This was one of the rare occasions when it was encased in denim rather than black leather. Nevertheless, I pushed my chair back with my feet.

"What do you mean, Steve? Did Dawn and Eddie actually . . . ?"

"Sure. She was looking for a place to show her stuff, to maybe make some contacts."

"So? Dawn's an asset to the club. She didn't have to sleep with someone to get a job here."

"That's what you think. Max wasn't sure he wanted her hanging around, so she played up to Eddie. The sucker," he added with a smirk. "Over Christmas the two of them went off together to one of those Vermont places. You know. Maple syrup and fireplaces and all that. You tell me, how much time do you think they spent cutting figure eights on the pond?''

This helped me understand what was going on with Eddie. I suspect that we've all been dumped in one way or another, but who wants to admit it? And Eddie, I well knew, would be even more reluctant to admit it than the rest of us.

There was one thing Steve had said that I didn't understand. I smiled, trying to make this creep think I actually enjoyed talking to him.

''Why didn't Max want to have Dawn around?''

That got a double-wide smirk out of Steve, but no answer.

''And so what happened with Dawn and Eddie?''

''What do you think? He's broke, he's struggling. Not to mention that he's Chinese. Dawn's got her eyes on bigger and better things. That's what it comes down to.''

Steve's view of Dawn didn't leave much room for hugs and kisses. I wondered, briefly, if he was one of Dawn's castoffs, but that seemed unlikely. He had nothing she would want.

''Have you known Dawn a long time?''

My question was a long way from innocent, but it must have sounded that way because Steve's head was in the middle of a nod before he caught himself.

''Nah.''

That ''Nah'' had almost been a ''Yeah.'' After hearing Amanda's confession, I'd suspected that the Breen brothers and Dawn went back a long way. Now I was certain. I put that information into a mental file. My spying heartbeat may have been faint, but it hadn't disappeared.

Every time the club's door opened, Dawn tensed. And every time it shut without John Daly walking through it, she tensed even more.

''He's supposed to be here. My nerves are shot.''

The pink polish on Dawn's thumbnail was shot, too. She'd been going at it with her teeth for twenty minutes.

"He'll show up, but I'm going to have to go."

A tinge of anticipation had marked the start of Ball-room Dance Night over an hour earlier. The almost im-mediate arrival of the Broadway director and his two-man, three-woman entourage had heightened the mood. Passing on the relative luxury of the Celebrity Lounge, they'd pulled extra chairs around what I now thought of as the emperor's table. On and off over the next hour, Dawn had sat with them. Max also came to the table, but there had been no sign of John.

Dawn had made some halfhearted noise about intro-ducing me to the director, but it never happened. That was okay. Unlike Elsie, I'm not much of a celebrity groupie, and my days of trying to impress directors were over. I had stayed that evening to see Dawn and John dance, and especially to see if they would have the desired effect on the director, which must make me an event groupie.

Eddie's absence from the club was understandable. When he'd returned briefly earlier that evening, the shiner John had given him was blossoming. In a manic mood, Eddie might have worn a black eyepatch and pulled off a swashbuckling routine. He'd been bitter, though, and ducked his head when I tried to take a look at his eye. "It's nothing," he said harshly. "Don't make a big deal of it. It's not your business."

I was on the train by nine thirty. As the wheels rumbled over the tracks, my first open-call Broadway audition came back to me.

I'd been nineteen and terrified. The other dancers were older, cynical, smoking cigarettes. Every time the voice called out that dismissive, "Thank you," I expected it to be for me, but I was one of the dozen lucky ones that afternoon. If I hadn't been, maybe I would have stopped trying right then and there. Who knows? The show closed after a six-week run, and then, for longer than I care to think about, there was nothing. But, if John Daly was the one who lit the Broadway fire in me, it was that first success that really got it going.

I thought about Dawn—her excitement, her nervousness—and about John, too. He'd get to the club. Most likely he was already there. He made it to Long Island to teach senior citizens. He would travel any distance from his apartment, even on the coldest night in years, for another chance at success.

14

THE LIGHT ON THE ANSWERING MA-
chine was blinking when I got home. I
rewound the tape until it clicked. The
first call was from Sam. "It's about
seven o'clock. Give me a call." My
mother had called after that. "It's eight-
thirty. Where are you?" She thinks that
if I'm out by myself after dark, I've
fallen into the hands of an axe murderer.

Between those two calls a third person had dialed our number. The tape
clicked, but for a few seconds nothing
came through the speaker but the hollow noise of an open
line. Finally a peculiar muffled sound came through the
receiver. It was human, I thought, but it wasn't a word.
It was a grunt, a slur. Another click followed immediately.
The caller had hung up without saying anything coherent.
Nothing out of the ordinary for my old neighborhood. I
thought nothing of it.

At a little after eleven, when I was dozing off, I was
jolted awake by another call. My heart jumped a little, but
I was still alert enough to grab the receiver on the first
ring.

"Hello?"

"It's Eddie, Bonnie. I want you to know I'm sorry.
Really, really sorry."

"Sorry for what?" He sounded drunk. I lay back onto my pillow. Moses' eyes half-opened and he scooted closer. I rubbed his head behind his ears. Instant ecstasy. His eyelids dropped and a purr rumbled in his chest.

"I'm just sorry for everything," Eddie said. "My whole sorry life. I'm an asshole. A fool."

"Of course you are, but no one's going to hold it against you," I responded sleepily. "You were upset . . ."

"Everything I touch turns to garbage, including relationships. I'm a fool. I hope you can forgive the way I acted. It's just that . . . you know . . . this business with Dawn and T'Bird got me so upset. At Christmas, Dawn and I were together and . . . well, I thought I'd died and gone to heaven. Now I find out she'd rather be with that wino. It's eating away at me."

"Are you at home, Eddie?"

"Yeah. Sitting here all alone."

"Are you drunk?"

"Not really. I'm just looking at my life honestly. This whole business has shown me how I rate. I'm less than a wino. I'm nothing."

Oh, please! His voice was thick with self-pity.

"Snap out of it, Eddie! You've got a good business that's probably going to pay off in the long run, a partner you can work with, and a landlady who gives you credit. Not to mention relatives who lend you money, friends who care. . . . "

"The bottom line is, I act like a fool, and I get what a fool deserves. Just hope you understand that I'm sorry."

"I get the idea. Now why don't you go sleep it off. Things will look better in the morning."

"Umm," he moaned. "I'm not sure I can face another morning, Bonnie. The thing is, I'm not sure my life is worth living without Dawn."

"Good night, Eddie. And I hope you have some aspirin in your medicine cabinet."

Six hours later the phone rang again. I was sleeping so soundly that at first I wasn't sure whether the bell was real or part of a dream. I'd been in a deep sleep and my mind was muddled. A second later there was another ring. Stirring, I grappled for the receiver. This time I wasn't so agile and the phone toppled to the floor. As I retrieved it, my bleary gaze passed over the only light in the room—the face of the clock. Five A.M. Damn!

"Eddie? If that's you, you *are* a fool."

For a moment there was dead silence on the other end of the line.

"I'm trying to reach a Bonnie Indermill."

"What?"

"This is Officer Goode, NYPD, Tenth Precinct. I have a report here of an unidentified male on its way to the City Morgue. . . . "

He spoke quickly and in a monotone. I had trouble understanding him.

"Pardon me?"

"A body. Male, unidentified."

There was a break in the burst of words, but what he was trying to convey didn't get much clearer for me.

"It seems that the only ID he had on him was yours. Looks like—" There was another pause. "I'm just reading the report here. Seems like the guy had your business card. Finkelstein Boys. That mean anything to you?"

"Yes."

"Body's on the way to the City Morgue now. You want to see if you can identify him? Any time after nine A.M."

His words were coming too fast. A body? I tried to make sense of this, but on top of being half asleep my heart had started racing.

"I might not know him. Anyone could have one of my cards."

"The report indicates that the card was found inside an article of leather clothing."

My stomach lurched. Eddie. *I'm not sure my life is worth living without her.*

"Is he an Oriental?"

"It doesn't say. Hey—"

The officer called out to someone, and a second later came back on the line.

"Nobody around here saw the deceased. He must have known you, though. Looks like he was going to call you or look you up or something."

"Why do you say that?"

"It says here that your business card was tucked inside a leather glove."

I squeezed my eyes shut, trying to block out a mental picture of Eddie's expensive leather gloves. Oh, God! Why hadn't I taken him seriously?

The overnight freeze had added a sheen of ice on top of the packed snow already blanketing the city, and driving into Manhattan was a challenge I wasn't prepared to meet. The seven twelve A.M. train, when it finally arrived at seven forty, was as frigid as an igloo, and during the slow ride I shivered from cold and fear. Eddie had committed suicide. Why hadn't I paid more attention when he called? Why hadn't I read between the lines?

New York City's morgue is on First Avenue near Thirtieth Street, south of Penn Station and on the other side of town. An overheated subway brought me within six blocks of the place. After that I was on foot, picking my way over ice slicks. I was running solely on nerve, and by the time I stood facing the building it was already depleted.

I'm not sure what I had been expecting—maybe gargoyles nesting in soot-blackened turrets—but the simple modern building with the stripe of blue tile trim on its façade looked completely innocuous. Inside, a receptionist sat behind a counter. When I gave her my name she responded efficiently and without any emotion. "Ah, yes."

She didn't look sympathetic or unsympathetic. She looked . . . businesslike. Maybe she'd gotten used to the bodies and the people who come to identify them, or maybe her unfazed manner was a defense. Picking up the phone, she pressed a button, asked for a Mr. Patel, and gave him my name.

"Someone will be with you soon," she told me, nodding toward a waiting room.

Like the building itself, the waiting area was simple, but not sinister. Gray light shone through the curtains that were drawn across the windows, and black vinyl chairs formed a square around a glass-topped table. I was the only person waiting, and as I perched, weak-kneed, on the edge of a chair, I wondered if it would be better if the other chairs were occupied. Would there be comfort in the company of other frightened strangers? Probably not. I was better off alone. Just the impassive woman at the desk and me.

It wasn't long before Mr. Patel hurried into the room. He was very young and, unlike the woman at the desk, a little ruffled, not only in his manner but in his clothing. I'd expected hospital whites or a green scrub tunic, but Mr. Patel wore a suit of ocean blue, made of a synthetic fabric that gleamed under the fluorescent lights.

He introduced himself as an identification clerk, and waved a brown hand toward me.

"If you would like to come with me."

"Like" had nothing to do with it.

Mr. Patel had a quick, jaunty walk, and following him from the waiting area, through a set of doors and into a hallway, I became absorbed in the way his trouser legs clung to his black nylon socks. I noticed that he had amazingly small feet, that his black loafers had tassels.

My obsession with the identification clerk's clothing was my defense mechanism. What this stranger wore, no matter how peculiar, was safe. When my eyes wandered into dangerous territory I quickly focused back on his outfit. Everything else around me was too threatening.

I've seen lots of movies. I knew what to expect. Massive, body-sized drawers, or gurneys with white-sheeted shapes lumped on them like laundry pulled from dryers and piled on ironing boards. The terrible smell of decay, partly cloaked by antiseptics. A sour lump had formed in my throat and there was a hard knot of dread in the pit of my stomach.

I did not want to see Eddie Fong's body under one of those sheets. Eddie had his faults, but who doesn't? He had been my friend.

As Mr. Patel opened a second door I concentrated on one of his loafers. It squeaked.

The room I followed him into felt chilly. An unwitting glance showed me that it was much too small for a gurney, and that there were no massive drawers built into the walls. Other reluctant peripheral glances revealed that I was in an ordinary-looking office. One small wood desk, a couple of wooden chairs, and a two-drawer file cabinet.

Mr. Patel indicated that I should sit, then took a file folder from the cabinet.

"If you will take a look at these photos of the deceased," he said in a voice that was almost lilting. "They were taken early this morning when the deceased . . ."

"Photos? I don't have to look at the body?"

He shook his head. "Oh, no. We haven't done that in years. It was rather"—a look of repugnance crossed his face—"barbaric."

Never mind that it was looking at photos spread across a desk that had gotten me into this situation in the first place. I was so relieved that I willingly—almost eagerly—shifted my eyes toward the 3-by-5 Polaroid snapshots.

"It appears as if this male Caucasian froze . . ."

Caucasian. The word sank in before my eyes focused on the pictures, and my mind wobbled at the edge of exhilaration. "Caucasian?"

"Yes," Mr. Patel all but sang. "Caucasian male, approximately forty years . . ."

My relief was so tremendous, a hysterical laugh burst from me. A second later, tears flooded my eyes as the puffy face in the pictures swam before me. I wiped my eyes with my fingers to clear my vision. This couldn't be. Blinking, I pressed my knuckles hard on the side of my head and gasped. "Oh." It was a moment before I said, "His name's John Daly."

"You wake me in the middle of the night, make me identify his corpse, but you won't let me see his possessions or even tell me where they are?"

The businesslike woman behind the desk was implacable. ID Clerk Patel, less stoic, was trying to explain, but from the excited pitch of his voice he may have thought he had a lunatic on his hands.

"Please try to understand," he said in his quick, formal English. "In cases of suspicious death, until the report of the Medical Examiner is complete, personal property found on or with the deceased is kept under lock and key. The clothing Mr. Daly was wearing is being held here at the Medical Examiner's office, and property Mr. Daly was carrying which may relate to the investigation of the circumstances surrounding his death is in the possession of the police officer in charge."

"Suspicious death? What's suspicious about freezing?"

He didn't respond. After the chilly office, the reception area seemed ghastly hot, and a wave of fatigue hit me. If I sat in one of those black chairs now, sleep might be instantaneous.

Worn down, I almost gave up, almost decided to go home and cry into my pillow for a while and be finished with this. John deserved better, though. I dug my address book from my bag.

"I need to use your phone. This is a police matter."

The strength in my voice surprised me. Mr. Patel took a step back and waved his hands as if trying to shoo me from the room, but the receptionist wasn't impressed.

"In the corridor there's a public . . ."

"Kindly dial this number. It's for Captain Lee, NYPD Organized Crime Control."

The woman tilted her head and squinted as she read the number. I thought she might argue, but after giving me a hard look, she lifted the phone. Rank definitely has its privileges.

The little pile of belongings on the police officer's desk made me incredibly sad. It shouldn't have been that way, I kept thinking. Looking at the rich-brown leather gloves, I remembered the afternoon when John picked up Eddie's expensive gloves and caressed the leather covetously. So he'd gone out and bought a pair of his own.

Sergeant Nolan, the detective in charge of the investigation, was about as stiff an NYPD cop as I've run into. He was tall and narrow shouldered, and perhaps to counter those shoulders, he had a tendency to puff his chest out, roosterlike. He had an investment-banker-type haircut, a severe gray suit, and a white shirt that went with this personality: starchy. His navy blue necktie was knotted high and hard, and his Adam's apple bulged over it.

"If you and Captain Lee can wait until we get the autopsy report, we'll have a better idea of the time of death, but from the condition of the decedent's body it appears that he had been dead for approximately eight hours when he was discovered. Apparently rigor mortis had set in. The outside temperature and the decedent's build must be taken into consideration, of course. Rigor sets in more rapidly in thin people than in heavy ones. Daly was a slender man. The Medical Examiner's office will consider that."

John Daly's body had been discovered at about two A.M. by a security guard from the Javits Convention Center who was making his rounds.

"There's a half-finished pedestrian walkway under Eleventh Avenue," Nolan explained to me. "It runs between the Convention Center and a vest-pocket park across the street. It looks as if Daly slipped on ice while he was trying to make his way down the steps. The Convention Center was closed, and he probably was looking for shelter in the tunnel. He may have knocked himself unconscious, or possibly he couldn't get back up the steps. In any event, he froze to death.''

"Then why the fuss about letting me see his possessions? Especially since my business card was one of them.''

Nolan ran his hand across his mouth and made a hissing noise behind it before answering. "The fuss is because there may be questionable circumstances.''

He pursed his lips, determined to make me work for my next morsel.

"Such as?''

"Such as the fact that Daly had no wallet and no cash on him, which could indicate that he was the victim of a robbery. Do you happen to know if Daly ordinarily carried a wallet?''

I nodded. "I remember him putting my card in a leather billfold. What are some of the other questionable circumstances?''

Nolan took a look at the report on his desk, but he appeared to be familiar with it and I got the impression that he was trying to decide just how much he had to tell me.

"A small amount of blood was discovered on the wall and ground near a public telephone at the corner of Thirty-fifth Street and Eleventh Avenue,'' he finally said. "That's directly across from the park where Daly's body was found. There was a gash on Daly's head, just behind his right ear. The blow that caused that gash probably did not kill him—again, we won't know until we have the Medical Examiner's report—but if the ME's office ascertains that the blood near the phone is Daly's, then it appears that he somehow injured himself or that, perhaps in the process of robbing him, an unknown perpetrator inflicted the wound.''

My mind jumped back to the incoherent message on my answering machine the night before. I told Nolan about the muffled grunt and the dial tone that followed it.

When he had written down the information, he looked at me curiously.

"You have any idea what time that call was made?"

"Yes. My fiancé left me a message at about seven, and my mother called at eight-thirty. This call came in between those two."

Nolan took down that information, and then asked if John Daly and I had been close friends, so close that if he was in trouble John would have called me.

"Not really. I'd only known him for a couple of weeks. We taught a dance class together."

"So you have no idea why he would have been trying to get in touch with you? You know he had your card tucked into one of his gloves. By the way, the gloves were in his pockets rather than on his hands."

I shook my head. "Not a clue."

Nolan stared down at the other things that had come from John Daly's pockets, and then bit into his lower lip for a moment. "And you're working with Organized Crime Control?"

Nolan couldn't figure out my place in this. Why would someone with the status of Captain Lee order him to reveal vital information to a non-NYPD, non-status type like me?

"Yes. I'd like Daly's apartment keys if that's all right." If it wasn't all right, I was prepared to give Lee another call, but Nolan didn't fight it.

"A forensics team went to Daly's place a little while ago, after you identified the body." Nolan fished into one of the plastic bags. "They didn't find anything suspicious. I'll go to that club . . . The Dancing Fool . . . as soon as we're done here."

I took the keys from Nolan. "Please don't mention to anyone there that I'm connected with the Organized Crime Control unit."

He stared at me for a second and then said, in clipped tones, "I don't need to be told that."

The perforated quarter and chain that John had worn

around his neck had slipped onto the desktop. As Nolan scooped them carelessly back into the plastic bag, my gaze was drawn once more to the third plastic bag on the desk. It was hard for me to believe, but there it was and there was no avoiding it. When John Daly had been pulled from the tunnel under Eleventh Avenue his pockets had contained, in addition to the new leather gloves, the apartment keys, and some small change and subway tokens, one almost empty half-pint bottle of cheap blackberry-flavored brandy. Seventy-proof.

I slipped the keys into my pocket. "You'll let me know the results of the autopsy as soon as you have them?"

"That's up to the DA's office. As long as Captain Lee clears it with them, you can have anything you want."

15

I GOT JOHN'S ADDRESS AT THE PRE-
cinct. He'd lived on West Forty-fourth
Street, only a couple of blocks from the
club.

The relentless cold, the continual
mess falling from the sky, the treacherous patches of ice on the sidewalks—
winter was really getting to me, and
probably to everyone else. The entire
population seemed to move with the
same head-down posture, the same
short, flat-footed steps. Fear of sliding.
I no longer glanced into faces or looked at window dis-
plays. I watched my feet.

Apart from keeping you upright, there's something else
to be said about walking around that way: It gives you
time to think. Making my cautious way toward Forty-
fourth Street, I thought about John. My initial shock at
seeing his photo at the morgue had faded. I would mourn
him later, but now my mind was on the way he died.

No one would know for certain until the autopsy was
complete, but the logical assumption, the only assumption,
was that after eight sober months John had started drinking.

I tried to put myself in his place, to imagine his state
of mind the evening before. He was ready to make a big

move, trying to jump-start his career. Had he fallen victim to a massive case of butterflies? Cool as he was on the dance floor, confident as he might have been with Dawn as a partner, John still would have been nervous about meeting the theater people. At least once before, in a similar situation, he'd gotten drunk and blown it. Those butterflies can hit anybody, hard.

On top of that, there was the fight with Eddie. John was nominally the winner—he got the girl, and the other guy got the black eye—but John didn't strike me as someone who had had many fistfights in his life. The situation might have unnerved him and added to his performance anxiety. Buttoning his ruffled shirt, fastening his bow tie, his hands may have trembled. *A drink will help*, he might have said to himself.

When I tried to take things further, to imagine what John had done after getting himself dressed, I ran into trouble. The night had been bitter cold, yet here was a man who appeared to have walked away from his destination—the club—rather than toward it.

Dodging some nasty ice in a gutter, I noticed a wine bottle that had frozen into it like an Ice Age artifact. There was no scarcity of liquor stores in his neighborhood, and John undoubtedly knew them all. I imagined him hurrying into one of them, hat pulled low, face hidden by a scarf, not wanting to be recognized. Then, outside the store, he takes one quick slug from the bottle to calm the butterflies. But it had turned into two slugs, and three . . .

Or maybe he hadn't bought the liquor in his immediate neighborhood. Maybe a desire for anonymity was what turned him south toward Thirty-fifth Street. The one thing that seemed certain was that, somewhere between his apartment and the tunnel running from the Convention Center to the vest-pocket park, John had gotten hold of that bottle of brandy.

Where, actually, had he drunk the liquor? Had he ducked into a doorway? Or had he finished off most of the bottle on the street?

I tried taking this reconstruction to its next logical step.

Drunk and feeling guilty, knowing he'd messed up, John had tried to call me. But why me? Why not Dawn? She was the one he had left chewing her thumbnail. And why try me at home, but not at the club?

Because he was drunk, and no one can say why a drunk does anything.

I had a nagging, nasty feeling that the blood around the public phone would turn out to be John's. It seemed odd that he'd been sober enough to dial my home number correctly, but too drunk to leave a message, but it was possible that he'd fallen and cut himself before he could say anything into the phone. And then, once he'd picked himself up, he'd either forgotten about the call, or changed his mind about it. He'd wandered across the street and into the park. But why hadn't he put his gloves on?

Because he was drunk. That simple fact answered a lot of questions.

Okay, but what if John hadn't injured himself at the phone booth? Assume that someone else injured John as he was trying to reach me, took his wallet, and then forced him across Thirty-fifth Street into that park and then into the tunnel.

That made more sense to me, but who was this phantom someone? A drinking buddy who got greedy? Or a mugger?

When I reached Tenth Avenue at Forty-fourth Street and turned toward John's apartment house, my train of thought was interrupted. I'd been here before. A few days earlier I'd followed that low-end street peddler up this same block, but from the opposite direction. It had been late afternoon then, and already growing dark, but today the sun shone hard, the way it sometimes does on cold days, and diamond-bright shafts of light glinted off the packed snow. The red bricks of John's building were etched clearly against the pale sky. His building bordered the alley where The Dancing Fool's old office equipment had been discarded. The Dumpster was still there, and still overflowing. It was no coincidence that John had lived next door.

The steps leading to the front door were treacherous, and making my way up them I clung to the iron railing. In the little entryway were some battle-scarred mailboxes and a row of buzzers. John's name was on one of them, Apartment 4B. Since the police had already been there, the super probably knew that John was dead. I debated ringing the super's buzzer, but decided that could wait. After trying a couple of keys, I found the one that let me into the building.

The stairs were like those in every other tenement I've been in—steep and lopsided with a wobbling banister. On the second floor salsa music blasted from Apartment 2A, which also sported what looked like a decade-old Christmas wreath on its door. I hurried past the noisy apartment and looped around to the next flight of stairs.

A rusty metal bucket with a mop poking from it, and a leggy, parched philodendron shared a corner on the landing at the top of the third flight of stairs. There were three apartments on the floor, with 4B at the building's side. I expected the apartment to be empty but knocked first anyway. When there was no answer, I unlocked the two locks and turned the knob.

There was nothing for me to feel guilty about, but when a door behind me opened without warning I jumped and probably looked as if I'd been caught breaking and entering.

A young woman with short, spiky dark hair, wearing a blue bathrobe and holding a towel around her neck, stared from inside the apartment next to John's. I recognized her immediately. Katharine Parker. A second later a man with red hair appeared behind her. He was about her age, and lean and shirtless. Maybe even pantless, but I didn't look down.

''Can I help you?'' she asked.

''No. That's okay. But thanks.''

Brad Gannett's girlfriend sure hadn't wasted any time

finding a way to console herself. But then, grief is a personal thing and mourning can take many forms. For Katharine Parker, it had taken the form of a young man with red hair.

I dived into John's apartment and shut the door behind me.

John had been living nicely. Not lavishly, but decently. I was glad to see that. The windows—new ones from the look of them—were spotless, and sunlight peeking under half-lowered wicker shades brightened the wood floorboards. The furniture wasn't terribly different from my own—inexpensive and mismatched—but the colors were subdued and pleasant. The rumpled brown corduroy sofa looked like a good place to stretch out and watch television. John had also owned a VCR, and a decent stereo system.

There was a bricked-up fireplace, and on the mantel over it, flanked by framed reviews of his shows, stood the actual Tony he'd won so many years before. It was smaller than I'd expected, and bright gold. I reached for it but pulled back. If it turned out that John's death was anything other than accidental, the police might print the entire apartment. The less of me they found there the better.

Some folded brochures advertising the production of *Picnic* at the Hell's Kitchen Actors' Workshop were stacked beside the Tony. Taking one from the top, I glanced through it. How awful. The production was dedicated to Brad Gannett, and John Daly was listed as the second lead. If nothing else, the Workshop's understudies were getting a lot of work. I slipped one of the fliers into my tote.

John's kitchen wasn't in the hovel category, and it was clean, but even by my Washington Heights standards it left a lot to be desired. Never mind what my elevated suburban standards thought of it. A thin stream of murky water leaked from the faucet into the sink, leaving a brownish stain across the scratched porcelain, and the gas stove and half-sized refrigerator probably predated my birth.

The most interesting thing about the kitchen, from my point of view, was—the point of view. The window looked directly out on the alley and the abandoned building on the other side of it. When I peered down, I saw the Dumpster. There was no screen to deal with, and when I unlatched the window, it lifted easily. If John hadn't felt like walking down the alley, he could have tossed the adding machine and Dictaphone into the Dumpster from up here.

Using a paper towel to shield my fingers, I opened the small refrigerator and pushed aside the quart of milk and the orange juice. There were two apples and a container of low-fat cottage cheese, but the only part of John's diet I was interested in was liquor. I didn't find any. When I'd finished with the refrigerator I went through the metal cabinets mounted on the kitchen wall. Again, no liquor. There was a small garbage can lined with a plastic bag from the A&P under the ancient double sink. In it I found crumpled paper towels and an empty tuna fish can, but not a hint of liquor.

The bedroom was at the other end of the apartment. Like the rest of the place, the room faced the alleyway, but the two windows did let in a lot of light, and from the proper angle John might have been able to catch the sunrise.

There was no gate on the fire-escape window, which was surprising. Though unguarded fire-escape windows are not unknown in Manhattan, they aren't terribly common in neighborhoods like this one. I looked at the frame around the window and saw holes in the plaster. Some sort of gate had once been in place there. I wasn't sure what to make of that. Maybe nothing at all.

Like the rest of the apartment, the bedroom was neat, which was a good thing because the least mess in a room so small would have caused chaos. Double bed, small chest of drawers with a mirror mounted over it, a plastic cube for a night table, and that was it for furniture. Two framed posters from John's Broadway shows took up most of the wall space. Thrown over the bed was one of those inexpensive Indian spreads that were popular about the same time as love beads and Nehru jackets. The spread had faded to a pale purple, as if it had been washed a hundred times.

Standing in this room, I was struck by the difference between John's apartment and Dawn's. She lived only a couple of blocks north and east, but it seemed, for me at least, a million miles away. John had lived in this dumpy old place in the full sense of the word "lived." Despite all his problems, despite his shambling lifestyle, he'd made a nest and occupied it and kept it clean. Dawn's apartment, in contrast, was like a tree branch. She was perched there, poised to fly on.

John's wardrobe was hardly extensive and I looked through the small clothes closet quickly. Again there was no sign of liquor. Before I shut the door, my eyes were drawn to the shoes paired in a row on the floor. Sneakers, loafers, and the winter boots John had been wearing most of the time. Where were the new shoes that had cost him so much? Was it possible he'd been wearing them when he left his apartment the night before? If he'd only planned to walk the couple of blocks to the club, yes. But would he have worn those new shoes, unprotected, if he planned to walk down to Thirty-fifth Street?

When I finished with the closet I went through the dresser. Searching through John's underwear gave me a weird enough feeling, and when I opened a paper bag and found some fancy-type condoms—they were labeled "Pleasure Nubs"—I almost gave it up and skipped the two stacks of folded T-shirts in the top drawer. It's a good thing I didn't, because when I ran my hand under one of the stacks, a small piece of paper wedged between the soft cloth of the shirts and the bottom of the drawer stuck to my finger. As I withdrew my hand, the scrap of paper came with it.

It was one of those long, red-rimmed file labels that you see in offices everywhere, or at least part of one of those labels. Most of it had been torn away, and this little piece was blank. It was nothing more than a scrap, and ordinarily wouldn't have been worth a second look, but most of the video cassettes in the secure room at the club had these labels, and the night John broke into the club, he'd been in that room.

What had been on the missing part of the label? A number indicating the day of the month? Or the title from a triple X–rated video?

I stuck what was left of the label onto the Workshop brochure I'd taken and went on with my search.

John had kept his cash, such as it was, in the bottom drawer. There were a few loose dollar bills and one or two tokens.

Going through John's meager belongings was depressing, but what made me saddest was the box of photos I found when I wandered back into the living room. The sturdy white box—it was about 10-by-12 inches—was on the coffee table. At first I thought it held stationery, but when I flipped it open there was John's likeness looking up at me through a clear plastic envelope. Head shots. There were six of those envelopes in the box, and each showed John in a different pose: smiling, pensive, stern, debonair, hair mussed, hair combed back. You'd never suspect that the subject of these photos had made a wreck of a large part of his life. John had photographed like a real leading man.

As I looked through the pictures, the grief I'd been keeping at bay came from out of nowhere. It had as much to do with finding the photographer's receipt at the bottom of the box as the photos themselves. The day before he died, John had paid almost five hundred dollars for something he'd never get to use. That struck me as so terrible that I sank onto the sofa and sobbed out loud into my hands.

The sound of a key turning in the apartment door startled me, but I wasn't able to pull myself together before the door opened wide.

" 'S'cuse me, miss. Tenant next door called and said I might find you up here."

He was a light-skinned Hispanic, middle-aged with a comfortable middle-age spread. In one hand he had a key ring, and in the other a toolbox.

I didn't have any tissues so I swiped at my face with my left hand. "Are you the super?"

He nodded. "I'm Pedro. Want to fix that sink before it gets worse." He took a couple of steps toward the kitchen, but then turned back. "John told me there was a new woman in his life. I'm real sorry about your loss. He was a good man. Good tenant, too. Always paid on time, and never any trouble 'cept once or twice when he was drinking."

My loss? For a second that threw me, but when I lowered my hand the super's eyes were clinging to my engagement ring. I didn't set him straight. He might try to get me out of the apartment before I was ready to go.

I followed him into the kitchen. He had stooped in front of the sink and already had the cabinet door open.

"Thanks, Pedro. Could I ask you a couple of questions?"

"Sure. Don't know if I can answer them, but . . ."

"Why isn't there a gate on the fire-escape window? There are holes in the plaster for it."

"We had to take it off when we put in new windows last fall. John decided to leave it off." A small smile crossed his face. "Said he'd been looking through bars long enough, and he didn't have anything worth stealing, anyway."

"That makes sense. Next question: Had John been drinking lately?"

Pedro tilted his head quizzically, which was understandable. If anyone was in a position to know whether John was drinking, it was his fiancée.

"The thing is, the police say he might have been drunk when he died."

"Cops! They're always lookin' for an easy answer. John went to his AA meetings almost every day, sometimes twice a day, when he wasn't working. Last night when he left here, where do you think he was headed? Straight to St. Ann's."

"Where's that?"

"A block over, between Eighth and Ninth. AA meeting down in the basement every night at six."

"You're sure that's where John was going? Did he tell you that?"

"He didn't have to. He walked out of the building at about ten to six, turned left, and said 'See you later.' I knew where he was going. You shouldn't believe what cops say. They lie worse than anybody else just to make their jobs easier."

Half disappearing under the sink, Pedro banged around for a few minutes. "Have to go downstairs and shut off the water," he said when he crawled out. "I'll be back in a while."

"I may be gone, but I might want to come back."

"That's okay. Rent's paid. For next month, I mean. John put the check under my door yesterday. You being his fiancée, you feel free to stay here. I know you got his affairs to take care of."

"Yes, I do," I said out loud when the super had left the apartment.

John had paid his rent and he'd paid for head shots. He'd gone to his AA meeting, and immediately after that he'd gotten drunk. It wasn't impossible, but I didn't believe it.

Trying to think my way through John's last evening wasn't going to be enough. If I wanted to find out what had persuaded—or forced—John to go ten blocks out of his way and into a tunnel, I had to try to retrace his steps.

Before I left his apartment I slipped two of John's new head shots into my tote. Outside his building I turned left, as John had done the night before.

My first stop was St. Ann's, on the other side of Ninth Avenue. It was a big stone building, more solid than graceful. Someone had shoveled the steps to the main entrance, but the door itself was locked. Wandering around to the side of the church, I found a street-level door. It looked promising—light shone from a barred transom over it—but this door was also locked and my knock got no response. There was, however, a plastic-coated bulletin board mounted on the wall beside the door, and among the announcements of bake sales and after-school programs was one for AA. Meetings nightly at six, followed by Gamblers Anonymous at seven. How long did the meetings last? And had John actually made it to the meeting the night before? AA, from what I understood, didn't give out members' names. If that was true, they certainly wouldn't identify John to me, but maybe Detective Nolan would have some success.

In Manhattan, stores tend to line the avenues, leaving the streets for apartment houses, churches, and schools. There are exceptions, of course, but I decided to stick to the avenues in my liquor store search. Otherwise I'd be forever. After leaving St. Ann's, I walked down Eighth Avenue all the way to Thirty-fifth Street, crossed Thirty-fifth to Ninth Avenue, and then walked back up to Forty-fourth. In that nine-block square, there were six liquor stores. I showed John's head shots to clerks in all of them. No one recognized him until I was almost back where I'd started.

In a small mom-and-pop liquor store on Ninth, not more than a block from John's apartment, a woman with beautiful black hair and tired dark eyes nodded when she saw the photos.

"Oh, sure. He's changed lately but I know him. We always called him T'Bird."

She held the photo toward a grizzled man who was sitting behind a machine that dispensed New York State Lottery tickets. "You know him. He comes in a lot."

The man's eyes flicked briefly away from the newspaper he was reading, focused on the photo, then shifted to me.

"I'm a cop," I said.

It wasn't all that much of a stretch but the man snorted. "And I'm the Pope."

The woman tapped the photo with her fingernail. Her ornate gold wedding band caught my eye. "He was in yesterday," she said.

"Yesterday evening?"

As she nodded, her hair bounced on her shoulders. Making a comb of her fingers, she carefully smoothed it. A small vanity, but if she was married to the man at the Lotto machine, she deserved all the vanities she could get.

"I think so, but I can't be positive. I take my lunch here, my dinner here. After a while I don't know from time."

"He bought his usual," the man put in churlishly.

"He didn't buy just his usual," the woman snapped back.

My reaction to that information was pretty ridiculous when you consider that John was dead, but I wished he'd gone out fighting. "He bought a half pint of brandy?"

The man turned back to his newspaper without answering. The woman glared at him for a moment, then looked at me.

"T'Bird hadn't been drinking for a long time. He bought a couple of QuickPix Lotto tickets for Saturday's drawing, like he always does. And he got one for his girlfriend."

A bell over the door jingled as two ragged men walked into the store. They emptied their pockets of small change and meticulously spread the coins across the counter. I waited until they paid for a bottle of cheap wine and left.

"Was T'Bird's girlfriend with him?"

The woman shook her head. "She was outside, double-parked in a cab. Someone started blowing a horn and T'Bird said he had to hurry. He said, 'And give me one for my girlfriend out there.' "

"So you didn't see her?"

The man made a nasty noise at the back of his throat. He hadn't looked up from his paper, but there was an ugly smirk on his face that had nothing to do with the news. "That's what she's after. She's afraid her man's cheating on her."

"I should be so lucky," the woman said.

"He didn't say anything about where they were going, did he?" I asked.

"No. I got busy or something and that was the end of it."

I thanked both of them for the information, but the man ignored me. On my way out of the store I held the door open a second longer than necessary.

"You're letting the heat out," the man grumbled.

"Sorry." I let the door swing shut.

The cabbie pulled to the curb catty-corner to the Convention Center and looked over his shoulder. "This is where you want to get out?"

Closed warehouses lined one side of the street, and on the other was the deserted and unappealing park. Shoppers and people looking for an early dinner out were several blocks east, and though it was rush hour and traffic was heavy at the intersection, there was no sign of life at the huge Convention Center across Eleventh Avenue.

"I'll just be a minute. Please wait for me." I was out of the cab before he could argue.

A yellow crime-scene ribbon blocked access to a public phone on the northeast corner of the intersection. On the pavement under the phone there was a splattering of brownish dots. Daylight was fading and I didn't cross the ribbon to take a closer look, but this was probably the blood Nolan had mentioned.

At a lull in traffic I made a run for the park. A westbound driver blasted his horn, and probably spent a few seconds cursing crazy Manhattan pedestrians.

Nolan had called this place a vest-pocket park, but for

me the word "park" implies grass and trees. Even in the summer there would be no grass and trees here. Everything in this tiny park—ground, benches, towering hunks of modern sculpture—was concrete, and every horizontal surface was icy, whipped by wind from the Hudson. In spots the ice had cracked, perhaps under the weight of the cops' feet early that morning, or maybe John's feet the night before.

As I started exploring, the street lights flickered on and cast an eerie yellow sheen across the frozen surface. I made my way cautiously, taking those short steps that had become second nature, and in the center of this concrete park, maybe fifty feet from the street, found the entrance to the tunnel where John Daly had died.

What John had slipped down wasn't actually a stairway. It was an unused, unfinished escalator. A wire mesh fence that had blocked access to it had been torn free. A corner of this fence swayed in the wind, and though it didn't offer much stability, it was better than nothing. Gripping the wire, I stepped as close to the entrance as my nerve let me, and stared down.

The half-dozen metal escalator treads that were visible were covered with ice. What lay beyond and below them was obscured by darkness. I didn't dare try to make my way down.

Backing away from the tunnel, I was struck by the utter desolation of this place. The park was so exposed and so uninviting that it was hard to imagine anyone seeking shelter here. John, a man who had liked his creature comforts, had found a miserably uncomfortable place to die.

As I made my way toward the street, I wasn't paying enough attention to those short footsteps. I put one foot down where it shouldn't have gone and ended up doing a desperate little dance trying to stay upright. It didn't work and before I could even think about the best way to fall, I was on my hands and knees. I reached the relative safety of the curb in that same position.

My driver was half out of his cab, staring. I couldn't

read his expression. Trying to preserve some dignity, I struggled to my feet and made my way across the street.

"Thanks for waiting. Penn Station, please."

"Checking out the park for ice skating? That triple-axle of yours is a beauty."

It had been a long, bad day. I was tired and sad, and my knees hurt. I shut my eyes and ignored him.

Sam called early that evening and said they had decided to work through the weekend. That way the move would be finished by the middle of the week. That was good news. The house was lonely at night.

A little later, when I had fed myself and Moses, I called Lee and told him what I'd learned that day. John had not been drinking, and he had been going to AA. He had paid his rent in advance and he had plunked down $500 for head shots. He'd bought lottery tickets for himself and for an unknown woman. For me, all of these things said that he'd been moving forward with his life. I also told Lee that John had surely broken into The Dancing Fool, and that there was a chance he had taken one of the video cassettes from the secure room.

Lee, as always, was doubtful.

"You should know something, Miss Indermill. After I talked to you this morning I checked out the deceased. A year ago Daly spent the night in jail on a drunk and disorderly charge, and in California he was arrested twice for driving while intoxicated. Certainly, the death of a third person involved with The Dancing Fool may suggest more than coincidence, but if there is a link, well, I don't know how you're going to find it."

This wasn't encouragement Lee was giving me, but it wasn't necessarily discouragement, either, and when we'd hung up I realized that for the first time Lee hadn't said a word about contractors, or about my fixation on show biz types.

16

I WALKED INTO AN IMPROMPTU WAKE the next day at the club. For Eddie, it almost turned into another fight.

Max had been stocking the register with cash. Tossing aside a paper band from some fresh bills, he spread his hands expressively.

"The thing that surprises me the most is that you're so surprised, Dawn. I'm sorry about John, obviously, but what did you expect? The guy came from the gutter, and he went back to the gutter."

"You've got a lot of heart, Max."

Dawn was on one of the bar stools, wearing, appropriately, black—tights, boots, and a long, fuzzy sweater. It wasn't exactly your usual outfit for mourning, but as I said, grief is a very personal thing. And she was grieving. Whether it was for John or for the unpleasantness in her career path I wasn't certain, but her voice was husky and her eyelids so swollen that the cornflower-blue irises were almost invisible. What made the biggest impression on me, though, was her complexion. She probably hadn't slept well, maybe not at all, and it looked as if she'd applied her makeup with a heavy hand. Her skin was chalky and dry, and there were fine lines crossing her forehead that I'd never noticed before. For the first time since we'd met, Dawn looked her age.

She had turned her face down as if to study the bar's shiny surface, but her eyes shifted toward Max. "Thanks for being so nice. I won't bother asking you to go to the funeral with me."

I leaned against the coat-check door and started unzipping my boots. "Have you heard anything about a funeral for John? I'd like to go."

Dawn shook her head. "But there's got to be something, hasn't there? They wouldn't just"—she took a sharp breath, then choked back a sob—"throw him in the ground."

Steve, who was changing light bulbs, a job which no doubt challenged him, paused. "Come on, Dawn. Don't cry. If there's a funeral, I'll go with you. Max is right, but hey! The poor guy's dead."

He sounded sympathetic enough, but his eyes were glued to the risky territory where Dawn's legs disappeared beneath the fuzz of her sweater. Business as usual with Steve. At least that's what it seemed like until he started goading Eddie.

"It's not like I had any beef with John," he said. "We got along fine. I'm not ashamed to pay my respects."

If Eddie hadn't been there, that might have rolled past the rest of us. But Eddie was there, crouching on the bandstand fooling around with wiring for the mixer that the disc jockey would use later that night. Steve's words hung in the stale club air, a fat, malevolent cloud ready to burst.

"What's that supposed to mean?" Eddie asked after a moment.

"Nothing, except you're the guy John beat up. It's understandable why you wouldn't want to go to his funeral. When I think about it, though, you might like seeing him buried." Then Steve chuckled. "Maybe you even helped him fall down that escalator."

Escalator. My spying mind pounced on the word. Nolan had referred to steps. A small thing, but interesting.

Eddie was rising to his feet. "John didn't beat me up.

He got in one lucky punch. And I never saw him again after that, so don't start any shit about me helping to kill him.''

The vein in Eddie's temple was twitching. Max stepped in quickly.

"When you're through there, Steve, why don't you go upstairs and open a case of Scotch."

Max the peacemaker.

"Bummer about John, huh," Steve said as he walked past me.

"Yeah. Bummer."

Eddie watched Steve until he had disappeared up the stairs, then went back to fiddling with the wires. Max went downstairs but he left the register open, which meant that he'd be right back. Dawn seemed content to stay put at the bar, but if I was going to try to get anything out of her I didn't want to do it with anyone else around.

"Want to get some lunch, Dawn? We could get something to bring back, if you'd like." I slipped my wallet into my pocket and tossed my tote on a chair.

Swiveling the bar stool, Dawn looked at me as if I were trying to communicate in a foreign language. "I couldn't eat a bite," she finally said, but she slid off the stool and peered at me through those swollen lids. "I'll walk with you, though. Some fresh air might pick me up. I don't know how I'll ever lead my aerobics class this afternoon."

Having another of Jaguida's grease-laden meals was tempting fate. And tempting fat. But when Dawn and I left the club, I turned toward Tenth Avenue as if I'd been programmed.

The wind gave meaning to the word "bracing." It drove us every step of the way as we walked with it at our backs, and opening Jaguida's door was a battle. When the battle was done, though, and I stood before the counter in the steamy room, the smell of grease and the splattering sounds from the kitchen were almost reward enough.

God knows what goes into Rumanian chicken, but I ordered two pieces of it anyway—white meat—and the biscuit and mashed potatoes that went with it, adding piously, "No gravy, please." A minute after I ordered, Dawn touched my arm and said in a choked-up voice, "Ask them to make it two, Bonnie. Only I want the gravy."

Oh-oh. If Dawn didn't watch it, she might end up looking like the woman on her Louisiana driver's license. I called toward the kitchen. "Jaguida? Would you make that two orders, one with gravy. No. Make *both* of them with gravy."

"Yeah, yeah."

"We should eat here," I said. "This will be a mess to carry back. Okay?"

Dawn looked around the cafe with a grimace. Of the seven tables, four were empty. The wild-eyed old man had his usual table at the back of the room.

"This place is depressing, but I guess the club's even worse right now."

I assumed that meant yes. "Jaguida. We've decided we'll eat here."

As Dawn and I sat down at the window table, Jaguida came out of the kitchen with cups of tea for us. I half expected this hostess-with-the-mostess to be a little testy about our change in plans, change being something that she didn't take well, and her smile, though it wasn't one that would have stirred a poet's soul, was a relief.

"So Eddie must have hit the daily double."

"What?"

"He walked in here this morning and paid me most of what he owed and said he'd have the rest of it tonight. Two months' rent he was behind, not to mention all the meals he's talked me out of."

Dawn's eyes flashed angrily toward Jaguida, but she didn't speak until the woman had shuffled back to the kitchen.

"We found out about John yesterday, around noon.

This cop—Nolan—came to the club and talked to us. And last night there's Eddie at the club flashing around a fat wallet, buying drinks for people he hardly knows. I wanted to kill him, Bonnie. It was like he was celebrating John's death.''

"He wouldn't do that."

She went on as if she hadn't heard. "You know what I kept thinking? First Eddie picked that stupid fight with John, and John won, and now John's dead and his wallet's missing and Eddie's got cash for the first time in months."

The cash had come from the New York City Property Clerk, but Dawn didn't know that. "I'm sure the money Eddie's spending wasn't in John's wallet. Eddie's been expecting money from a legal settlement."

Dawn sipped at her tea. "Maybe you're right. John probably wouldn't have had enough in his wallet to pay two months' back rent. But I called Nolan anyway."

"You did what?"

"Called Nolan. The cop. When I got home last night, I was so mad about the way Eddie was acting that I called Nolan and told him about the fight Eddie picked with John. I told him that Eddie was jealous and making crazy threats. The thing is—"

Jaguida set two steaming, heaping plates in front of us. She didn't bother with niceties like bread plates, and the biscuits were already saturated with gravy.

"You want butter?"

Dawn and I agreed that our biscuits were just fine the way they were. Once again, Dawn was quiet until Jaguida had returned to the kitchen.

"I don't know how things would have worked out between me and John personally. Okay, so we'd spent a couple of nights together and they were good, but I've had good before. The big thing is, the two of us had just started something that might actually have been great for our careers."

Hesitating, she stirred her fork into the mashed potatoes. "I've been trying to make it for a while, Bonnie. I'm not as young as you might think. And suddenly, with John there was a real chance. I blame Eddie for ruining it. Eddie . . ."

After taking a mouthful of the potatoes, she dug into the chicken. It was a minute before she went on.

"I made a mistake with Eddie. We had a brief . . . and I do mean brief . . . thing at Christmas. You know how lonely the holidays can be. Anyway, I didn't take it too seriously. But Eddie! He got so possessive I could hardly believe it."

"Maybe you should have told him straight out you weren't interested."

That got me a calculated look. "I wanted to keep the job at the club. It was getting me a little exposure. More than I'd get from waitressing and leading aerobics classes. Max wasn't crazy about me being there."

"Why not?"

Dawn looked down at her plate. "Max and Steve and I go back farther than you think. Their father and I had a . . . relationship. It went on for a while, and lately he's helped me some financially. Don't get the idea that I'm taking advantage of some pitiful old man, Bonnie. In one way or another I've earned every penny. Max and Steve's father was a . . ."

While she searched for the right words any number of them went through my mind: criminal, mobster, murderer.

"Well, he could be unpleasant," Dawn said finally, "but he's gotten much nicer."

I suppose that looking the Grim Reaper in the eye can make one . . . nice.

"Anyway, I thought Eddie would get over his infatuation after a while, but it doesn't look like that happened. Even if he didn't push John down those escalator steps, he pushed him over the edge . . ."

I interrupted her. "What makes you think it was an escalator, Dawn?"

"Isn't that what it was? That's what Steve just called it."

Nolan hadn't used the word "escalator" around me, but maybe he had used it in front of them.

"John was tough in a lot of ways," Dawn continued, "but he was fragile, too. Nolan said that John had been drinking. That was Eddie's fault."

"We don't know that. When you saw John later, after the fight, did he seem overly upset?"

The forkful of chicken Dawn was about to bite into stopped short of her mouth. "I didn't see John Thursday evening. Why do you think I did?"

I shook my head. "There's a rumor that John was with a woman."

She didn't ask where I'd heard that rumor, which was just as well. I couldn't have told her how deeply involved I was in this.

"John and I left the club together, but that was it," Dawn said. "I went home to change clothes and take a nap. He wanted to go back to his place and cool off. And then he had an AA meeting to go to."

"Was he seeing any other women that you know of?"

"No. I mean, he had some women friends from his workshop, but nothing heavy." She brightened briefly. "It might have been Elsie."

"You think so?"

"Maybe. John spotted her in the neighborhood a couple of times this week. We were joking about her stalking him."

For someone who couldn't eat a thing—who claimed to never eat much—Dawn was doing quite a job on her chicken. Between bites, she suddenly said, "Do you think maybe Elsie killed him?"

"Right now they're not saying anyone killed him."

"Well, if anyone did, my money's on Eddie. Eddie hated John. Elsie's just a little strange."

"Elsie's profoundly strange." And, awful as the idea was, I was going to have to track her down.

I asked Dawn if she'd tried calling John from her apartment Thursday evening.

"No, because by then he would have been at AA. Six o'clock every night. He was supposed to meet me at the club at seven thirty."

Her Rumanian chicken was now history, and the heap of mashed potatoes was shrinking. Catching me looking at her plate, she forced a smile. "I didn't have dinner last night. You want to know what I did? After I called Nolan?"

"Sure."

"You know how I can see some of the theaters from my window? I sat there staring down at them. Friday night, and they were all lit up. I got depressed and started thinking about giving it up, settling for some regular job and some regular man. I'm getting tired of living like this, Bonnie. Afraid to gain a pound, afraid to have a drink because my skin might not look so young the next morning. Maybe I should find myself a moving man and move to the suburbs like you," she added, taking a pointed look at my ring.

"Marrying Sam isn't 'settling.' "

It came out more defensive than I'd intended.

"I'm sorry, but Bonnie you've got to have some idea what I'm talking about. Ten years ago you didn't have your sights set on the suburbs, did you?"

This certainly wasn't the dewy ingénue I'd had lunch with a week before. This was a woman who had been around for a while, and was growing tired. This was Ella baby, nee Dawnella Starkey. Strangely enough, I liked this newer—or better put—older, tougher Dawn more. The young, perky, clean-scrubbed Dawn hadn't had much soul. This one did.

When we got back to the club Max and Eddie were gone. Dawn collected the bits of her wardrobe she needed to teach her aerobics class. I walked with her to the door, and then went to retrieve my tote from the chair where I'd left it earlier.

It wasn't there. For a moment I was baffled, and anxious, too. My wallet was safe in my pocket but my house keys, my apartment keys . . .

Steve had turned on the television behind the bar and was staring at it, mesmerized.

"Did you see . . ." I began, but then spotted the bag on the floor beside the chair. As I picked it up, Steve grunted, "Huh?"

I couldn't tell what he was watching—the set faced away from me and the sound was turned low—but his mouth was open slightly and his eyes didn't waver from the flickering images.

"Nothing."

As soon as I got back upstairs, I called Elsie's home number. She picked up on the first ring.

"Elsie. This is Bonnie. You probably know about John."

"Of course I know. In my position, I was one of the first to hear."

What position? For a nutty second I wondered if the long-defunct John Daly Fan Club had some muscle with the NYPD. Elsie set me straight.

"We have reporters who monitor the morgue continually. As soon as someone identified John's body I heard about it. I wasn't surprised."

"You weren't?"

"No. Not after . . . But I shouldn't talk to you. I'm a material witness."

Whatever she was talking about, there was the strangest note in her voice. Pride, almost.

"Material witness to what?"

"Sergeant Nolan—Isn't he nice!—said that I shouldn't discuss my information with anyone."

"But he didn't mean me. Sergeant Nolan and I are working together on the investigation."

Elsie, who I admit with great reluctance wasn't a complete and utter idiot, hooted. "Why would he work with you, a known thief?"

"Known to whom?" I demanded hotly.

"Well, Sergeant Nolan mentioned you and I felt it was my duty to tell him everything. After all, he is a law officer."

And you're an asshole! Amazing the effect this woman had on my disposition. I took a deep breath and thought hard before opening my mouth again. Even if she was the woman John had bought the Lotto ticket for, Elsie wasn't going to offer me any information. Not willingly, at any rate. But I'd discovered this one thing about her: She had a price.

"Gee whiz, that's a darned shame," I finally said in language she wouldn't find offensive. "Because I've got access to John Daly's apartment, and knowing your interest in him I was planning to take you on a tour, even though I'm under strict orders not to let anyone in there."

Elsie and I were friends again.

Ten minutes later I walked out of the ladies' room in the Celebrity Lounge with my boots on my feet, my tote over my arm, and the knowledge that Elsie had been waiting in front of St. Ann's in a cab when John's AA meeting broke up, and had offered him a ride home.

The Celebrity Lounge was dim, and light from the television downstairs reflected on one of the walls. I wasn't especially interested in Steve's viewing tastes, but whatever he was watching sure was keeping him quiet. It was idle curiosity that made me walk to the railing and look down.

Without my glasses the figures on the screen were blurry. I'm not blind, though. There was one thing—several things, thinking back on the moment—that I made out quite clearly. The people cavorting on that television screen were, as Amanda might have said, "in the altogether," and what's more, they were all . . . friendly.

From Steve I wouldn't have expected *Wall Street Week* or the Weather Channel, or even one of *Masterpiece Thea-*

tre's racier productions. On the other hand . . . How did that couple on the screen ever manage to get themselves into that position?

I quietly dug my glasses from my tote, but it probably wouldn't have mattered if I'd sounded like a backhoe digging through concrete. Steve was so absorbed that he never turned his head.

It was a video cassette he was watching. With my glasses on my nose I made out the bright indicators on the VCR. What's more, I could see what that couple and their friends were doing and how it was being done. There were four of them in the film, all looking very happy, despite the fact that some of the positions they had gotten themselves into would have taxed the abilities of a yoga master.

The centerpiece of the film, the thing the action appeared to revolve around, apart from the humongous bed with red sheets, was a smashing redheaded woman. A little overweight and big-haired by New York City standards maybe, but gorgeous to the rest of the world, I'll bet.

Oh, Dawn. Dawnella. Ella baby. What interesting things you have done in the name of your career. Compared to this film, Amanda's romp with the Canadian businessman was about as wild as a sewing circle.

I try not to be judgmental. You've heard the expression "There but for the grace of God go I"? It's true. Many men and women who rummage around the edges of show business hoping to make it, myself included, get wind of these film "opportunities" from time to time. Most say, "Not for me, thank you," but some of us say, "Sure. Can't hurt." And who's to say Dawn had been wrong? The people on the videotape didn't look unhappy and neither did the moron sitting at the bar leering at them.

As I headed toward John's apartment, I did more of that heavy, cold-weather, foot-watching thinking. "Can't hurt," I'd said to myself moments before, but maybe

Dawn's fringe acting career had hurt someone. Maybe John Daly . . .

Suddenly the circumstances surrounding John's death were so clear that I could have been reading them from a list.

It begins with Dawn. Thinking that her relationship with John will lead to Broadway, she tells him about these films—most likely there was more than one. Better he know now than get a nasty surprise later, she figures.

John is concerned about the tapes, and wants to get them back. With or without Dawn's knowledge, he takes her keys, sneaks into the secure room, and takes what films of Dawn's he can find.

He watches the tapes, and begins to question his involvement with Dawn. He's on his way back up. Does he need a lover/partner with this sword hanging over her head? And if she's done video porn, what other kinds of things has she done?

As the Broadway director's visit to the club approaches, John is already anxious about the tapes and Dawn. The fight with Eddie increases his anxiety. He meets briefly with Elsie—God only knows what that did to his nervous system. Terribly upset then, John goes somewhere he won't be recognized and buys the bottle of brandy. When he realizes he's had too much, he tries to call me. Why me? Why *not* me? He's drunk. He doesn't have to make sense.

When he's unable to reach me, he finishes off most of the bottle and accidentally cracks his head against the phone booth wall. Drunk and despondent, and maybe delirious from the blow on the head, he wanders into the icy park and slips down the steps of the abandoned escalator, where he freezes to death.

By the time I turned down Forty-fourth Street I had it all figured out.

ELSIE WAS GETTING OUT OF A CAB when she spotted me. Her greeting wasn't as enthusiastic as it had been when we'd met at Dawn's apartment, but it wasn't as sour as it had been in the health food store, either. She gave me a simple "Hi, Bonnie," and I mistakenly thought this was an Elsie I could endure for a while.

"What do you think of John's building?" A 35-millimeter camera was strung around her neck, and as she spoke she raised it and focused on the building's nondescript front door. "Does it say anything to you?"

What a funny question. "Nothing special. It's not too good a building, but not bad, either." Starting up the stairs, I added, "About average for the neighborhood."

She snapped off two shots, then lowered the camera and shook her head. "I'm looking for quotes for my series. That's not good enough."

"Sorry. What series?"

"I'm doing John's biography. It was going to be a book, but now that he's dead I'm trying to get the paper to run it as a series. While he's hot."

"I hadn't realized he was."

"He will be when I get through with him," Elsie said

confidently. ''Don't get me wrong, Bonnie. This will be a serious biographical work about a serious artist. I won't do a trashy star bio.''

I picked up a note of reproach there. Maybe she knew that I love trashy star bios.

''That's a big undertaking.'' I unlocked the door in the vestibule and preceded Elsie into the building.

''There's no one better qualified. There are blanks to be filled in, but I know more about John's life than anyone else. My knowledge is encyclopedic.''

That might have been true, but Elsie didn't know much about people, and with her personality she might have a hard time getting anyone to help her fill in those blanks.

At the top of the first flight of stairs she paused and took a long, deep breath. Someone was cooking with curry, and the air was close and thick with the smell.

'' 'The sounds and smells of exotic, faraway places greet you when you walk into the building where John Daly spent the last days of his life,' '' she said, raising her voice to be heard over the beat of bongo drums coming from the apartment with the wreath on the door. ''What do you think of that for a first line, Bonnie?''

I shrugged. ''That's not the way I'd go, but it's your series.''

We continued up the staircase, the railing wobbling under our hands and the stairs creaking beneath our feet. By the time we reached the fourth-floor landing Elsie was red-faced. Someone had been doing some heavy spraying for roaches and the exotic smell of faraway places had been overpowered by the acrid smell of Raid.

Panting, Elsie nodded. ''You're right. That's too soft. I need something tougher. A 'mean streets' kind of opening.''

I stopped abruptly in front of John's door. ''And here is the rent-controlled apartment John held on to for more than twenty years.''

Elsie's lids dropped over her cow-brown eyes. ''If only these walls could only talk. I could do something like,

'The touchstone in John's life, through drunk and sober, up and down, was the rent-controlled. . . . ' "

I jangled the apartment keys. Elsie opened her eyes slowly, and then glommed onto the key ring as if it were the Hope Diamond being waved in front of her.

"That sounds good, Elsie."

I held the keys up and jangled them again. She moved closer but I shook my head. "But you're not getting inside until we talk some more."

"I already told you about picking John up in the cab."

"You waited for him after his AA meeting."

"It wasn't like I was . . . pestering him."

In a pig's eye.

"The thing is, I'd told John about my idea for this book. He and I would collaborate. It would be his autobiography, as told to me. He hadn't said yes, but he hadn't said no, either. I knew he went to St. Ann's every night at six. It was too cold for me to walk, so I got a cab and had it wait until the meeting was over."

"What time was that?"

She hesitated. I flipped the keys in the air and caught them.

"About six forty-five. I wanted to discuss the book, but John was in a hurry and didn't have time to talk right then. He had to go home to change clothes."

"Was John wearing his boots?"

"Of course," she snapped. "What a silly question. It was freezing. Anyway, he got in the cab, but then he asked the driver to let him out at a liquor store a block away so he could buy a Lotto ticket. He told me not to wait but I waited anyway. When he came out of the store he handed me a Lotto ticket, and then he walked off toward his apartment, and . . . and that's all I'm supposed to say." She jutted her chin defiantly.

"I understand that, Elsie, but if you want to get into this apartment you're going to have to disobey Sergeant Nolan. After all, I'm disobeying orders by letting you in," I said, though it was only common sense I was ignoring.

For a second there was no reaction from Elsie; then it came all at once, the same red-faced fury I'd seen in the health food store. Even more alarming, she moved closer to me, until her face was inches from mine. I scooted around her, but there was nowhere to go except up against the banister. Undeterred, Elsie stuck with me, and as I tried to keep my distance, the railing wobbled frighteningly. I glanced through the flimsy posts, and the floor below looked a hundred feet away.

"I'm sick of being pushed around by everybody," she shouted. "Sick of it!" She stamped her foot hard, like a temperamental child. "My boss. You. I'll get into that apartment one way or another!"

Who knew what this woman was capable of? Not wanting to find out, certainly not while I was backed against a banister that wouldn't hold my weight, I changed my approach.

"You might be able to, Elsie, but don't you want to see it now, while the walls can still talk about the real John Daly?" I nodded toward the bucket and mop in the corner. They hadn't changed position since the day before, and maybe not since the year before, but she didn't know that.

"Apartments don't stay vacant long. It looks like the super's ready to get in there and start cleaning up for the next tenant. The 'essence' of John Daly is going to be mopped up and washed down a drain."

Her lower lip quivered as if she might start to blubber any second.

"So what's the information that makes you a material witness?" I asked.

"I'm not supposed to talk to anybody. . . . "

"Inside this door is the kitchen John Daly cooked in for twenty-two years. The table where he ate his meals, the bedroom, the very"—I paused to get the full effect out of this—"pillow where he rested his head."

When she sighed and the blood left her cheeks, I thought I had her. Elsie was a tricky devil, though, and it was a mistake to underestimate her. Her eyes narrowed and so did her lips. I'd seen that expression before. It was the one that meant her little weasel mind was churning away. Sure enough, she didn't want to give until she got.

"If you're really working with Sergeant Nolan," she began, "then you must have access to information that I don't."

"No other deals, Elsie. You want to get inside this apartment, you tell me what you know."

She didn't respond right away, so I moved toward the stairs. She made a grab for my arm but I slipped past.

"Eddie Fong did it," she blurted.

"What?"

"It was Eddie. Eddie's a murderer. He killed John, and I'm a witness."

She might as well have punched me. Almost unable to get my breath, I whispered, "You saw Eddie kill John?"

"Not actually kill him, but I know he did it because I saw him attack John. From behind, like a coward."

"When was this?"

"After John walked away from my cab. He was partway down the block when a man in a black leather jacket ran up behind him and started yelling. John turned and raised his hands in front of his face to protect himself. I opened the cab window and screamed, 'Get away from him,' and then the man in the leather jacket looked at me and said some words that I won't repeat. It was Eddie."

"And then what happened?"

"Eddie crossed the street. Before he did, though, he threatened John. I was close enough to hear exactly what he said."

"Which was?"

"He said, 'We're not through with this.' I wanted to make sure John was okay, but he hurried off before I had a chance to talk with him." Elsie shook her head sadly. "I never saw John again, because Eddie killed him a little while later when he left his building."

On the surface, that was a leap in logic, but if Elsie

was telling the truth, and I couldn't imagine why she wouldn't, then Eddie had lied about not seeing John again after their fight at the club.

Elsie looked pointedly at the keys in my hand. "Now let's go inside."

So much for sad. The moment I had that door open, she shoved past me and rushed into John's apartment. In the center of his living room she stopped and turned slowly, rapt as a first-time visitor taking in the Sistine Chapel.

"I'm trying to get it all. I want to feel what John felt when he came home at the end of a day."

I'm not sure what John felt, but what I felt—and I felt it immediately—was chilly. The day before the apartment had been comfortable. I put my hand on the radiator, expecting it to be cold but it was warm to the touch.

"The super must have just turned on the steam."

Elsie was focusing her camera on the little Tony statue, and didn't pay attention. When the shutter had clicked a couple of times, I went to the fireplace and examined the statuette myself. Hadn't it been in the center of the mantel the day before, next to the pamphlets about the Actors' Workshop? Now it was to one side of the mantel and the pamphlets were gone.

"I'm taking two shots of everything, just to be safe."

Elsie headed into the kitchen. "Let's see what John ate. I'm not sure what can be done with that, but you never know. If there's one thing I've learned from the old witch, it's not to let any stone go unturned."

Or any package of margarine, or any container of aging cottage cheese either. This new, businesslike Elsie crouched in front of the refrigerator for a few minutes, then shifted her attention to the garbage sack under the sink. Watching her, I realized that I'd been waiting for an avalanche of wild emotions—tears, hair-tearing, the works. Instead, here was this anthropologist on a research expedition, digging through old campfires for shards of pottery and stripped chicken bones.

"And the bedroom's back there?"

Without waiting for my response, she tromped across the living room and flung open the bedroom door. The temperature in the apartment seemed to drop even more, but by the time my body had registered that information, Elsie was squeaking.

"Oh, my, my! What is this?"

Had she found the condoms in John's dresser drawer? I walked into the bedroom grinning, wondering how she was going to fit the Pleasure Nubs into her serious biographical work.

The source of the apartment's frigid air was instantly clear. A stiff cold wind blasted through a hole as big as a pie plate that had been cut from the fire-escape window.

The self-confident anthropologist of moments before was now white-faced and agog. "What does this mean?"

It didn't take a genius to answer that. It meant, for one thing, that John should have replaced his window gate.

Elsie raised her hand toward the broken window.

"Don't touch it," I warned. "There might be prints."

"We better call Sergeant Nolan. I'll bet it was Eddie." She glanced excitedly around the bedroom. "There must have been something here that tied him to John's death."

That had occurred to me too, but the last thing I wanted was Elsie as a partner. "I'll call the police. You'd better leave. You're not supposed to be here."

I hurried into the living room and faked a phone call to the precinct.

As you might imagine, the idea of leaving didn't much appeal to Elsie. It took some inventiveness on my part, including both a threat and a bribe, to get rid of her.

"This is bigger than you realize, Elsie. Even Sergeant Nolan doesn't know how big it is. If you don't go now, if I ever tell the story, it will be to your boss. If you go now, you'll get an exclusive if I talk."

She rolled her tongue around inside her cheek, making it look as if a good-sized boil were about to sprout there.

"An exclusive to what?" the crafty stinker wanted to know.

"The show biz secret that killed John Daly. My information would catapult you to the top of . . . celebrity columnists."

From the mouths of babes.

As soon as Elsie was out of my hair I put my gloves on and went through the apartment slowly and carefully. Even so, I spotted only a few things missing.

The thief hadn't been terribly interested in valuables. The loose cash had disappeared from the bottom dresser drawer, but the tokens were still there. The VCR, always a hot item on the resale market, was still on its shelf under the television, and the stereo hadn't been touched. That seemed to eliminate a random burglar.

So what had been taken? I've already mentioned the Workshop brochures and the cash. The condoms were gone, too.

A thief with a sex life and a thing for Off-Off-Broadway. A thief who didn't use public transportation. Weird.

What about Eddie? Well, in the time I'd known Eddie he'd never shown an interest in the theater. As for his sex life, from time to time he had one, but unless he was keeping a secret—something he wasn't good at—this wasn't one of those times. Eddie's no stranger to fire escapes, but would he climb one and break through a window to steal a couple of dollars and a pack of condoms? No. Eliminate Eddie.

That left . . . who? A fan? John's biggest fan—possibly his only remaining fan—had discovered the break-in, and had been as surprised as I was. Besides, any rational thieving fan would have taken the Tony from the mantel.

What did this burglary do to the logical theory I'd worked out less than an hour before? Maybe nothing. Burglaries are not unusual in Manhattan and, for that matter, neither are people with tastes for the unusual in sex and theater. Having a fire-escape window without a gate is like sending an invitation: "Welcome."

I called Sergeant Nolan first, and then I called Captain Lee.

"You didn't touch anything after you discovered the break-in?" Nolan asked.

"I was here yesterday. My prints may show up. And they'll be on the phone. But they won't show up on the window."

The fingerprint technician, who was examining the window with a magnifying glass, shook his head. "It doesn't look like we're going to find any prints here. It's clean."

In addition to the fingerprint man, Nolan had brought two uniformed cops, one of whom was photographing the apartment with an Instamatic flash camera. This seemed like a lot of attention for what was probably a routine burglary after an accidental death.

"Are you going to send someone to the Hell's Kitchen Workshop?" I asked Nolan.

He responded to that with a look of pure arrogance.

"The Workshop flyers are missing," I pointed out.

"According to you, so are some condoms. Where do you suggest I send someone to investigate them?"

Any answer I could possibly have come up with cannot be repeated here.

"I'll tell you what, Miss Indermill. You're the only one who saw the fliers and the condoms. You're on the payroll. You can take over that part of the investigation." He ran his fingers along the butt of the pistol slung low on his hip. "I'm concentrating my resources on a different aspect of this case."

"Which is?"

"Eddie Fong. I have a witness who saw Fong attack Daly on the street out here Thursday evening."

"Give that witness a Rorschach Test and see what you've got."

Nolan smiled. "She likes you, too. She said you have a bad habit. You like to take little things . . . mementos . . . from people you admire."

Jesus! He believed Elsie. That was why he was so nasty about the things missing from John's apartment.

"Elsie Scott is crazy, but that's beside the point," I said. "Since John died accidentally, froze to death . . ."

Nolan's smile broadened until he looked positively gleeful. "When Daly's body was taken out of that tunnel and brought to the morgue, the ME's staff was too busy to give him more than a quick look. Late yesterday, when things slowed down, the body was autopsied."

"And?"

"There was damage to the interior structure of the throat and larynx that wouldn't have happened to Daly in his fall down the steps. Also, a cap on one of his front teeth was loose. Since it turns out that there was more liquor spilled down the front of Daly's coat than there was in his stomach, there's a strong likelihood that somebody forced that bottle into his mouth."

For effect, Nolan raised his forearm and pressed it against his neck, then opened his mouth in an imitation of a man gasping for breath.

"This same somebody might have steered Daly toward the tunnel, and maybe even pushed him down the stairs. And I'm not the only one who suspects that. The ME is calling the death a murder."

Oh-oh. That meant that Nolan was probably going to call Eddie Fong a murderer.

Before leaving John's apartment, I asked Nolan about those escalator stairs.

"You keep saying John fell down steps, or stairs, but it was an escalator."

"It was the steps of a nonfunctioning escalator. An escalator moves. These steps do not move, and as far as I'm concerned, they are not an escalator."

It appeared that Steve and Nolan disagreed about this. It was a small matter of vernacular, and I couldn't make too much of it. Steve might have heard the word "escalator" from any of the cops working with Nolan. But I couldn't ignore it, either, because there was a chance that Steve had seen the escalator for himself.

18

JAGUIDA'S HAND WAS STEADY AS SHE poured coffee into the plastic foam cup but her eyes shifted nervously, even suspiciously. "So where's your friend Eddie hiding out?"

Every time Eddie sparked someone's suspicions he became *my* friend.

"What do you mean, 'hiding out'?"

She clamped a plastic lid onto the cup and hot black coffee oozed through a hole in the top, spilling over her fingers. Cursing softly, she wiped her hand on the leg of her sweatpants. Cleanliness wasn't a big issue with Jaguida.

" 'Hiding out' like in 'disappeared.' Gone. He was supposed to stop by last night and pay the rest of what he owes me but he never made it. Figures. You having a jelly doughnut with this, or a cream-filled?"

The morning offerings in the gray cardboard box looked fresh and wonderfully greasy. The restaurant's fluorescent lights reflected in the glazed coatings on the pastries, and a new temptation had been added: chocolate croissants.

I pointed at a jelly doughnut first, but then, not wanting to get in a rut, moved my finger to the largest of the croissants. "I'll have that."

"Why don't you have them both?"

"How big a pig do you think I am?"

She just smiled.

"Eddie's probably upstairs now," I said. "It's a little early for him."

"No." Jaguida slid the croissant into the bag on top of the coffee, where it would get nice and warm. "The thing is . . ."

I was the only customer in the place, but for effect she leaned across the counter and whispered. "A plainclothes detective dropped by here yesterday afternoon looking for him."

"And?"

"Eddie wasn't here. That same detective came back last night with two uniformed cops, but Eddie still wasn't home. Early this morning they showed up with a search warrant. . . ."

"You let them in?"

"What was I supposed to do? For all I knew, Eddie could have been dead in there. Of course," she added, "I was pretty sure he wasn't. When he left here yesterday, he looked healthy enough. He was heading to the Laundromat."

"How do you know?"

"He was carrying a laundry sack."

When I asked Jaguida if she'd noticed anything missing from Eddie's apartment, she shook her head.

"The cops went through his things, but I wasn't paying much attention to them. I was more interested in looking around at my things, making sure they were all right. Eddie rents the place furnished, you know. I got some objects d'art up there."

The thought of Jaguida's "objects d'art" was mind-boggling. She leaned farther over the counter and crooked a finger at me.

"Just between us, Bonnie, did Eddie steal that money he's been flashing around?"

"No. He did not steal the money." He'd stolen it once

before, but he hadn't stolen it this time. But what *had* he done?

By afternoon New York City was in the midst of a veritable heat wave. The temperature had reached the low 40's and the sky was blue. I celebrated the thaw by taking in a matinee.

The Hell's Kitchen Actors' Workshop had a cramped performance space on the ground floor of a six-story building near the river. The building itself was probably of the same vintage as the one that housed The Dancing Fool, and the frills that you find in Broadway theaters—chairs with padded seats, velvet curtains, glossy programs, usherettes in black dresses—were nonexistent. During lulls in the action on the stage—and there were lots of lulls—cars speeding along the Westside Highway were audible, and during one tender moment in the afternoon's performance the foghorn from a passing boat gave a lonesome cry.

There was, nevertheless, an upbeat feeling to the theater. The wood floors had been sanded and bleached, and the audience sat on long wood benches. There was no orchestra section and no balcony, and seating was democratic. The first people into the theater got benches within touching distance of the uncurtained stage. Since the semicircle of the stage was no more than a foot high, prompt theatergoers could imagine themselves almost part of the production.

Though the flier I'd taken from John's apartment had advertised *Picnic* for that afternoon, the company presented a modern-dress version of Chekhov's *The Three Sisters*.

There were a dozen people in the production and, to begin with, about thirty in the audience. These numbers weren't nearly as bad as John had claimed for the place, and not bad at all for a small theater blocks away from Broadway's bright marquees. Unfortunately, though, during the intermission at the end of the second act about half of the audience left and the numbers evened out. It's a kindness to call the Workshop's production ragged.

Katharine Parker played Masha, the middle sister, who, desperate for romance, deceives herself into believing that the boorish Colonel Vershanin is the ideal lover. This being a modern-day version of the play, when Katharine appeared on stage with her spiky hair, wearing a short skirt and sweater, there were no gasps from the audience. Early in the performance her gaze met mine. I knew she had recognized me, but she didn't look directly at me again.

I found her an adequate Masha, but not a very inspired one. As for the others, they were all right too, but frankly the entire production had an unpolished quality. The actors were too subdued, and didn't appear comfortable with their roles. At one point the man playing the brother, Andrei, had to be prompted when he forgot the pungent lines, "One shouldn't marry. One shouldn't, it's boring." At another, the romantic, brooding Vasili, who looked suspiciously like the bare-chested, lean young man I'd seen with Katharine in her apartment, made an uncalled-for exit from the stage and had to make a red-faced reentrance.

Finally it was over. The actors clasped hands and bowed bravely, and I applauded along with what was left of the audience. The actors left the stage and returned. More bows, but the applause quickly became sporadic until only the isolated hands of an older woman were clapping. She was probably someone's devoted grandmother. The rest of the audience was moving toward the exit even as the performers rose from their second bows.

Was it worth it for the actors? Did Katharine experience a performance thrill, an adrenalin rush? That's not as unlikely as it may seem. I've gone to the dressing room after appearing in some absolute bombs, feeling as if I was ready to storm Radio City.

As I've said, there was no curtain across the stage. The actors filed off through a door at the set's side. When the last of the audience, including the grandmotherly woman, disappeared, I got up and followed the actors.

The company was going quietly about its business. Everyone pitched in here, doing double duty. The tall, heavy-set woman who had collected my eight dollars at the ticket window was helping one of the actors stack scenery flats, and two of Chekhov's three sisters were moving furniture from the stage. One or two people glanced at me, but no one seemed to think that there was anything odd about my being there.

"Well, that was sure a roaring success."

The man who said that—and he *was* the fellow from Katharine Parker's apartment—was sitting on a folding chair.

"What do you expect?" someone else said. "It's surprising we could get out there at all."

"The show must go on," the tall woman said, but then she added, "I guess. We might have been better off canceling everything."

The man in the folding chair hid his face in his hands and groaned.

"Is Katharine Parker around?" I asked.

One of the actresses glanced my way and nodded, and the young man in the chair straightened. "She went into the dressing room."

There was no sign of recognition in his glance. "Are you a friend of hers?"

I shook my head. "I was a friend of John Daly's."

A man in a blue workshirt put down one end of the flat he was carrying. "It's a damned shame about John."

"I'd like to talk to Katharine, or"—I shrugged—"any of you, actually, about John."

"This is too depressing." That was the tall woman.

The fellow in the folding chair agreed. "I can't take it. Maybe you should wait for Katharine. She knew John best."

It appeared that Katharine had known several of the men in the Workshop best.

The tall woman was the first to notice my engagement

ring. "You poor thing! Katharine told us about you. You were John's . . ."

A door slammed nearby and seconds later Katharine walked into the area. She was smaller than I'd realized, and in her sweater and jeans she looked about sixteen years old and anything but a femme fatale. Spotting me, she said, "Oh, God!"

The next thing you know I was in the center of a touching, weepy circle of actors, getting more sympathy than I'd had in a long time, and certainly more than I deserved. When the hugging finally stopped I sought out Katharine with my eyes.

"My name's Bonnie. If you have a few minutes, I'd like to talk to you about John . . ."

"Of course."

". . . and about Brad Gannett, too."

The group froze. Okay, I'm exaggerating, but the touching moment ended as quickly as it had started. All those eyes that had looked at me so pityingly shifted abruptly away. The man in the workshirt and the tall woman picked up their section of the set, and the women moving furniture went back to work.

Captain Lee was wrong, and I was right. Something about Brad Gannett's death was suspicious.

Katharine grabbed a gray tweed overcoat from a hook on the wall. "I'd love to talk to you but I have to go to work. Let's get together some other time. See you later," she called to the young man in the folding chair.

She started across the stage. I fell into step beside her.

"Where's your job?"

"It's way over on the East Side," she said, making a huge gesture with her arm. Apparently this job was way *way* over on the East Side.

"I've got to go to the East Side, too. Want some company?"

"Well, actually . . ."

Outside the theater Katharine hailed a taxi and gave the cabby an address on Park Avenue. She wanted my company like she wanted twenty extra pounds on her hips, but I climbed in after her anyway. As the cab sped uptown she stared purposefully out the window.

"I understand you were Brad Gannett's girlfriend," I said. "I saw you on television the night he died."

"That's right, but let's not talk about Brad. I'm not coping very well yet."

"Then can we talk about John?"

Katharine shifted in the seat and looked toward me. "Sure. I'm sorry about John. He was doing so well. I didn't realize things had gone as far as an engagement, though, and I sure wouldn't have thought John had money for a ring like yours."

My diamond ring was certainly opening doors for me. I was almost as uncomfortable elaborating on my "relationship" with John as she was talking about Gannett, but to keep the conversation going I mumbled something about unexpected movie residuals.

"Oh, yes. Every actor's favorite mail." A smile played across her face. "You're certainly not what I expected."

"No?"

"John told me he was going out with a real showgirl type."

Which meant that I wasn't. Oh, well. *C'est la vie.* The cab was heading into Central Park when I tried again. "I was surprised to find out John had been drinking the night he died. Did you know about that?"

Katharine nodded. "A policeman dropped by the Workshop on Friday night. John's drinking surprised all of us. Sure, he was anxious about getting his career going again, but he seemed to be handling everything well. You meant a lot to him, too," she added kindly.

As we moved into the heavy traffic of the Upper East Side I was feeling guilty, but not guilty enough to give this up, or even to be particularly subtle about shifting the conversation back to where Katharine didn't want it to be.

"Did John ever talk to you about Brad's death?"

"Of course John talked about it. We all did. But John

was obsessed with the subject." She ran her hand through her hair. "He had gotten some nutty idea..." She paused. "John kept dropping hints that made me wonder if all those years on the bottle had messed up his brain."

"Hints such as what?"

"Oh, that someone had forced Brad to shoot himself. Not physically. Emotionally. According to John, a few days before Brad died, Brad said something to him about his future as an actor being in big trouble. But let's drop the subject, okay?"

After hearing that, I had no intention of dropping the subject, but she sounded as if she meant it, so I shut up and looked at the scenery.

To me, the most visually interesting apartment buildings in Manhattan are on the West Side. That's where you find the Dakota and most of the other rococo piles. On the East Side you find the fortresses that look as if they could withstand mortar attacks. The Park Avenue apartment building where Katharine told the driver to stop was one of those.

God help an inept spy who tried to sneak past its pair of doormen. One of them all but lifted Katharine from the cab, and gave me a helping hand, too.

"Well, this is it for me," Katharine said.

"Me too."

I stared at the massive structure's well-guarded lobby. Katharine was going to work, or so she claimed, but what kind of work did she do in a place like this? A list of the usual actress jobs ran through my mind: waitress, word processor...

"Are you ... babysitting?"

The corners of her lips twitched into a smile. "Sort of." She reached out her hand, took my reluctant one, and shook it firmly and with finality. "If you're staying in John's apartment we'll probably run into each other again."

With that, she marched past a second doorman, who tipped his hat.

So much for my interrogation skills. All I'd managed to do with my afternoon was watch a lackadaisical production of a play, hone my suspicions, and travel several miles out of my way. I'm not sure what I would have done if that second doorman hadn't called after my quarry, in a distinct Irish brogue, "You're later than usual, Miss Katharine. Those dogs must be desperate by now."

Dogs. She was a dogwalker. I grinned at the first doorman. "I'll wait here for my friend."

Moses doesn't care much for dogs, which is one of the reasons I've never gotten one, but I do like dogs. When you have a cat you can forget how nice it is to be utterly adored. Moses never looks at me with eyes that say, You are my everything. But if I ever get a dog, it will probably be a catlike dog, small, agile, and easy to scoop up after. It probably will not be a Dalmatian, and there's no way on earth that I'll ever live with two Dalmatians. As for the fat white poodle with the pink eyelids, the obscene-looking backside, and the eating disorder, he was appealing in a perverse sort of way, but I'm sure Moses wouldn't have thought so. I don't think that Katharine Parker liked him all that much either.

When her trio of charges pulled her from the building and she saw me waiting, Katharine's face became as stony as the building's façade.

"I don't have time for this. We're going for a walk before it gets dark."

The dogs completed the business portion of their walk with city-dog efficiency—find the right spot and do it—and Katharine had her scooper role down better than she'd had the role of Chekhov's Masha. Once all that was done with, she and her three charges took off.

Katharine was younger than I, and the Dalmatians must have been the canine equivalent of boisterous twelve-year-old humans. Anything less than a full-out run wasn't enough for them. I should thank that poodle for his refusal to go at any more than a waddling trot. There were long stretch leashes on the dogs, and as we covered the two blocks to Central Park, the Dalmatians strained at them, leading the pack. Katharine was in the middle, and the poodle and I brought up the rear.

We entered the park on a paved path near one of the playgrounds. The daylight was almost gone and ordinarily the park would soon have been deserted, but the sudden warm weather had brought out crowds who were reluctant to leave. Nannies still pushed buggies along the path near a pond, and the playground was filled with children.

I was huffing a little when we came to an overflowing garbage can and the poodle put his feet down, all four of them firm against the leash, and dug in. Katharine glared at him and said, "Fred!" sharply, but Fred, undaunted, buried his nose in a torn paper bag. For his efforts he was rewarded with some French fries smeared with catsup.

"Why are you doing this?" Katharine asked me. "There's nothing else I can tell you about John. I liked him, and I'm sorry he slipped down those stairs, but . . ." She shrugged. "I'm sorry. That's all."

"What about Brad? What can you tell me about his death?"

The two Dalmatians were circling around her, eager to be on their way. "Brad's death? It was all over the news. The whole world knows as much about it as I do."

"Do you think there might have been drugs involved?"

Katharine shrugged again. "I suspect Brad was just unhappy about something. Sometimes he slipped into these bad moods. The way his career was going I can't imagine why, but this must have been one of those times."

"And what about the other guy who was with you when you visited The Dancing Fool. Terry? He's dead too. Apparently some accident involving drugs. Did you know that?"

Even with daylight dimming, I could see the color leave her face. "No," she finally said. "But that's not so surprising, when you think about it."

"Why not?"

"Terry had a reputation. Drugs, and . . . oh, I don't

know. He lived somewhere near the theater, and had gotten to know a couple of the actors. Casually," she added. "I only met him that one time. Brad didn't know him well either, I don't think."

Where Brad Gannett was concerned, Katharine "suspected," she "supposed," she "thought," but as for hard facts she seemed to know even less about Brad Gannett than I knew about my so-called fiancé, John.

"If Brad was already depressed, might he have taken something that made things worse?"

The color returned to her face. "He might have, I guess."

For Katharine, talking about Brad and drugs was less scary than talking about Brad and Terry. Drugs can be a passing fancy, a nonfatal mistake. A stint at Betty Ford and all is forgiven. But someone like Terry . . .

"You guess? You shouldn't have to guess. You were his girlfriend, weren't you?"

She shifted the leashes nervously from one hand to the other but said nothing.

"Weren't you?"

"Of course."

The poodle had finished off the fries and was sniffing at a candy wrapper. Katharine glared down at him. "Drop it, Fred. Let's go."

The Dalmatians yanked hard. Katharine braced her feet to keep from being dragged toward the pond, and began shortening their leashes.

"Katharine? Were you really Gannett's girlfriend, because . . ."

Her hand, the one that wasn't gripping the leashes, balled into a fist. "Oh, why did I ever get involved in any of this," she said angrily.

"Involved in what?" I demanded. "There's something about Brad Gannett that you're hiding. I saw it back at the theater, and I see it now."

She started to turn away.

"Katharine? Was Brad Gannett interested in Terry? I

don't mean for drugs. I mean for sex.''

"Why do you care? It doesn't make any difference now. Brad's dead and so is his career. And John's dead too, and so are his nutty ideas.''

"That's exactly why I care,'' I said. "You probably don't know this, Katharine, but the police think John's death was a homicide.''

Katharine's body seemed to go slack and one of the leashes slipped from her hand. Bending to retrieve it, she said, "I didn't know that. Is something really going on? I mean, was John right?''

"I don't know, but your relationship with Brad is a good place to start.''

She shook her head. "There was no relationship. I was Brad Gannett's . . . beard.''

There are several definitions of the word "beard,'' but the way Katharine used it, only the theatrical one made sense.

"You went out with Gannett when he needed a date.''

"You've got it,'' she said. "Brad's career was taking off because of that ridiculous macho TV show. He was getting sacks of fan mail, all of it from women. He started worrying about being exposed as gay.''

She reeled in the leashes and started walking away. I fell into step beside her. "I'm surprised he hadn't been.''

"Apparently most of Brad's relationships with men were anonymous, one-night stands with strangers,'' Katharine said. "Sort of nonthreatening types, like Terry. Only people who were close to Brad for a long time knew the truth. If it had gotten out, his career—at least his film career as a romantic lead—would have been ruined. He needed a woman on his arm, and I didn't mind getting some exposure. It didn't seem like any big deal to go to a couple of parties and premieres with him. That is, until the police knocked on my door and told me Brad had killed himself. Before I could even think straight and get a story together, a dozen reporters were shoving microphones in my face. I ended up getting more exposure than I ever dreamed possible.''

"What about Terry? Was it his idea to go to The Dancing Fool that night?''

"No," Katharine said. "It was mine. John had talked about the club, and it sounded like fun. Terry was just this stoned, star-struck kid. He thought Brad was wonderful.''

Shortly after I got home, Detective Nolan called. He wanted to know if I had any ideas about where Eddie Fong might be. I had several ideas, all of them oceans away. I told Nolan, "No.''

A few minutes later I received another call.

"So you've got some mice in your apartment that you'd like to get rid of, Miss Indermill?''

"That's right," I said, surprised by this personal attention from my smarmy landlord.

"I'll tell you what," he said. "You get rid of the Chinese fellow you've got living there, and I'll get rid of the mice. And please don't try passing that one off as your brother. I'm not as stupid as you think.''

Slam!

19

THERE WAS NO RESPONSE TO THE doorbell, but when I pressed my ear to the metal door itself a familiar sound reached me: The teakettle, in my kitchen, was whistling.

"Eddie?" I called softly through the locked door. "Oh, Eddie. I know you're in there. You stole my keys out of my tote and I had to get the super to let me in the building."

Footsteps crept past on the other side of the door and tiptoed into the kitchen. The kettle's whistle grew faint and then was quiet.

I tapped with my knuckles and said, louder, "If you don't open this damned door I'll get the super to break it down!"

The spyhole in the door flipped up and a familiar brown eye, surrounded by a less familiar purple bruise, peered out.

"Are you alone?"

"Yes, but I won't be for long if you don't let me in."

Both locks were latched and the safety chain was on, and there was a moment of fumbling before the door swung open.

Eddie was a real march down memory lane for me, in

a blue terry-cloth bathrobe that had belonged to one of my previous boyfriends, and leather slippers that had belonged to another.

"Hurry up and get inside before those nosy old ladies across the hall see me."

"They've seen you," I said. "They reported you to my landlord."

Eddie rolled his eyes, and the one with the shiner looked even more florid. "That makes things interesting, doesn't it?"

I followed him into the kitchen.

"You want a cup of coffee? That's all you've got here, you know. There's zero food. If it wasn't for that Chinese carryout and the pizza parlor, I'd be starving to death."

"The police are looking for you, Eddie. You've got to turn yourself in."

He lifted the kettle from the stove. "I've been a fugitive from justice before. It's no big deal. When I traveled around the Orient it wasn't bad at all. I stayed in first-class hotels, ate in the best restaurants . . ."

"Maybe it's not a big deal for you, but harboring a fugitive from justice is a big deal for me."

As he poured the hot water into a mug he tried to put on a tough act, but it didn't work. "Actually, Bonnie, it is sort of a big deal for me, too."

When he turned toward me his eyes were glistening. It's awful to watch someone you know, someone who has always put up a strong front, break down. Eddie didn't quite go that far, but when he walked to the table in front of my living room window, he took a deep, shuddering breath.

I stayed in the kitchen for another moment and made myself some coffee, not because I wanted it but because I wanted Eddie to have time to compose himself. When I carried my mug to the table he was looking out the window.

"Great view you have here. And rent stabilized. You'd

be crazy to give this place up, even though you do have mice.''

Pulling out a chair, I sat down. "You can't stay here."

Eddie stared into his mug. "You wouldn't go to the cops. You're not like that."

"I'll go to the cops."

"You know, Bonnie," he said, finally meeting my gaze, "that's the problem with you. You cave in to authority. It must be something to do with your background. What else could it be? You're smart, you're creative, but someone shows you a badge and you wimp out. Your humanity disappears. Poof.''

I slid back the chair. "I'm calling them now."

I might have, too, but before I made it to my feet Eddie said, "Actually, that time I spent traveling around the Orient wasn't all so terrific."

"Really?"

"Well . . ." His gaze dropped back to the mug. "The truth is, none of it was terrific and some of the time things were . . . crummy."

The story that Eddie told me was the one I'd gotten from Lee, but Eddie filled in details that Lee either hadn't known, or hadn't shared with me. In Manila, before he got out on bail and ran, Eddie had spent a week in a 4-by-7 cell with a dirty mat for a bed and a bucket in the corner. "There were roaches bigger than the mice you've got running around here, and the temperature never went below a hundred. I can't go through that again, Bonnie.'' He swallowed some coffee, then looked me in the eye. "You can't let them lock me up. I didn't kill T'Bird."

"Then why did you lie about not seeing him after the fight? Elsie saw you confront him on the street after his AA meeting."

"Elsie's a moron!" he said. "Okay, I was over by St. Ann's, but I didn't go there to pick another fight with John. It just happened that when I saw him my temper got the best of me for a second."

"Then why were you near St. Ann's?"

Eddie scratched the side of his nose and rubbed at his purple eye. "Bonnie, it almost kills me to admit this, but I was going to my Gamblers Anonymous meeting. Three times a week. I haven't missed once during the last four months. You wouldn't believe how damned good I've been. And now, after all my effort, after the way I fought those devils that try to pull me into every Off Track Betting place that I pass, you're going to send me to jail."

I was on the verge of mentioning that the two things— Eddie's battle against the demon OTB and John Daly's murder—were unrelated, but before I could open my mouth his eyes grew shiny again.

"Have you ever seen any of those movies about prisoners in the Orient? *Bridge on the River Kwai*, *Escape from Bataan*, *The Deerhunter* . . ."

Oh, baloney. None of his argument made a bit of sense, but seeing him sitting there, a broken man . . .

I've said it before: I'm weak.

It was a while before I got on the A train for the trip downtown, but that was because the lines were long and the clerks overwhelmed at the A&P where I went to get Eddie some groceries. When I finally left Washington Heights, I wasn't entirely empty-handed, either. I had Eddie's word that he hadn't killed John. I also had his promise, sworn on his mother's grave, though for all I know she's still alive, that he would be out of my apartment in twenty-four hours.

That said, I wasn't feeling so good about the way things were going. I was a police spy who was withholding information from the police, an employee who was spying on her bosses, a tenant lying to her landlord, and a fiancée who was using her engagement ring to wheedle information out of unsuspecting people. My life was a sham.

By two P.M. the temperature had risen to a positively balmy 50 degrees and my dark mood was brightening. This heat wave was probably one of nature's tricks and it would be a while before I could put the snow shovel away, but winter was going to end. All over the city fur-lined snow boots were being replaced with rubber ones as New Yorkers coped with the rivers of melting snow. People stripped off down jackets and wool hats and lifted their faces up to the sun.

Still, we were a long way from the time when people who like to peel off their shirts in public could do it without getting goose bumps. Nevertheless, Steve was peeled right down to his pectorals.

As I walked toward the club I saw him in the driveway washing the Bronco. His chest and back were wet, and from a distance his skin glistened golden and smooth as a lifeguard's in mid-July. From closer up, the goose bumps covering his glorious self were obvious and the picture wasn't as pretty.

Seeing me, he made a cute move with the hose. I jumped away from the spray.

"It's not beach time for me yet, Steve."

"Sorry about that." He climbed into the Bronco and scrubbed hard at one of the side windows with a wet rag. The inside of the window was terribly smudged, and after a minute he gave up.

"Have to get something stronger to clean that. So Bonnie, it looks like your friend Eddie's skipped out on us. The cops have called half-a-dozen times looking for him."

"He's your friend, too. Aren't you cold?"

"Yeah, but I'm trying to catch some rays. I've been going to a tanning salon to get an undercoating, but . . ."

He gave the top of the Bronco one last blast with the hose. "This should do it."

Ice snapped, and we both looked up. A chunk of it had split off from the glacier coating the storage shed roof and was inching its way down the steep slope. Steve hurriedly turned off the water and began coiling the hose.

"I don't want to be under that when it falls."

He followed me through the door of the club.

"Where's Max?" I asked.

"He went to get a sandwich."

Once in the office, I could hear the ice cracking on the roof. The window remained painted shut, though, killing any possibility of fresh air.

I started going through what was left of the papers on the floor. The club's files and books were in shape, the checking account was under control, and the phone company was happy. My office job was winding down. My spying job, though, was incomplete. Brad Gannett's secret life might make hot gossip, but it wasn't going to mean much to Lee.

Steve finished up whatever he'd been doing downstairs. When he walked into the office he had the bucket and mop with him, and a bottle of ammonia under his arm.

"I sure miss T'Bird. Got to clean the johns myself. I'm not going to bother with the ones in the Celebrity Lounge. There haven't been any celebrities. Just you, and you're not that messy."

"Thanks. I'm no star but I'm clean."

He smiled. "Maybe I should get some more of that Giorgio perfume for you, though. That's the one you like, isn't it?"

"Sure." I like a number of perfumes, but Giorgio happened to be the only one in the Celebrity Lounge restroom that I'd used, and I hadn't used it since the first night I visited the club. Had I given myself such a heavy blast that Steve had been able to smell it?

"It's not the real thing," he added, "but you know that."

Steve was right. I'd examined the Marvelous Mimics labels on the bottles. But how did Steve know I knew?

He went about his cleaning and I pretended to go about my work, but my mind was on the ladies' room. Ladies' rooms, actually. It was no secret that the restrooms were being monitored by camera. Standing in the security room, I'd been able to watch Amanda putting on her lipstick two floors beneath me. But when I'd examined the perfume labels, Steve had been downstairs working the bar.

John had questioned the fact that the restrooms were being monitored, and Max had said that they kept an eye on things "intermittently."

Now, there's a difference between keeping an intermittent eye on something and examining it closely after the fact. Max had made it sound as if he and Eddie and Steve merely glanced at that monitor from time to time, as if they'd never bother replaying a tape unless the cash register came up short or unless the club's patrons came stumbling out of the restrooms high as kites.

"You know those videotapes from the surveillance cameras?" I asked.

Steve forced the mop through the bucket's wringer and slapped it onto the office restroom floor. "Yeah?"

His back was to me and I couldn't tell whether the subject made him nervous, but I wasn't going to get anywhere if I wasn't persistent.

"What do you do with them? You probably reuse them," I added, knowing that they did, "but you must play them back and watch them, too. Otherwise you wouldn't know which perfume I like."

I had kept my voice purposefully conversational, but when Steve turned toward me, his forehead was furrowed and there was a nervous-animal look in his eyes that I'd never seen before.

"Sometimes . . . just once in a while, because none of us have much time . . . we slip one in the VCR."

I flipped through some of the papers. "Why?"

"I don't know. I just do what Max says." Steve smiled, but the tension remained in his face. "He's the smart one. I'm the handsome one."

Footsteps—I recognized them as Max's—caused us both to glance toward the hallway. When I looked back at Steve the nervous-animal expression was even more pronounced. Before Max walked in Steve turned away and began mopping diligently.

Steve was afraid of his brother. I don't know why that surprised me. I was afraid of Max, too.

"So, Bonnie," said Max. "Your two-week sentence will be over in a couple of days. You've done a good job here."

"Thanks."

"We're going to miss you. You can still come in if you want. Once a week or so just to keep things together up here."

He was wearing that incredibly sincere expression that always made me feel like I was dealing with someone who had nothing to hide. If I was right, though, Max was hiding more than cheap booze.

"There's a lot that still needs work around here," he said. "If Eddie doesn't turn up pretty soon and clear his name, we're going to be needing someone to help with PR."

He had his jacket in his hand, and when he pulled the closet door open, Dawn's belongings—clothes, shoes, everything—spilled across the floor.

"And there's always this. Not that I would want to turn you into a cleaning lady or anything, but . . ."

I forced myself to smile. "That's the problem with small businesses. One minute you're the director of public relations, the next minute you're cleaning closets."

"Right, but look at this mess. We're still a long way from organized around here."

He gave one of Dawn's aerobics shoes a kick that sent it sailing like a hockey puck into the closet, then stooped and started shoving back the rest of her junk.

"Doesn't that damned gym give Dawn a locker? You teach a class, Bonnie. You get a locker at the Y, don't you?"

The second I said "Yes" I could have kicked myself harder than Max had kicked that shoe. John, who was easygoing enough to leave his fire escape window unguarded, had been awfully concerned about that locker out in Huntington.

Steve had finished with the restroom and was nudging the bucket toward the hall. "Yeah, Bonnie. It would be cool if you'd stick around. Max would find things for you to do."

Just before he disappeared through the door he flashed me a lascivious grin. "And if Max couldn't, I would."

Max remained crouched in front of the closet. His eyes were on the mess inside, but I had a strong suspicion that his mind was on a locker in a Long Island YMCA. The phone rang and I answered automatically. "The Dancing Fool."

"Miss Indermill?"

The voice was so familiar, but I couldn't believe he'd call me at the club. "Yes?"

"This is Captain Lee, but do not say my name. Are you alone?"

"No."

"Then smile and act happy, like you're talking to a friend."

Max was still stooped by the closet, but his eyes were on me, curious. Faking happy was out of the question.

"I've seen mice. There was one in the bedroom the other night."

"The police have lifted a fingerprint from Terrence Doyle's room that matches the prints taken from Maxwell Breen when he applied for his liquor license and handgun permit. At the least, there is clearly some drug business operating. . . . "

"No," I said, "That's not true."

"Please don't argue, Miss Indermill. You must leave The Dancing Fool as soon as you can without calling undue attention to yourself. These are very dangerous people, so don't make yourself conspicuous. We don't want their suspicions aroused. Once you're clear of the place, call me. Sergeant Nolan is in the process of getting a search warrant. When I know you are safe he will get the go-ahead to search the club."

"If you do it that way, you're not going to find any mice."

"Miss Indermill! You have your orders!"

Slam!

Max smiled. "Mice in the suburbs?"

I shook my head. "Mice in Washington Heights."

"Maybe you should get a cat. But you spend most of your time out on Long Island anyway, don't you?"

"Yes," I said absently.

"Speaking of Long Island, what are you going to do for a partner at that Y out where you work? I mean now that John's out of the picture."

"They'll find someone." It was three twenty-five. There was a four o'clock train that would put me in Huntington a little after five. A cab would get me there even quicker.

While Max's back was turned I opened my desk drawer and quietly flipped up the lid of the petty cash box. The money hadn't been touched. I removed the two twenties and the ten and slipped them into my pants pocket.

"These bills can wait until tomorrow." I closed the drawer. "I've got some errands to run this afternoon."

"Whatever you want," said Max. He had one of Dawn's aerobics shoes in his hand. "Why does she leave all this junk . . ."

Max seemed content grappling with the closet, but a minute later, as I was on my way out of the office, he stopped me.

"Bonnie? Where is that Y where you teach?"

"On Long Island."

"I know, but where? One of the guys who shows up on Sundays for Ballroom Dancing is looking for part-time work. He'd be terrific."

"It's in Hempstead," I said, though I wasn't even sure that Hempstead had a Y.

Once outside I ran to Tenth Avenue. As I flagged a cab, I glanced toward the club and saw Max and Steve climbing into the Bronco, and by the time I was in the cab and it started moving, the Bronco was making its way down Forty-fifth Street.

"I need to get to the train station in Huntington, Long Island, as quickly as possible."

The driver looked happy almost beyond words.

Hempstead is near the center of Long Island and Huntington at the north. As the crow flies, there are a good twenty miles between them. By car, there are even more, and crows don't run into heavy traffic, either. Max hadn't taken the time to make some calls and check my story, so I figured that I'd be okay. I didn't even consider calling Lee. Now I really was a rogue spy.

20

"BUT YOU CAN'T GO IN THERE," SAID the middle-aged man who had just pushed through the swinging door. "This locker room is for men."

To bolster his argument he nodded at the stick figure stenciled on the door. It was wearing slacks. Well, so was I. I flashed my engagement ring at the man, shameless—"I have to get his things. Only be a second"—and marched past him.

It was a little before five P.M., and too early for the commuters from the city to hit the Y, but the men's locker room wasn't completely deserted. A cry of "Whoa!" and the slam of a metal door greeted my entrance, and somewhere out of sight showers were running. I focused on the floor and kept moving.

"Locker eight," John had said. "Eight, sixteen, twenty-four."

The men's lockers were laid out like the women's, two rows high along two walls. I located John's on the nearest bottom row with no trouble. Opening it was another matter. The room was terribly steamy, more than the women's, and the lock so loose that it kept rolling past the exact numbers.

Eight, sixteen, twenty-*six*. Damn! I tried to lift the handle but it wouldn't budge. Eight, sixteen . . .

Bare feet padded on the damp floor nearby. An elderly man had emerged from the shower in a cloud of steam. Clutching a towel around his middle, he said, "Hey, lady. You're not supposed . . ."

"I'm not looking at anyone."

Twenty-four. The handle lifted.

There it was, as I'd been sure it would be. A video cassette with a torn red-rimmed label. The label scrap had the number "11" printed on it. February 11. The night of Brad Gannett's first visit to The Dancing Fool.

I put the cassette in my tote, slammed the locker, and spun the dial. As I straightened, a short, balding man in a sweat suit burst through the swinging door. His pugnacious expression and the golf club he had gripped mid-handle made it clear that he had been sent to get rid of the intruder by any means necessary. Holding the door wide, he pointed toward the stenciled stick man.

"Can't you read?"

I pointed down at my trousered legs, then hurried past him, up the stairs, and out the Y's front door.

The bright sun was dropping lower in the sky and my shadow on the pavement was long. I hadn't put my gloves on and my hands grew cold quickly. The temperature was dropping. Trotting to the Chrysler, I got in and started it and pulled out of the lot.

The first thing was to put some distance between myself and the Y. Then I'd stop somewhere, give Lee a call, and drive back to Manhattan to show him what I'd found.

I had turned onto the road that skirts the golf course, when the squeal of tires in the distance broke my chain of thought. Around the curve ahead, out of my view, a car was grabbing for traction on the bridge. A second later a dark green fast-moving Bronco wheeled around the curve and came toward me.

I hardly had time to panic before the Bronco was passing. Steve was driving, and when our eyes met, his were grim. Max was beside him riding shotgun. In this case that was surely more than a figure of speech.

Before I reached the curve I glanced into the rearview mirror. The Bronco was making a U-turn. An hour earlier I could have counted on encountering a school bus and some car-pooling moms on the road. An hour from now there would be a stream of commuters. But for the moment the road was deserted.

Once around the curve I was headed west. The sun beat hard into my eyes, but there was no time to look for my sunglasses. Squinting against the glare, I pressed my foot on the accelerator. The car picked up speed and the gentle snow-coated hills of the golf course flashed past in a blur.

When I reached the stand of trees I took another look in the mirror. The Bronco was closing the space between us. It was no more than fifty feet behind as I approached the bridge at the bottom of the hill. I broke into a sweat. Just before I reached the bottom of the slope the whine of the Bronco's engine grated the air.

I hit the accelerator and went into a skid. The Chrysler slid to the right and everything I'd ever known about how to steer out of a skid vanished from my memory. The front bumper slammed into the bridge's iron railing, but before I was thrown forward the airbag built into the steering wheel exploded, pinning me to the seat. It might have been the shock of the accident, or perhaps it was the airbag pressing into my chest that made breathing hard. I took a couple of shallow, panicky breaths before I looked out the window.

The Bronco had stopped on the road. Max was making his way on foot along the side of the bridge, using the iron railing for support.

My car blocked the bridge entirely, and luckily it had come to a stop with the passenger side facing my pursuers. I struggled from behind the airbag and opened the door. The ice on the bridge glistened in the low sunlight, and my knees were trembling as I stepped across it. I held my breath until I reached the roadside and safer footing.

Max had gotten as far as the middle of the bridge. He

was moving carefully around my disabled car's rear fender. Steve was just behind him.

"Do you have something that belongs to me, Bonnie?" called Max.

He hadn't come all that way to retrieve the contents of the petty cash box. I kept moving.

"It's a good thing we stopped and called a couple of Y's. You would have had us driving all over Long Island. Give the tape back to me and it will be over."

Right. The way it had been over for John when he got hold of the tape.

In the tree limbs overhead a branch cracked. Steve must have looked up at the sharp sound because I heard him call, "Watch out."

Fortunately, Max's eyes never left mine.

A big chunk of dense ice and snow had accumulated near the end of a branch. Maybe it was the fluctuating temperatures of the last twenty-four hours, or maybe its time simply had come. The chunk fell, and most of it landed on Max. He was bare-headed and the icy downfall must have been a shock. A small, surprised "Uh" was all he managed before his feet flew from under him and he landed hard on his back.

I heard the groan of a big, sluggish engine fighting the hill ahead. A school bus came over the rise, and I couldn't have been happier if it had been a beautiful big gold nugget rolling my way. I ran toward it, waving my arms. By the time the driver pulled to the side of the road and opened the door for me, the Bronco was gone, and so were Max and Steve.

21

THE LIFE AND DEATH OF A DANCING Fool, by Elsie Scott, has been running in the paper for the past week. The series began last Sunday with John Daly's birth to Irish immigrants—"to hook in the Irish crowd," Elsie told me—and quickly moved on to his Broadway triumphs. By midweek everyone on the New York City subway seemed to be reading about John's years in Hollywood. Elsie, whose canniness is a continuing wonder, interviewed many film people and both of John's ex-wives, and got some riveting material.

I won't go into any of that here. If you haven't read the articles, you can satisfy your curiosity by watching the TV miniseries that's in the works.

The last installment of the series appeared in this morning's paper. The police source mentioned is Sergeant Nolan. I'm "Ms. X," described as a "source close to Daly during his last days." Anonymity was my wish, as well as Sam's and Captain Lee's. Lee wouldn't even let me mention my involvement with the NYPD.

Here, hot off the press, are some excerpts from today's installment.

Ms. X wasn't initially suspicious when she saw that, in a snapshot, Brad Gannett had raised his glass to cover much of Terry Doyle's face. Her suspicions were piqued later. Why had Gannett been so belligerent on his second visit to The Dancing Fool? Was it drugs he wanted from the "ponytailed bozo"? Drugs had been a problem in Max Breen's L.A. club, and Breen's paranoia about the room with the safe and the security monitor added to Ms. X's suspicions about drugs.

She was wrong. It wasn't drugs Max Breen was hiding in that little room. What he was hiding was in plain sight: a tape made on February 11, the night Brad Gannett first visited the club. Gannett appears for only a few seconds on the tape, but that brief appearance would have ruined the career he'd been building. That segment of the tape, which this reporter has studied at length, shows Gannett and Terry Doyle embracing in the club's Celebrity Lounge men's room.

How did John Daly find out about the tape? According to Ms. X, Gannett had revealed to Daly that his career might be in "big trouble." When Daly, who had never liked Max, realized that the restrooms at The Dancing Fool were being taped, he became curious about the February 11 tape. Daly's friendship with Dawn Starr gave him access to the club's keys. Once he got hold of the tape and watched it, he understood why Brad Gannett had shot himself. Ms. X suggests that if Daly had been less aggressive in the way he began dealing with Max, he might still be alive.

Max and Steve Breen were taken into custody at their father's home in New Orleans the day after the incident at the bridge. Max, through a lawyer provided by his father, continues to claim he is innocent of all charges. According to a police source, however, Steve, who has not been allowed to speak to his brother, confessed to the blackmail scheme almost immediately. Steve said that the club needed money, and Max felt that confronting Brad Gannett with those few seconds of videotape would be an easy way to get it. Unfortunately, Gannett chose another way out.

When Max learned that his fingerprint had been found in Terry Doyle's room, he claimed that he and his brother had paid a "social call" on the young man. However, Steve, who is said to have "gone to pieces" without his brother's guidance, admits that he and Max dropped by Doyle's room to "get a take" on Doyle and find out how much he knew about the blackmail scheme. Both of the Breen brothers continue to deny any part in Doyle's death, and the way Doyle died was consistent with his lifestyle and could have been an accident. Ms. X continues to believe that the brothers murdered Doyle, but without either a confession or further evidence, we may never know Doyle's entire story.

Since Gannett was accompanied by Doyle on his second visit to the club, we can assume that Doyle knew about the blackmail scheme. Why did Doyle call Max and Steve later, though? Did he plan to try some blackmailing of his own? Ms. X, who spoke with Doyle, thinks not. She claims that Doyle sounded confused and hesitant, but not confrontational. It is Ms. X's feeling that Doyle would have been harmless to the Breens, and that he might simply have been trying to make sense of Gannett's suicide.

After consulting at length with his own lawyer, Steve Breen confessed some involvement in John Daly's death. According to Steve, he drove Max to Daly's apartment at Max's insistence. Steve thought his brother wanted to talk to Daly, and claims he was surprised when Max forced Daly into their Bronco at gunpoint. Again at his brother's insistence, Steve drove to a deserted area a dozen blocks south of the club, and held Daly while Max attempted to pour liquor down his throat. Daly apparently put up a tremendous struggle inside the vehicle and ultimately broke away from the brothers.

Here Ms. X again enters the picture. Daly, knowing she was curious about Brad Gannett's death, tried to reach her by phone. Before he completed the call, however, the Breens caught up with him. There was another struggle, and Daly was injured. Steve says that he remained with the car while his brother forced the now-groggy Daly across the street and into the park. When Max returned alone a few minutes later, he told Steve that he'd left Daly "sleeping it off at the bottom of an escalator." Though Daly's missing wallet has not been recovered, police theorize that Max took the wallet before pushing Daly down the escalator so that the crime's motive would appear to be robbery.

The break-in at Daly's apartment was Steve's doing, but again he insists it was his brother's idea. Max was desperate to recover the tape. Max also is alleged to have told his brother to take anything from the apartment that linked Daly with Brad Gannett. All Steve found were the brochures with both actors' names listed.

Where Daly's death is concerned, Max Breen again denies everything, but a search of his Bronco, which was found in the long-term parking lot at Kennedy Airport, turned up several of John Daly's fingerprints and hairs. This evidence appears to strengthen the prosecution's case against Max Breen.

Had John Daly lived, what would he have done with the tape hidden in his locker? Maybe nothing. Ms. X has suggested that once Daly got all the publicity he could from The Dancing Fool, he would have turned the tape over to the police, but Ms. X,

*a star-struck woman who once hungered after a
stage career, may be looking at John Daly through
the proverbial rose-colored glasses.*

*And so, the life of John Daly, a poor player who
strutted and fretted his hour upon the stage, ended
ignominiously in a tunnel under 11th Avenue. We'll
miss you, John.*

Strutted and fretted? And Elsie has the nerve to call me
star-struck? I suppose I should be grateful that she didn't
say that my story was a tale told by an idiot. She could
have and the paper would have printed it. Elsie's being
touted as the New Reigning Queen of celebrity gossip.
Who would have thought it?

Eddie hasn't done as well. He tried to keep The Dancing Fool going and might have made it, but one night last
week the City Fire Marshal showed up unannounced. In
the marshal's report, the old furnace was called "a disaster waiting to happen," the absence of a sprinkler system "unacceptable," and that rusted window gate upstairs
"dangerous." This is nothing that money won't cure, but
with Sally the Shotgun's sons out of the picture, the building's rent has skyrocketed. I have no idea what Eddie's
going to do, but when I saw him the other day the ponytail
was gone and he had *The Sunday Times* want ads under
his arm.

I tried calling Dawn a couple of days ago but her phone
has been disconnected. Maybe she's gone back to Louisiana, or maybe she's gone somewhere else to reinvent
herself. I hope she does okay. I like her.

As for me, the dial on the scale finally stopped bouncing at a number beyond merely shattering. I am the new
Reigning Queen of low fat. My mom and Amanda and I
went to look at wedding dresses, and if I'm going to get
into a size eight, it's either diet or liposuction.

The first time I got married I wore pure snowy white.
This time maybe I'll go with off-white.